The Picture Jumper

Mary Missig

Published by Mary Missig, 2022.

THE PICTURE JUMPER

First edition. October 10, 2022.

Copyright © 2022 Mary Missig.

ISBN: 979-8215986035

Written by Mary Missig.

Chapter 1

Questions Unanswered

~LINCOLN~

During the prior few weeks, Lincoln Peterson had conjured the courage to ask his mom two simple questions. The mystery of the past year had to end.

"Do you remember what today is? Can we talk about it?" he asked, tapping on her bedroom door and guiding it to a forty-five-degree angle. The drag marks left a small section of the shag carpet groomed like a slice of pizza.

"Of course I remember. But there's nothing to talk about. Everything's fine. We've all moved on," she said, not even turning around.

Lincoln heard the sound of her voice, but he couldn't believe her words, which railroaded through his chest. His bony twelve-year-old shoulder blades clamped the frame of her bedroom door.

His mom, makeup applied and the linger of her citrus shampoo in the air, stared into the mirror above her dresser and tugged at her blazer collar to lay flat. "Do you need something?" She turned to him as he stood frozen. "Are your grades slipping or something?"

He turned his bottom lip inside out and nodded no. He was almost as tall as she was in her patent leather pumps, as she brushed past him, headed to the stairs.

Today was supposed to be different—April 5, 1996, the one-year anniversary of Dad's accident. He had trouble calling the occasion his dad's death, but at least he tried to remember. Shouldn't his mom at least try to care? Just for her son? Especially today? He just wanted to know what had happened.

"We're leaving in five minutes. You'd better be in the car," she said as she descended the first few stairs. Her long blond hair bounced as she moved.

He waited until she was all the way downstairs to jump onto her bed. He buried his head of wavy blond curls in the pillow. *Ahhhh*! The soft cotton muffled the hot breath of his scream. He punched his hands and kicked his Converses into the worn-out mattress.

Out of breath, blood pulsing, he tossed the pillow aside and sat up.

In this very bed, his dad used to cuddle him on Saturday mornings when he was a little boy in his footed pajamas. Dad's legs were so long, he'd bend his knees to create an easel, prop up Lincoln's favorite book, *Euphonia and the Flood*, and read. "If a thing is worth doing, it's worth doing well." He heard his dad making his voice high and shaky, impersonating Euphonia, in contrast to his normal deep voice. Resting on his dad's strong, sparsely haired chest, feeling the vibration, was rhythmic and soothing.

Worth doing well. The motto was one his dad lived by and one that he lived by too. But somehow his mom thought talking about Dad wasn't worthy? Nothing about her in the past year made sense to Lincoln.

He looked at the rumpled covers from his kicking. Guilt bubbled in his stomach for perpetrating violence in this sacred place. He smoothed the bedspread and jogged downstairs. Being late would just give his mom another thing to yell about.

As the neat rows of corn and soybeans blurred out the window like an animated flim, the cassette tape ejected. His mom pulled it out, flipped it over, and inserted it into the tape deck of the Oldsmobile.

No surprise to Lincoln, they'd be listening to the Air Supply *Greatest Hits* album again for the umpteenth time. He didn't know why she couldn't listen to anything else, but this was something he didn't question. There was no logical answer.

His mom coughed and sipped from her thermos to clear her throat. "This won't take long. I need to make sure this house out on Locust Bend Road is ready for the open house tomorrow."

Ever since Dad was gone, she toted him around the rural outskirts of the county to all her realtor houses. If he wasn't at school or practice, he had to be with her. She said he helped make the spaces seem more kid-friendly and gave her better odds at the potential buyers making an offer. He thought she just didn't want to be alone and wouldn't admit it. Life had changed so much. She wouldn't ever talk about Dad or the accident, but their lives were dictated by his absence.

He studied the shrinking scar above her right eye. A blemish that couldn't be concealed on her otherwise perfect face. After the accident, she'd needed fifteen stitches there and twenty-one more across various parts of her body. Luckily only the glass got her—at least, that's what his Grandma Arletta had said.

. . . .

April 5, 1995

Lincoln heard a rap at the front door around 10:30 p.m. His parents had told him "10 p.m. lights out" before they left. But he didn't feel safe going to bed alone with the thunder still hammering. No use pretending to be in bed now. His curiosity walked him to the front door.

"Hey baby, git yur coat." Grandma Arletta's sweet southern accent had an unusual bitterness. He wondered why she had an accent and no one else in their town did. She'd only told him she'd grown up in Georgia and moved after her habit of talking was too hard to break.

She stood on his front step wrapped in a shawl as the wind whipped and the rain spat into her bloodshot eyes. He snatched his sweatshirt from a pile on the dining room table and threw it over his head.

"What's wrong?" He shielded himself from the downpour and lent an arm to help her dodge the puddles in the driveway.

With her short, stout body seated behind the wheel of her basil green station wagon, she focused on him.

He could tell the moisture on her face was not just rain.

"Dere's been a tear-bul accident. We gotta git to da hospital." She turned the ignition.

"What do you mean? Are Mom and Dad okay?" The thud of his heart outsung the splatter of the rain on the windshield.

"Baby, we don't know yet. But I thought ya shud be dere." She squeezed his hand and squeezed the rosary draped down her bountiful chest.

He nodded and focused straight ahead, blinking to fight off the tears. Pins and needles tickled the inner recesses of his nose. Hot sweat beaded on his forehead. He slinked his hands inside the sleeves of his sweatshirt to rub it all away. He tensed his whole body.

"It's okay ta be scared, ya hear me?"

He cocked his head to the side.

"I can tell yur tryin' ta put on dat strong face. Dontcha even think of it again."

He let out a long breath and his muscles relaxed.

"Dat's better, baby. Ain't gonna help no one if ya not being truthful. I know yur parents don gone telling ya not to lie to others and so on, but the biggest lie ya can tell is to yurself, 'bout yur feelings."

"Okay, Grandma."

She patted his shoulder.

"Dat's my gran baby."

· · · ·

"My son, Beau Peterson, and his wife, Deb Peterson, please," Arletta said.

Lincoln stood close to her at the ER reception desk, as if he could absorb her warmth.

"Come with me, ma'am."

They followed the nurse through a maze of curtains.

Time stopped—and whizzed by him.

Arletta gripped his forearm as she hobbled to keep up.

"Debra Peterson is here." The nurse pulled back the curtain and left.

"Mom!" He lunged to hug her.

"I'm fine," she said.

Burrowed in her chest, the silence subdued him for a moment until thoughts crowded his mind. He rose to find her tired eyes, just below her gauze-wrapped head. Her lip was cut and crusted with blood.

"Where's Dad?"

He watched her eyes pinball around the room. First to the ground, then at him, then at Arletta, and back to him.

"Oh dear lord, my baby!" Arletta clutched her rosary as her knees buckled.

"Grandma, are you okay?" He guided her to the foot of the bed, so she could lean against it.

Arletta grabbed his hand and nodded at his mom. "Ya gotta..."

His mom closed her eyes and put her head back. She took a deep breath. She opened her eyes as slowly as the exhale.

"Lincoln...Dad got hurt...really bad." She re-closed her eyes. "He...didn't...."

Her body convulsed trying to hold in the tears.

Pain tunneled through every bone in his body, entering but immediately exiting.

"I bet he was brave. I bet you were brave too," he said.

. . . .

"Lincoln!"

The floorboards of the Locust Bend Road house rattled under his feet.

"Lincoln, come quick! Hurry!"

He flung the Game Boy toward his bookbag. Bullseye. The bag swallowed it. He scooped up the bag.

Crack. A flash of white lightning lit up the dark hallway.

He froze atop the stairs.

Boooom, the thunder replied.

He skittered his Converses downstairs.

On level ground, he saw her locked toe-to-toe with a furry gray mouse. The mouse lifted its tiny arms and fidgeted with its face.

"Do something," she mouthed at him.

"I have an idea. I'll be right back."

"Where are you going?"

He bounded up the stairs and rummaged through his bookbag. *Bingo*, he still had his Gatorade leftover from baseball practice yesterday.

"What're you doing?" His mom tiptoed away from the mouse. The mouse stood its ground.

"Give me a second." He poured the lime green fluid down the kitchen drain. "Is there any food around?" He peered into the empty refrigerator.

"No—why would there be?" His mom glared at him.

He walked behind her, surveying. There had to be something.

"Hey, are those apples real?" He pointed to a bowl on the dining room table.

"Those are for the open house."

"Not all of them."

He grabbed one and put the plastic Gatorade bottle on the table. Sliding the hunting knife his dad had given him on their last fishing trip out of his back pocket, he sawed the top of the bottle off and put a slice of apple inside.

"Come here, little guy." He coaxed the mouse into the bottle and held the top firm. "I'll be back."

"Where are you going in this rain?" His mom's voice faded behind him.

He pulled his hood up and jogged across the soggy yard to the back property line. The mouse escaped as he opened the bottle. He watched it scurry into the woods, with the half-eaten apple slice gripped in its jaw.

Back inside, the house was quiet, eerie. Goosebumps sprouted on his damp skin.

"Mom?"

She sat in one of the dining room chairs, hunched over, clenching his hunting knife.

"Mom, are you okay?"

He inched closer.

She didn't move. She stared at the knife.

"I can't do it!" she screamed.

Lincoln jumped back.

"I can't! I can't!" she yelled. Her breath quickened. "I can't!"

Sweat dribbled down his temples.

"What?" he asked.

"I can't!"

"What can't you do?" he said, inching closer.

"I caaaan't!!!"

Her scream curdled his blood.

"I can't! Why did we have go out?!"

Lincoln stood in front of her, but kept his distance.

She kept screaming, but she didn't look at him.

"Mom?" He waved his hand in front of her face.

She kept screaming. "I can't!"

"Okay. You can't," he whispered. "Why don't you take a deep breath?"

She kept screaming. Louder and louder. Her eyes glazed and fixated ahead.

He covered his ears. Tears tingled in his eyes.

He stood there, waiting.

In a few minutes, her voice grew hoarse.

Ah-huuugh. Ugh-huuuh. Ack. Ack. Ack. She coughed. Hard. Hyperventilating, she turned in her chair to put both hands on the table. The knife still locked in her fingers.

Lincoln leaned in and swiped the knife. He let out a sigh of relief as he folded it and returned it to safety in his pocket.

He paced the length of the hall between the kitchen and the dining room a few times and then peeked his head around the corner. She was resting her head atop her folded arms on the table.

He floated his hand above her shoulder. "You okay?" His sweaty palm landed on the foam pad of her suit jacket.

She shuddered and looked up at him, eyes glazed.

"Oh. I didn't see you there. I must have dozed off."

He looked at her, teary-eyed.

"I'll be right back," she said.

• • • •

~DEB~

She went to the half bath for a tissue. Her nose was sniffly. Maybe she was catching the cold that was going around?

She flipped the light. Her reflection haunted the mirror. Tired flesh. Runny mascara. Hollowed cheeks. Had she been crying and not even remembered it? Did Lincoln see her?

She hunched over the sink and plunged her hands into the rush of warm water. She cupped the water and splashed her skin. Burying her face in the towel, she rubbed her flesh raw. As she smelled the laundry detergent, she stopped. She held herself in the cushioned darkness. When would it all end?

Always keep fresh towels in the guest bathroom.

Her mother's voice echoed the chambers of her mind. The phrase made her think...

Would Lincoln remember anything she'd taught him? Would she ever be able to tell him what happened? Would he think she was a good mother? The questions swirled in her head.

"Mom?" She heard Lincoln's voice behind the door.

She threaded the towel on the rack and opened the door. Lincoln stood before her.

"Would you come help me?" She put on a straight face and led him to the dining room. "Let's finish up this job so we can go home."

All the walls of the dining room were draped with heavy plastic sheeting and the room smelled of fresh paint.

"We need to pull all this plastic down. The open house is tomorrow."

She watched Lincoln, as he shoved his hands in the front pocket of his baseball team sweatshirt. He lived in that sweatshirt. She had to peel it off him whenever it was time to do the laundry. His number five silkscreened on the back, his dad's old number.

"It'll only take a few minutes."

She wrestled the piece of thick plastic sheeting closest to her. The edge released from the ceiling and buried her to the ground.

• • • •

~LINCOLN~

"I got it." He hopped across the room. He held up the plastic canopy until she escaped.

"Damn lazy painters. I knew this was going to happen." She dusted herself off.

He stood still, studying the paint-streaked cardboard protecting the floor.

"Good thing I decided to give everything one last check before the open house tomorrow." She relaxed her shoulders.

He bent over, collected full armloads of plastic sheeting in his skinny arms. The room whooshed and crinkled, as he cleared the mess. He knew the work would fall to him.

"Thank you," she said. Then she pointed to a piece he missed under the table.

He retrieved the stray piece.

"All done." He stood with hands on hips.

"Yep." She confirmed with her own inspection of the room. She walked toward the front door. "My, it's really coming down out there."

He followed her, then stared out the curtain-less window. The "For Sale" sign wobbled as the wind gusted.

"I didn't bring an umbrella," she said.

"Guess we'll have to make a run for it?" He opened the front door. The rain whipped his freckled face, not yet riddled by adolescent acne. He yanked his hoodie over his wavy curls and beelined to the Oldsmobile.

He stood at the locked passenger door and looked back. His mom's heels pranced across the milky puddles in the loose stone driveway. She fumbled the keys in the car door as the rain matted her flowing blond mane.

Soaked, he jumped in and shivered in the front seat.

"Thanks for helping," she said as she slid in and pulled her door closed.

Lincoln nodded.

They backed down the driveway. The rhythm of the windshield wipers, two beats faster than the rhythm of the Air Supply song.

"Mom?"

She didn't answer. She looked straight at the road, her elbows locked and hands anchored at ten and two.

"What happened back there?"

She kept silent.

"At the house..." he continued.

"You mean the mouse? How did you know about building a trap like that?"

"You know...Dad." He knew the moment he brought him up, the conversation would end.

She stared at the road.

He looked down at his soaked shoes.

"I mean, after that..."

"Can we talk about this later? I need to focus on the road."

Lincoln sat still. The force of the rain sounded like a million nails on the car roof. The droplets raced across the side window. He watched, imagining them as his tears, washing away the past. Washing away the pain. Wishing his mom could do the same.

• • • •

~DEB~

She pinned her eyes on the slick road. The temperature was cold enough that the rain could turn to sleet. Her heart thudded against the seatbelt snug to her chest. She felt heat in the underwire of her bra. The yellow stripes on the road paced by her like a treadmill.

A small bump. The wheel inched a degree to the left.

Another bump. The wheel recoiled.

She pumped the brakes. The darkness surrounded them, except for the two beams of light leading them through the storm. She hoped the rain would stop for the open house tomorrow.

As she gripped the wheel, her wedding ring dug into her finger. She swore she'd never take it off. She didn't know how to be anyone but married to him. Death wouldn't do them part.

On the shoulder. Two white eyes of a small rodent.

She inhaled. Her taut grasp shot her arms straight.

The danger passed.

She exhaled. She wanted to be home.

Since the accident, the smallest spit of rain put her on high alert. Her mind flooded with visions. The car spinning. The crash a foreboding destiny never fulfilled.

This was how she felt most of the time. Trapped. In a nightmare that would never end. A nightmare where her husband never returned.

• • • •

April 14, 1995

~LINCOLN~

Lincoln clawed at his neck. The tie itched and choked. His mom insisted he wear it despite his reluctant pleas.

He sat next to his mom but left a large space between them. The first pew sparse. Reserved for the immediate family. His grandma, Arletta, plump and huggable in a burgundy floral church dress, to his opposite side. His grandmother, Helen, petite and formal in a long black dress with her gray hair in a tight bun, opposite his mother. The four of them. That was it.

He wanted to cry. But he was too busy thinking. What would life be like without his dad?

He didn't remember much from the ceremony. The priest talked. Adults he didn't know wept in the pews behind him. Sad songs were sung as the organ echoed the tune from the loft above the parishioners. The town was small, only three stoplights, but people had come from all over to attend.

He had wanted to talk at the funeral. To tell everyone how much his dad meant to him. What he'd taught him about life. All the good times together fishing and playing baseball.

He looked at the priest and pictured himself standing at the altar. All eyes on him. The butterflies rushing through his insides—but he'd stop and take a deep breath. He'd feel his dad looking down on him. He'd orate the most brilliant eulogy. And when he was done, he'd feel his dad smiling down on him. But none of that happened. His mom had not allowed it. She wanted the family memories to be kept private.

During the receiving line, his best friend Trent offered a hug with his impressively growing wingspan. "Not here," Lincoln had said.

Trent walked away with a forehead of distraught wrinkles and slumped shoulders. Trent had known Beau too. He had been the boys' peewee football coach. The thought didn't occur to him that maybe Trent missed him too.

Lizzy, a new girl in his class, also showed up. She didn't have the right to be there. She didn't know his dad.

"I'm so sorry," Lizzy said. She found him outside after the congregation spilled onto the quiet street lined with Victorian and craftsman houses in hues of weathered whites and creams.

"Thanks." The words left his mouth like a robot. He stared at the ground.

"My gran-mama died two years ago, and it was hard for me. Let me know if there is anything I can do." Lizzy's voice was soft and sweet, matching her deep brown, teddy-bear eyes.

"Okay." He walked away.

He was in another universe. The day was moving on without him. His dad would soon be in the ground. He had no control. He wasn't really mad at his mom. Or Trent. Or Lizzy. He was mad at his dad.

• • • •

~DEB~

The funeral was not the hard part for Deb. No, she knew how to suffocate her feelings. The customs were a playbook she could execute. She could carry on with small talk, nod politely as the bereaved went through the motions to offer condolences, tune out the barrage of reminders that her husband had—as many described it and she hated the term—"passed away." To her, his death was immediate and brutal. "Passed away" was soft and gentle.

She prided herself on how well she acted the part. The strong widow. She'd made all the arrangements. She invited Lincoln's entire sixth grade class to make sure he had support. Sadly, only a few showed up. She envied the parents that could shield their children from the sorrow of death.

No one could tell she hadn't slept since the accident. That she cried so hard she threw up. That she worried she'd never be able to face the truth.

"I'm sorry for your loss. I know how hard it can be. I lost a lot of friends in the war," said a man in a dark blue suit with an American flag tie pin.

She nodded and stared at the unfamiliar man. There were many people at the funeral she didn't know. A friend of his maybe?

"You know, it's okay to cry. There's not a dry eye in the place." He paused. "Except for you." He reached to hold her elbow, but the crowd swarmed around them and swept her away from the man.

But her thoughts couldn't let go. He'd said the most real thing to her she'd heard all day. She thought it odd not to wear black. She hated that she noticed this man. His suit stretched at all the right places to indicate a strong chest and biceps underneath, all while her husband lay in the coffin ten feet away.

• • • •

The drive home from the Locust Bend house was twenty minutes. To Deb, it seemed like two hours. The torment of the rain. The wall of silence wedged in the center console. Her own son, a stranger. In the past year, they had grown farther apart, not closer together.

The moment she stopped the car, Lincoln darted inside.

She clutched the wheel. She watched the door between the garage and the kitchen slink itself closed.

"Goddamn rainnnnn!"

She unleashed a harrowing scream, knowing her voice wouldn't carry into the house.

"Ahhhhh!" she belted from the bottom of her belly. Purging. The emotion cut her throat.

She swallowed the cold air and stared at the steering wheel. It stared right back. Silence surrounded her. Mocked her.

She rested her elbows on the wheel in defeat. A single tear dropped into her lap on her peach skirt. As soon as she wiped it away, a new one appeared. She pounded the wheel until her arms jellied. She exhaled. Her chest heaved as she struggled to regain her breath.

She looked right and imagined him sitting beside her. He always had to push the seat back after she had driven his car. He was six feet tall. He would make fun of himself and say his "stilts" got in the way. His chest and shoulders were muscular and wide, but his legs were skinny. That didn't matter. He could run like the wind. He won state his senior year in the 400-meter dash.

Her heart slowed. She looked at the empty seat.

She thought about the pressure of driving all over hell's half acre and back selling house after house. She thought about the staring mothers, whispering behind her back at after school pickup. There were whispers everywhere she went in the small, all-white Christian town of Brightonville about how she "wasn't right." Whatever that meant.

She dropped her hands. The car still running. The idling of the engine like her mind, functioning but not going anywhere.

A flash of light. She flinched.

She noticed the porchlight glow outside the garage. She glanced in the rearview mirror to confirm. Lincoln must have turned it on. Her heart warmed a few degrees. She'd never seen him do that before.

She switched off the ignition and closed the garage door. She flung her bag over the padded shoulder of her damp peach suit jacket and slogged into the house.

She went straight to the kitchen. From under the sink and behind all the cleaning supplies, she pulled out a bottle of vodka. With the bottle in hand, her mind settled and she swayed to the living room. She plopped her frail body on the sofa. Had it only been one year? The memories of that night still seemed alive and young. She wanted the day to be over. The vodka stung her esophagus.

"Uhh, uhh," she choked. She shouldn't have yelled so much in the garage.

Another swig.

She felt ashamed hiding the hard liquor, but she didn't want Lincoln to find it. Not because he might drink it, but because of what he'd think of her.

Chapter 2

Grand Gestures

Clad in a dry white T-shirt, Lincoln hopped on the couch to browse *Sports Illustrated* and wait for his mom. What was she doing sitting in the car in the garage? After skimming the cover story about how the Cleveland Indians were going to win it all, he tossed the magazine on the end table. The Red Sox had a good chance too. They had the "Rocket," Roger Clemens, on the mound and Mo Vaughn and Jose Canseco going long at the plate. He walked out to the kitchen.

The door to the garage was closed, so she was still out there. He switched on the porchlight and went up to his room.

In his drawer, under his socks, he dug up the picture of his dad and him on their last fishing trip. The framed picture was a birthday gift from Grandma Arletta that his mom only let him keep because he promised he would keep it out of sight. He cradled it in his hands.

"Dad, what happened? Why won't Mom tell me?"

A tear dripped down his cheek.

"She's freaking out now. Today she lost it. I've never seen her this bad before."

He slumped over and shook his head.

"Please, I have to know what happened."

A teardrop splashed on the glass.

Thuuuuummp. His bookshelf rattled as the thunder clapped.

• • • •

Buuuzzzz.

He rolled over and smacked the snooze button on the alarm clock. Spring break was over. He grumbled at the thought of going back to school.

He trudged around getting ready. He'd have to see everyone again and talk about his break. All he had to say was he had pre-training for baseball and trolled along with his mom at a bunch of houses.

He stood in front of the mirror. Did he look okay? His chin felt soft. He wished for stubble. He tucked and untucked his shirt.

Downstairs, he found his mother. She lay passed out on the couch, a half-empty vodka bottle tucked under her arm. He knew she enjoyed wine from time to time, but vodka was new.

He slinked the bottle loose from her arm and returned it back under the sink.

In the kitchen, he prepped his breakfast. He tore open an oatmeal packet. The mix slid from the paper sleeve and left a cinnamon cloud in its midst. He dribbled some water from the faucet until it was the right consistency. He liked it thick. He watched the bowl spin in the microwave as the oats bubbled up.

Beep! Beep! Beep!

He grabbed the hot dish.

He heard his mom rustle on the couch. "What're you doing?" She appeared in the doorway and pushed her tangled hair away from her face.

He dropped the dish on the counter. A few stray hot oats specked his forearm.

"Just making some oatmeal. I have school today."

"Jesus, the noise! It's too early!" She held her head with two hands.

He braced his back against the counter.

She was upset and there was no reasoning with her.

He wished with all his might to be anywhere but there. He wished he could go back in time, have a quieter breakfast like a Pop Tart instead of oatmeal. He wished his dad would walk in. He'd take her hand. He'd soothe her. She'd listen.

He wished hard. He wished for anything but the present.

He stared at the picture on the kitchen wall, a watercolor of a quaint Parisian cafe. Three circular tables under a red and white striped awning. The tables dressed in crisp beige linens. Each adorned with a bottle of wine and a breadbasket. Each with two chairs side-by-side facing the busy street, enticing the next passersby to take a seat.

He'd never been to Paris, but he wanted to go. His dad always reminisced about their Paris honeymoon. They'd bought the painting there. It was an original. They stood for an hour in the Montmartre district watching the emergence of the colorful scene. The painter, Esme, had been setting up his easel in that courtyard for nearly twenty years. He held the paintbrush like an instrument. The colors bled in perfect symphony, transforming the blank space. Welcoming you to walk right in.

"Go on! Get out there before you miss the bus!" She waved at him. "I'm not driving you if you miss it!"

He kept staring at the painting. He couldn't take his eyes off it.

"Did you hear me?"

He nodded. But he felt weird. His knees wobbled. His eyelids dropped. His body felt like when he tried to stay up late as a kid to watch the ball drop at midnight. Summoning all energy to awakeness, but the warm wash of sleep buried him under a wave of dreams.

The kitchen went black.

He held his breath.

Thud-thud-thud-thud. He felt his heart in the back of his throat.

He tried to swallow.

The ground shifted under his feet. He punched his arms to each side into the darkness.

Balance. Breathe. It's okay.

Is it okay?

He thought of his dad. Treading water in the deep end of the community pool. His dad's arms outstretched, waiting to catch him from his first jump. Lincoln's scrawny arms clutching the railing.

Do it.

Do what?

Lincoln squeezed his eyes open and shut. Hoping for light.

And then he saw—

He was at the café. Sitting at a table with a wide-angle view. In Paris.

"Holy shit!" he blurted and then covered his mouth.

A young couple sitting next to him gave him a dirty look.

"Uhh…" He bowed his head, attempting an apology. *"S'il vous plait,"* he said, hoping a French *please*, the only French he knew, would be a close enough substitute for *sorry*.

The couple twitched their noses and turned back to their table.

Lincoln touched the tablecloth. He picked up the utensils. He touched his face.

Was this really happening? Or better yet, what was happening?

"Monsieur, puis-je pendre votre commande?" The waiter whisked by and released a fresh croissant from his tongs into the breadbasket on the table.

Lincoln held up his hand to signal he needed a few minutes. Or maybe a bit more? What was happening?

He took a sip of water. The wetness cooled his nerves.

He scanned his surroundings. The scene was magnificent. There was so much life, so much color bustling down the cobblestone streets.

He was in another world. He hoped he could stay.

From the corner of his eye, a stream of orange. Across the street, he saw a man chasing down a woman's scarf. The wind leafed it up and down.

The chasing man came closer. Dad?

He squinted and studied the woman. Mom? She had the faint resemblance. Maybe when she was younger?

A chill shimmied his spine.

Was it really them? What if they saw him? What did all this mean?

The scarf landed in front of a cheese shop and settled against the windowed front door with a chain of bells hanging from the handle. The shopkeeper came out and wound it around his hand, the wind threatening to steal it a second time. He looked around and saw the chasing man a few trots away.

Lincoln sighed. The chasing man was not his dad.

A hot rush tingled his skin. A cool tear slipped down his cheek. He picked up the menu, burying his face inside. An envelope fell into his lap.

Lincoln brushed the tears from his face. He placed the menu on the table.

The envelope looked old and delicate, like an artifact from a museum. He slid his hand across the paper. It was real.

He turned it over. There was a circular wax seal—navy blue, with a dove in the middle. He peeled away the seal.

He reached inside. There was a notecard with the word *Dinner.*

What could this mean? Dinner at the café? Or maybe something more?

A surge ran through his body. He felt alive. He felt like he hadn't felt in a long time.

"Monsieur?" The waiter returned.

He shoved his hands under the table, gripping the envelope between his sweaty palms. His heartbeat accelerated.

His eyelids felt heavy again.

The colors faded.

Gray.

Black.

The fatigue pulled him.

He closed his eyes.

Darkness surrounded him but he wasn't scared.

He opened his eyes.

His head popped backwards.

He saw his mom again and shoved the envelope in his back pocket.

"Listen to me and get out that door now!"

He took a quick bite of oatmeal. His tongue burned. The oatmeal felt like it had come right out of the microwave and time had stopped.

"I'm going." He scraped the rest of the gooey mess into the trash, put his dish in the dishwasher, and headed out the door.

He shivered at the end of the driveway.

What had just happened?

He didn't know whether he wanted the bus to come sooner or later. Being outside was a nice dose of reality. The cool spring air was a nice slap in the face; the groundhog had seen his shadow this year. He watched each breath become a faint cloud.

The cold front that had blown in overnight had turned the wet front lawn into frosted green ice picks. He ventured off the driveway and listened to the crunch under his feet.

Craaa-nk.

The garage door lifted.

Lincoln skittered back to the driveway.

He didn't expect to see his mom leaving so soon.

He saw her tousled hair and sunglasses through the windshield. She sped by him.

Lincoln waved, hoping she would wave back.

She didn't.

He watched the exhaust puff from the Oldsmobile, the fog surviving only a few moments before it evaporated into the cool air. The car gained speed and distance down the rickety country road, growing smaller and smaller until it was swallowed by the horizon.

• • • •

~DEB~

She guzzled her coffee. Anything to take away the pounding. And the guilt.

Seeing Lincoln at the end of the driveway struck fear in her heart. She felt horrible for snapping at him. He was just trying to make himself breakfast. He was so responsible, she didn't appreciate him enough. Her anger sometimes spewed out of her without any control over the tiniest things. And did he see her passed out on the couch? What had happened to the vodka bottle? She knew she needed to do better.

There was no sun, but she put her sunglasses on. She needed something to help her get past her son.

She punched it down the driveway.

Lincoln waved as she passed. She tried to put her coffee down and wave back, but was too late.

As she drove into another endless gray overcast day, she tried to push down all the emotion. She passed the sprouting cornfields dotted with misshaped puddles from the overnight rain. Even the untidiness of the stagnant water sparked her anxiety.

There was a farmhouse to stage that morning before heading to Locust Bend for the afternoon open house. The farmhouse was far from ready. She had a big day of preparations and pageantry ahead.

The large farmhouse, located on the outskirts of town, near the county line, was an hour drive away. She cranked up the volume on the cassette deck and ran through her mile-long to-do list in her head.

She needed to supervise the cleaning crew. The staging furniture was scheduled to arrive. The gardeners hadn't trimmed the dead branches from the majestic oak. The tree was the centerpiece of the front yard, but with all those sick limbs it didn't look royal yet.

The first few chords of "All Out of Love" came on. Her to-do list vanished.

This was their song.

• • • •

August 8, 1977

"Soooo, you can't tell anyone...," Beau said. She glanced at his strong forearm leaning in front of her to open the car door.

"What?" She pushed her Farrah Fawcett-winged bangs to the side.

"A buddy at school had tickets to see the new band, Air Supply, at that dive, The Turning Key, but he can't go, and I bought them off him. I know it's short notice, but I was wondering if you'd like to go? It's next Friday."

"Sure, wow, never heard of them, but that sounds really fun." She tucked her floral print satin wrap dress under her knee-high boot covered legs and slid into the front seat.

"Oh that's wonderful," Beau said. He smiled and closed her door.

She studied him as he walked around the hood of the car. He was tall, but his legs looked even longer in his bell bottom jeans.

"You really know how to flatter a girl, huh?" she said as he sat down.

Beau gazed at her, resting his chin on his arm, outstretched from the wheel.

"I mean you're a curious mix of affability and audacity. This is our first date and you're already asking me out on a second date before you even know me. What if I hog all the popcorn at the movie, or even worse, I'm secretly a serial killer?" She giggled and tucked her purse under her leg.

"Well, you can have all the popcorn you want and no one as pretty as you can be a serial killer." He smiled. "I've seen you around campus a few times. To be honest, I've been meaning to ask you out for a while. It just took a bit to work up the nerve. And maybe I've been a little busy studying. Senior year is kicking my ass."

She laughed. "Yeah, I guess I'm still in the 'enjoying college' mode. Being a sophomore is probably the best year. Things aren't so new and you don't have the pressure of graduation yet."

"I'm so torn over whether to apply to med school or not. I think I'd rather just get started helping people and go the paramedic route."

"I can see that about you. I think you'd be really soothing with people in an emergency."

"Thanks. So what are you majoring in?"

"Communications. I want to be a journalist."

"Oh yeah? That's really great. Do you write for the school paper?"

"As a matter of fact, I do. How did you know?"

"I can see that about you." He winked.

. . . .

~DEB~

The song ended. She shivered. The heat from the vents in the Oldsmobile blew faint and weak against her Ann Taylor black cardigan. Why didn't she grab her coat?

"I don't know what I'm doing," she whispered.

She hadn't even realized she'd said the words out loud.

She took a big deep breath in and exhaled with a ponderous sigh.

"I think I need help."

A small ray of sunlight shot through the dreary ashen sky before she finished her sentence.

She pumped the brakes. But the car coasted through the sunbeam.

Every bone in her body surrendered.

She didn't know who she was talking to.

But she knew. Deep down she knew.

Maybe he could hear her? He could help her. He could make everything better.

She couldn't do this alone. She needed him.

Chapter 3
Resistance

~LINCOLN~

Lincoln heard the gasp of the school bus edge closer. The ironic vehicle meant for many starts and stops struggled to be nimble.

The door slid open with a mechanical sigh. He scurried up the steps. A wave of heat welcomed him. Thank God the heater was working this week.

"Morning," he said to Ms. Lohusky, the bus driver. She nodded but kept her eyes on the road. She scared most of the kids with her deep voice and husky build, but Lincoln tried to appeal to her good side.

He puttered down the aisle.

"Hey, Prez!" Craig called from the middle section.

"Hey." The bus jolted back. Lincoln grabbed the seat. Ms. Lohusky was in a rush today.

His friends called him Prez. He didn't mind the nickname. He appreciated they hadn't chosen something more embarrassing like Lincoln Log.

He took a seat across from Craig.

"How was your break?" Craig asked.

Craig flipped the page in the textbook splayed across his lap. His skinny legs struggled to hold the book steady as the bus rumbled along.

Lincoln had known Craig since nursery school. He was his oldest friend. Craig wasn't the most popular kid in junior high, but Lincoln didn't care.

Lincoln didn't know how to answer Craig. Last spring he'd went on a fishing trip with his dad.

"I'm sorry. It must have been hard without your dad. I didn't have that good of a break either." Craig smiled. His jagged braces peeked through his chapped lips.

"What are you studying?" Lincoln asked.

"Brushing up on my fractions. There is a quiz this week for extra credit."

"Well, I didn't get the memo."

"I can catch you up real quick."

"Thanks, man. I'm okay." Lincoln never worried about his schoolwork. He managed to get the A without hours of arduous studying or extra credit assignments.

"Okay, if you say so." Craig pulled out his Walkman and buried his head in his math book.

Lincoln leaned his head against the window. He watched the frost-covered muddy fields pass. In the fog-glazed glass, he outlined the word "help." Then wiped it away before anyone noticed. When would his life stop unraveling?

His stomach tensed and his thoughts circled. He rubbed the envelope in his pocket.

What was happening? The way his mom looked at him at the show house. The glaze over her eyes. She didn't want to see him. She wanted to see Dad.

He felt invisible. Unwanted. A bother.

But on the flip side, he felt invigorated.

Was it a dream? Did he really travel to Paris? Would he be able to do it again? Imagine the places he could go.

The bus pulled up to Jefferson Junior High, part of the abnormally prestigious public school system serving a wide radius of rural farmland. The school district was well funded due to the dairy and meat processing plants near the river. Many who lived in and around Brightonville had been there their whole lives, having inherited farms and wide swaths of property from European ancestors who'd come through Ellis Island to find a better life.

The school building resembled an old courthouse—monumental with concrete pillars and arches over the windows. Kids filled the sidewalk at the height of the morning rush. They funneled up the staircase and into the double doors.

"Prez! You gotta see this." Trent held up something in his hand, his biceps budding in the curve of his extended arm.

He headed toward Trent's locker. Craig followed.

Jacob Johnstone, but everyone called him JJ, grabbed the baseball card from Trent.

"Hey!" Trent said, waving his empty hand.

"I wonder why his parents didn't name him 'Juicy' instead of Daryl?" JJ said.

"Hand it over, JJ. Strawberry'll probably be a Hall of Famer. Here, look." Trent snatched it. He turned the card over, pointing to the stats.

"His .525 SLG percentage is impressive," Craig chimed in, leaning over to see. He loved baseball stats as much as he loved math.

"Who asked you?" JJ reached out to shove Craig. "What do you even know about baseball? You don't even play, shrimp!"

Lincoln stepped in front of Craig and prevented the contact. "JJ, knock it off."

"Do you even know what SLG stands for?" Trent asked.

"Stupid Loser Guy." JJ rolled his eyes. He lifted his baseball cap and rubbed his head, exposing the racing stripes sheared into the sides of his buzz cut.

Trent glared at JJ as the bell rang. "Let's go," said Trent. "You got saved by the bell. You better take that hat off too. Mr. Hudson will ream you out for that."

"You guys go ahead—I'll catch up." Lincoln watched as the three boys shuffled along to first period and disappeared from the hallway with the rest of the students.

Lincoln put the envelope in his locker. But he couldn't close the door. He stared at it in a trance. He knew he needed to get to class but he couldn't stop thinking about what this could mean. *Dinner.* His parents had gone to dinner and only his mom returned.

"Excuse me."

The voice startled him.

"What're you doing out here?"

Lincoln slammed his locker. He knew the grumpy, raspy voice.

"I'm talking to you, Mr. Peterson." Mr. Hudson marched toward him, but his command didn't match his stature. He was a few inches over five feet and balding with thick-rimmed glasses.

"I don't feel good," he said.

"Where's your hall pass?" Mr. Hudson shoved his hands into the pockets of his khakis and bent over.

"I don't have one." He turned his head to avoid Mr. Hudson's breath. The pungent remnants of a dinner with heavy garlic and a poor job of morning brushing.

"Okay, you know what no hall pass means...," Mr. Hudson said.

He noticed a picture across the hall. Would it work?

He took a deep breath.

He stared at the black and white photograph. It depicted the school founding ceremony. The school looked the same, but everything else was different. A big crowd. Men in suits. Women in fancy dresses and hats. Model Ts lined the street.

He stared so hard he felt cross-eyed. The picture blurred.

He heard Mr. Hudson's muffled demands. "I'm not going to ask you again..."

But he couldn't unlock his eyes from the photo.

His body wouldn't let him. His knees buckled.

He took a deep breath, which turned into a yawn.

His eyelids got heavy.

The picture faded from blurry to black.

He held his breath.

Black.

Numb.

He squeezed his eyes shut, counting ten Mississippi before he'd try to open them.

Open.

He blinked his eyes, adjusting to the light.

There was the school. There were the Model Ts.

Lincoln felt a tap on his shoulder.

"That's your new school, young man."

"I go to Jefferson already." Lincoln looked up. He saw an old man wearing a top hat with round spectacles.

"That's impossible. The inaugural school year doesn't start for another week." The man scratched his chin.

"Oh sorry, I mean..." Lincoln stumbled. His throat tightened. Why did he say he went to Jefferson?

"Son, where are your parents?"

"I don't have any." The statement felt true enough to say.

"I'm sorry, son." The man stepped back and paused. "I didn't mean to upset you. Say—let's go watch the ribbon cutting." The man reached his arm out to lead him to the action.

Lincoln wiggled away and ducked into the crowd. He didn't know what to do. But maybe there was another envelope to be found?

He saw a group of kids crouched on the sidewalk. There was a circle chalked on the ground. They flicked marbles back and forth.

He imagined playing marbles with his friends. Wearing pressed collar shirts. No TV. No video games.

What would those kids think of TVs? When were TVs invented anyway? He kept walking.

Approaching the front of the crowd, Lincoln's heart pounded faster. He put his hand over his heart and felt it skipping irregularly. Time must be running out.

Lincoln stumbled through the crowd, with his eyes feeling heavy, bumping into various people.

"Sorry," he managed to mutter as he nearly knocked over an older gentleman.

"Son, are you okay? I wondered where you wandered off to. I was looking for you." The man was the same man in the top hat and spectacles from earlier.

Lincoln froze.

"Patience, son. It's going to be okay. Here." The man handed him an envelope.

"Thank y..." Lincoln's voice faded. He rubbed his eyes. He felt a rush of fatigue.

He slipped the envelope into his front pocket.

His eyelids dropped.

Darkness.

Quiet.

Just the sound of his breath.

He waited.

Black.

Gray.

Light.

He was back at his locker. Mr. Hudson came into focus. Nothing had changed.

"Did you not hear me? I said get back to class."

Lincoln didn't move. He felt like he'd just run a marathon.

"Oh hi, Mr. Hudson. Lincoln." Principal Murphy nodded at each of them. "Shouldn't you both be in class?" Principal Murphy's tone was playful. Lincoln had never seen him yell before, though he wasn't hoping he ever would.

"Yes, that's exactly where we were going." Mr. Hudson shot Lincoln a threatening look.

Lincoln pretended like he didn't see. He let out a deep sigh.

As he walked to his first period math class, he felt the envelope in his pocket.

He knew he should go to class. Detention was waiting for him if he didn't.

He ducked into the boy's restroom. He swung the door of the first stall open-and-shut in one swoop.

He pulled out the notecard. *Car.*

This *had* to do with his dad's accident.

Dinner. Car.

He shoved the envelope in his pocket and ran to class.

JJ winked at him across the room as he snuck into his seat. He looked straight ahead.

"Thanks for showing up today, Mr. Peterson." Ms. Gardner, wearing a knee-length, pleated beige skirt with a red sweater, winked at him.

She adored Lincoln. His mom had leased her an apartment a few years ago. She'd moved to town after graduating with her teaching degree.

He appreciated the leniency. He sat up straight and smiled.

As Ms. Gardner continued about how they'd be covering simple interest calculations, his mind drifted. He replayed the events of the magical morning over and over.

What had happened? Was there something wrong with him? Was he drugged?

Tiny beads of sweat perspired across his forehead.

Could he tell anybody? Would anyone believe him?

Maybe this was all a dream?

"Okay, now here's the worksheet for today. You'll have the last fifteen minutes of class to complete it." Ms. Gardner passed out the worksheets to the first student in every row.

Lizzy turned around and handed the stack to him with a smile.

He nodded, took one, and passed the stack along.

He tried to pay attention to Ms. Gardner, but he couldn't hear a word she was saying. His mind was in another world.

"Hey, Lincoln."

He felt his desk jiggle.

"You're supposed to do the worksheet now," Lizzy whispered.

"Oh, thanks," he mumbled.

He scanned to evaluate the difficulty level. He hadn't been paying attention, but he understood. The sight of numbers snapped the cyclone of what-if thoughts. He breezed through the problems and turned in his worksheet before everyone else.

"Hey, Prez, you okay? You looked kinda sick during math today. And how come you were late? You're never late." Trent pulled at his bookbag strapped to his broad shoulders. He was growing so fast he needed a bigger one.

"Oh hey, Trent," he replied, disoriented and lightheaded.

"You wanna come to the batting cage before practice? Me and the guys are gonna go hit some balls since the eighth graders have the field first."

JJ slapped his locker shut. "Let's go, Prez, time to hit some baaawls!"

"Hey, man, you could have slammed my hand. That's my pitching hand even!"

"What? You're fine," JJ quipped.

"Whatever..." Lincoln lowered his voice. "I don't feel that great.... You guys go." He brushed the hair from his forehead, which was hot to the touch.

"Okay, feel better, man." Trent gave him a soft pat on the back. "Sorry about JJ."

"He's just being a dick. Why do you hang out with him so much?" Lincoln asked.

"I don't really—he always hangs around me," Trent said.

Lincoln turned around and closed his locker. "See ya tomorrow."

"Okay, yeah. And hope you feel better and..." Trent's voice faded.

He didn't hear the end of Trent's sentence. He was already around the corner.

"Hey, Lincoln."

The words startled him. He stopped just in time to avoid running into Lizzy Robinson. She had on a cropped denim jacket over a blue checked dress. Her fluffy bangs and gold hoop earrings framed her bright white smile.

"Hey, Lizzy. Sorry, didn't see you."

Usually that would have been the extent of their conversation. Lizzy hadn't really approached him since he'd been short with her at the funeral. He felt bad but hadn't apologized.

"It's okay." She paused and looked down. "Hey, is everything alright? I mean, you seemed a little flustered in math today."

"It was nothing." He started to walk away.

"I know it was somethin'." Lizzy jogged a few steps to catch up with him.

"Why do you care so much?"

"Sorry. Just thought you might want someone to talk to, that's all." She blushed and held his gaze.

"Well..." He stopped.

He didn't know Lizzy that well. Maybe he should give her a shot. She seemed gentle and safe. She had a cute little smile. The way she looked at him made the tiny hairs on the back of his neck stand up.

The longer he stood there, the more he wanted to blurt out his secret. Tell her about his mom. Tell her about his unexplainable adventures. The envelopes. All of it.

But he couldn't. His mouth wouldn't open.

"Okay...well maybe another time then...when you're ready. I'll be waiting." Lizzy winked.

• • • •

~LIZZY~

Her heart fluttered. She watched Lincoln's every step until he was out of sight. She couldn't believe he stopped for a minute to talk. He'd been such a zombie for the past year. She had gotten the message loud and clear to stay away, and she respected that and gave him his space. Maybe something happened over spring break and he was finally ready to open up?

"Hey, Lizzy."

The call echoed down the emptying hallway.

"Are you coming or not? We're about to start." Rachel, the Student Council president, stood with one stubby leg outside the classroom down the hall with her hand on her hip. She tried to compensate for her short height with her bossy attitude.

Lizzy jogged a few steps. "Yeah, coming."

Rachel had swooped Lizzy under her wing when Lizzy moved to the school the previous year. Lizzy had become part of the popular crowd whether she liked it or not.

"C'mon, Secretary, you gotta take notes," Rachel said to her as she took her seat at the circle of desks.

"Motion to start the meeting." Jeremy, the curly haired, comic book-obsessed vice president, said.

"Second." Lizzy raised her hand.

"Okay, first order of business. The spring dance is coming up and we have a small budget for snacks. Anybody have ideas?" Rachel twirled the stray hair not pulled back tight in her ponytail.

"What about some hummus and veggies?" Lizzy said.

"Ewww, we don't eat that kinda stuff here. You still haven't shed your big city stuck-up tastes." Rachel curled her nose and the rest of the council followed.

"Okay, it was just a suggestion to offer something healthy."

"We're kids. We don't need to worry about that stuff," Cindy, the treasurer and only child of the richest family in town, said.

"How about pizza?" Rachel raised her hand. "All in favor?"

Everyone in the room raised their hands.

She jotted down the vote, 5-1.

"Pizza it is!" Rachel said. "Okay, next order of business."

Rachel cornered her in the restroom after the meeting. "Hey, what was all that hummus stuff about? You gotta stop being so prissy and uptight if you wanna keep hanging out with us."

"Sure." She was exhausted of trying to keep up with what she was allowed to say or like.

"So is your mom still up your ass about that A- you got on the math test?" Rachel peered in the mirror, reapplying her lip gloss.

"Oh yeah..." Lizzy cringed. "Actually I didn't tell her. She'd ground me."

"Damn, look at you keeping secrets. I thought you were too good for that."

"I'm not too good. And don't even try to tell me you never kept a secret from your parents."

"Haha, yeah." Rachel zipped her makeup bag shut. "It was prolly a smart call. Just hope they don't find out." She walked out.

Alone, Lizzy sighed. She needed new friends. Maybe even a boyfriend. She pictured her and Lincoln at the end of school dance and smiled at her reflection in the mirror.

. . . .

~LINCOLN~

"Hey, Lincoln..."

He turned around to see who wanted him now. He just wanted to go home.

"Oh, hi." He stood straighter, realizing it was Principal Murphy.

"How are ya?" He put his hand lightly on Lincoln's shoulder, towering above him. Principal Murphy was an ex-Army Ranger. His tone was too chipper for Lincoln's state of mind and state of body to handle. His stomach flowed back and forth like a ship at sea.

"I'm okay."

"Don't you have baseball practice tonight?"

"Oh yeah. I do." Lincoln looked down. "I'm just not feeling that good. I need to get home and lie down."

"Oh, I'm sorry to hear that, sport. Hope you feel better, son. But I also want you to know you can talk to me if you want. I know it's been a year...since your dad passed." Principal Murphy paused and took his hand from Lincoln's shoulder. "But it's a new year...a chance at a fresh start. We just want to make sure you're still participating in your activities and keeping up with your friends..."

Lincoln didn't know what to say. On the one hand, what Principal Murphy said was true—and he desperately wanted someone to talk to and it was nice he remembered the anniversary. But on the other hand, this was his principal, his scary muscle-bound ex-Army principal. And then if he had a third hand, how dare he get involved with his social life, and who was "we"?

"I'm sorry if I overstepped. I just care about you. Okay?" Principal Murphy broke the silence, but Lincoln's eyes were still glazed over in thought. "Feel better, okay?"

Lincoln gave him a little nod so they could both go their separate ways.

• • • •

~DAN~

Principal Dan Murphy sighed and pushed the sleeves up on his white collared shirt, revealing his chiseled forearms and a sliver of a tattoo, as he watched Lincoln go. He'd held a fellow soldier's hand as he died in his arms and could bench press 300 pounds, but he still didn't feel strong enough to talk to a child who had lost a parent.

He'd risen to principal in only five years, but most parents didn't trust him. He'd started as a sixth-grade social studies teacher right after he returned from the Gulf War and was promoted to vice principal when Mr. Foster, who was so old he had his own stories to tell the kids of the Great Depression, retired. Most of the parents were older than Principal Murphy, making establishing his authority difficult, despite his charming good looks and physical prowess. This first year as principal had taken a toll.

When he returned to his office and sat down at his desk, he heard a loud *bang*.

• • • •

September 2, 1990

The explosion came from behind.

His body launched twenty feet in the air.

He landed in a pile of broken cement and rubble, inches from a lethal rebar pipe, wrapped in a cloud of thick smoke. The bar reached to the freedom of the bright blue sky.

Pain clenched and throbbed in his back and head.

He couldn't move.

A warm stream of blood trickled down the back of his neck and pooled onto his chest.

He saw himself as a little boy, his dad pushing him on the swing in their backyard, his tiny pudgy legs reaching for the same blue sky. This was it, he thought.

• • • •

He shook his head.

"Sorry about that, Mr. Murphy." He heard the voice of Linda, his secretary, near the printer. "I dropped the lid."

He put his elbows on the desk and held his hanging head. He rubbed his fingers over the scar on the back of his neck.

Chapter 4
Brushes with Failure

Lincoln burst through the back door and beelined to the dining room. He'd conjured a plan on the bus ride home.

He wedged himself behind the cherry wood hutch that held his mom's good china. He lifted an old, tattered blanket, revealing a dusty box of family pictures in the corner. There wasn't enough room to pull out the box, so he pushed with his shoulder and guided the heavy cabinet forward a few inches.

The box was among the few artifacts he managed to save when his mom cleansed the house of all visible memories of Dad for the auction.

Although the house was empty, Lincoln handled the box like a ticking bomb. If his mom caught him with something that reminded him of Dad, he was cooked meat.

He took a deep breath and shuffled through the photos. He stopped when he reached one of his five-year-old self. A mini-Lincoln and his tall, strapping dad stood on the dock overlooking their backyard creek. Lincoln had a fishing pole in one hand and a fourteen-inch channel catfish in the other. The smile plastered across his face paled in comparison to the one on his dad's.

His dad was always so proud of him and never ceased to show it. His dad had run inside to ask his mom to take the photograph. Lincoln's first catch, a moment his dad lived for. His dad made a big fuss over any of Lincoln's firsts—his first time riding a bike, his first baseball mitt, his first perfect score on a test. He probably made a big deal out of a bunch of firsts Lincoln was too young to remember, like his first word and first step.

He'd give anything to relive that Sunday afternoon.

Sliding the box aside, he sat Indian style on the floor. He fastened one hand on each side of the framed photo.

He extended his arms.

He closed his eyes.

He held his breath.

He wished with all his might.

He counted ten Mississippis.

Eyes open and...

The dining room. The picture in his sweaty hands. Nothing had changed.

"Dammit." He put the picture in his lap and slouched over, listening to his breath for a minute. What would his dad think if he gave up?

"No, this has to work." He gripped the picture so hard his arms shook. Tears bubbled up. He heard the thump of blood pulsing through his veins as his lungs froze.

He gasped. He couldn't hold his breath any longer. His arms went limp. The tears released.

A teardrop landed on the glass, right on his dad's chest.

Maybe if he couldn't see his dad, his dad could at least feel his pain?

He heard a rustle near the front door. The sound could have just been the big oak tree's branches swaying in the wind, but he hurried anyway. He put the picture back, covered the box, and whipped it behind the hutch.

He got his jacket and jogged to the creek. He sat on the dock and dangled his legs above the water, searching the muddy depths for fish. The water swirled and a couple of fish gills breached the surface. His dad might have gazed at one of these same fish. But not for long. The fish that were alive a year ago when Dad might have seen them would eventually be caught or die.

The things that overlapped with his dad's life were fading away. Each day there was less and less of him to feel connected to. Without the picture of his first catch, he might not have remembered the look of his dad's smile. The memory would always be there, but the aesthetics that amplified the emotion of the memory would have been lost. He couldn't believe his mother had been so careless with irreversible decisions.

He skipped a rock across the creek as the sunset approached. He daydreamed about the googly-eyed look Lizzy had given him after school. He wished he could talk to his dad about it. He'd never had a girl like him before and he didn't want to mess it up.

"Lincoln?"

He heard his mom shout from across the long yard.

"Lincoln, are you down there?"

She called again so he waved his hand at her, hoping she'd go inside and let him be.

"Okay, come inside now. It's getting dark and cold."

He moved like a rag doll; every movement zapped his energy. He trudged the long walk up the hill to the house. He was surprised to see her waiting when he arrived.

"How was your day, honey?"

"Fine." He slid past her, sucking it in even though he had plenty of space to pass.

• • • •

~DEB~

Fine.

The word popped the balloon of hope inside Deb's chest. As Lincoln brushed past her, she wanted to reach out, to give him a hug, to tell him everything was going to be okay, that she missed his dad just as much as he missed him, that the two of them could get through this together.

But she couldn't. She couldn't raise her hands. She couldn't say a word.

The day had been a tough one for her. The staging furniture hadn't arrived. The tree-trimmers had argued about their invoice. She had to pay them cash out-of-pocket to make up the difference. No offers at the Locust Bend open house. The pressure never ended. She never felt like she could breathe.

She was a slave to her sadness and the daily need to survive. Emptiness filled her. Happiness, peace, and love were things of the past. Lost. To be forgotten.

With vodka bottle in hand minutes after she arrived home, she'd strolled around the house, looking for a place to land. To sink into nothingness. She sat at the dining room table about to knock back two fingers from the bottle, when she saw a handprint in the dust on the floor. Edged right up against the molding.

She plunked the bottle down on the table and bent to her hands and knees. As she studied the handprint, she noticed a short trail in the dust; the hutch had been inched forward. She peered against the wall and spotted the box in the corner. Her adrenaline kicked in and she had no trouble pushing the hutch out in order to reach the box to uncover it.

Her heart spun at the sight of the pictures. His face. Lincoln as a baby. Lincoln as a boy. His face. Her face. Her smile. His smile. She flailed and covered the box.

What was she doing?

• • • •

~LINCOLN~

"This is a great extra room on the main floor that you could use for an office..."

He heard his mother's voice float up the stairwell, but his gaze remained glued to his Gameboy. The bed in the master bedroom was where he'd landed to pass the time. He hung his elbows over the front of the bed and the toes of his Converses punched into the pillows.

Another Saturday afternoon showing houses with his mother. He outright hated it at first, and they fought about it, but he learned to stay out of the way. Soon he looked forward to it as a time to retreat on his own, a time to be with his mom when she was halfway happy. But he would never tell her that.

"And here is the master bedroo—m." Deb stopped mid-sentence. She pulled the door shut. "Why don't I show you the other bedrooms first?" Her voice fluttered to an awkward high pitch.

The click of the shutting door snapped Lincoln out of his Gameboy trance. He jumped off the bed. He knew he was in deep trouble. Why hadn't he taken two seconds to take off his shoes?

He peeked around the corner of the master bedroom door. He watched his mother lead the young couple past a head-pop into the half bath and into another bedroom. This was his chance. He dashed across the hallway and pulled the door shut to the half bath.

"Let's take a look again at the master..."

Lincoln heard the group divert away from him.

"And that's all that's worth looking at up here.... Let's go back to the kitchen and look over some of the numbers...." He heard his mom's voice fade as the group departed the second floor.

He sat still, not knowing what to do.

"Lincoln, are you in there?" There was a tap on the door.

He froze at the sound.

"What did I tell you?" Her whisper remained low so not to alert the potential buyers, but her tone stung with outrage.

His glance drifted to the unlocked door. He reached up and pushed in the button. The little spring inside the door handle clicked.

"I thought so! Come out here!" He flinched at her hushed shouts.

He knew there was no sense in disobeying her further; it would only lead to more trouble and yelling. He gingered the door open and stood inside the bathroom, keeping distance between them.

"I can't believe it! I just can't believe it!" She tried to keep her voice only detectable to him. She shook her head, but her irate eyes remained steady, laser-focused on him. The vexed glare pinning him to the wall. "Look, I have to sell this house. Do you understand that? And I can't have you messing that up."

"I'm sorry." He bit his lip. He didn't know what else to say. He screwed up and felt terrible.

"Sorry? Is that all you can say!" Her eyes rolled into the back of her head.

He hesitated and remained silent.

Out of the corner of his eye, he saw a painting of a beach across the hall. He fixated on the picture, drowning out the lecture.

"I'm speaking to you, don't you hear?" She pointed at him, the gold bracelets on her arm clanged together.

He nodded on instinct, but nothing registered. He held his breath.

He focused on the picture. He would do anything to stand on that beach.

The sun. The sand. The water.

The scene flooded his mind.

Everything was quiet.

He only heard the hum of his heart.

The whistle of his lungs.

A rush of energy ran through him, like a ghost.

His eyelids drooped.

White.

Gray.

Then darkness.

He opened his eyes. His sight refocused.

He stood at the water's edge, with beach and ocean stretching as far as he could see. He was barefoot. The warm sand cushioned his toes. The light sea breeze misted his skin. He was so thankful he'd escaped—at least for the moment.

He skipped toward the water and ran into a wave. The force of the ocean plunged against his legs, a warm and tropical rush. He dove underneath the surface and through the clear blue-green water spotted a school of tiny fish in the distance. He waited for a moment to see if they would come closer, but their path veered back out to sea and he came up for air.

Refreshed, as the breeze kissed his wet skin, he took a seat on the warm sand. The tang of the salt water lingered on his lips. He watched the waves form and toss a wall of water with white edges before dissipating and retreating beneath the undertow. He'd never been to the ocean before; all he wanted to do was stay, but he felt his heart accelerating and a faint tingle in his toes.

With a sparkle of light from the sun's reflection, he noticed a small bottle floating at the water's edge. The next wave pushed the bottle past the foam tide and it stuck in the gooey, wet sand. He ran to snatch it before it washed back out to sea. There was something inside.

He smashed the glass against a log of driftwood stuck in the sludge. Shards dispersed upon impact, and he jumped back. He fished the envelope from the wet sand before it got soaked. He saw the same navy blue wax dove seal on the back and his heart lurched in mild pain. What did this mean?

He opened the envelope and pulled out a note. *Rain.*

He looked to the cloudless sky and put the envelope in his pocket. He gripped his tightening chest.

The sun faded.

His eyelids dropped.

He felt tired.

Darkness.

Then light.

He found himself back in front of his mother.

"I said I'm speaking to you!"

He blinked. He eked out a nod.

"Go wait for me in the car! I have to salvage what's left of this."

He slinked to the car. After he closed the door, he let the tears fall. He kept watch out the window for his mom so he knew when to stop. But for the moment—crying felt good.

• • • •

~DEB~

"I'm sorry to keep you waiting. Let's take a look at those numbers." She entered the kitchen with the best smile she could paint on. But after all her efforts, the perspective buyers decided they needed more time to sleep on it. She knew in her gut that the couple would not make an offer. They must have seen Lincoln on the bed or heard her scolding him.

Her previous track record of success didn't guarantee anything. To Deb, this was not just a job; it was the only thing keeping her going. Of course, she wanted to do better, and she needed the money, but she needed something where she would be held accountable. She needed others to know if she had gotten out of bed that day—she needed them to *care* if she'd gotten out of bed that day.

Standing alone in the foyer, the failure squeezed her throat. She'd lost the deal. She'd lost her son. She'd lost her husband. She'd lost herself.

She never thought she wanted kids. But kids meant everything to him. After he got his paramedics license, they moved out of the city to Brightonville, and started trying. She got pregnant quickly and she gave up her dreams of becoming a journalist. There were no important stories in Brightonville anyway.

While she loved Lincoln with every inch of her heart, there was always something she couldn't put her finger on. Motherhood didn't come natural to her for some reason. Like the universe knew her original wishes and there were no second chances.

. . . .

June 12, 1988

Oooowww!

Deb flipped the faucet off and looked at Beau, who put down the dish he was drying.

Lincoln came running into the house from the backyard. Blood streamed down his knee.

"Baby, what happened?" She bent down and extended her arms.

He ran past her and into the tall legs of Beau.

Beau craned over and embraced his crying son. "Hey, Link, that looks like it hurts. Can we take a look at it?"

Lincoln snuffled. "Okay." He pointed to the gash. His arm floating up and down with his heavy cries.

"What happened?" Beau asked.

"Well, I was climbing."

Lincoln's chest heaved in between the tears.

"In the tree."

Heave.

"And I stepped on a branch."

Heave.

"And it."

Heave.

"It snapped."

Heave.

"And it cut me."

Heave, heave.

"Oh my, that must have hurt a lot," Beau said.

Lincoln nodded, wiping tears and snot all over his forearm.

"Let's first take a deep breath."

Lincoln looked up and focused on Beau.

"That's good. In 2, 3, 4. Out 2, 3, 4."

She stood up and put her hand over her heart. She was crying inside—for the salve of her husband, for the hurt in her little boy's knee, and for the longing to be a part of it.

* * * *

"Why can't I do this?" She wept for a few minutes, then picked up her briefcase and locked up the house.

Walking out to the Oldsmobile, she saw Lincoln's head bob down, as she came into his view. The sight made her feel worse. Her own son—afraid of her.

She hopped in and glanced at Lincoln as she reached across her lap to fasten her seatbelt. She saw his red eyes and his blush, moist cheeks and felt as if she was looking in a mirror.

"I overreacted. I'm sorry for getting so angry with you, hon." The words seeped out of her unconscious. When she heard the audible sound of her own voice, her body clenched up with guilt. She lost control once the sobbing started.

* * * *

~LINCOLN~

Lincoln reached in the back seat, grabbed the tissue box, and offered it to his mom. This was the first time she'd cried in front of him. What had changed?

She looked up from crying, but his gesture only accelerated her tears. A new batch rained over her face. Taking the tissue, she took a deep breath in and blew out with such gusto that he jumped back a little.

"I'm sorry too. It was stupid to lay on the bed like that." He sniffled. The fountain of emotion splashing out of his mom saturated his pride.

She reached her hand and steadied herself on his shoulder. Her head hung over and her other hand pressed against her chest.

"Are you okay?" He worried, as her breaths shortened. The staccato punches of her exhales turned the atmosphere in the car sour. He grabbed her right hand and put his other hand on her back. "Sit up. Take a deep breath in."

He knew exactly what to say after watching his dad calm down random strangers all the time—when they were on vacation, when they were grocery shopping, or once when they were at his baseball game and a kid on the other team got hit in the head with a high fastball.

"Now, a deep breath out. In and out, nice and slow. I'm right here." He squeezed her hand. "You're doing great."

She squeezed his hand back.

"Thank you." She took a deep breath in. "You're just like..." She couldn't say it.

When they returned from the showing, Lincoln scurried to his room. He pulled out a bright orange Nike shoebox from his closet, removing a pair of old baseball cleats. He found the envelope from the first picture in his dresser drawer and dropped it, along with the second and third envelope, into the shoebox.

So far he had: *Dinner. Car. Rain.*

These were parts of that night he already knew. He wanted to know more about what his mom wouldn't talk about. He put the cover back on the box and shoved it under the bed.

He rolled onto his back on the floor and stared at the ceiling. He imagined the roof lifting up and seeing his dad floating in the clouds, looking down on him.

He wondered what his dad thought about the pictures, the envelopes. Did he know? Did he see Mom cry? Did he know what would happen next?

• • • •

~DEB~

As Deb dressed for bed, the telephone rang. She finished putting on her robe with the phone ringing and ringing, hoping the caller would hang up, but it kept ringing. She picked up the receiver.

"Who is this?" Her adolescent tone couldn't have sounded more annoyed.

"Deb?"

She recognized the voice on the other end of the line, Arletta.

"Arletta, why are you calling? It's late. I have nothing to say to you."

"Excuse me, I'm sorry. I should've known betta than to 'av expected a warm welcome."

She rolled her eyes. "You still haven't said why you're calling."

"I want Lincoln ta come ta church wit me tomorr-aw mornin.'"

"No. And I don't care how many times you ask. The answer is still going to be no." She slammed down the phone.

• • • •

~ARLETTA~

The shrill dial tone sang in Arletta's ear. She unclenched her fingers from the receiver, laid it to rest in the cradle, and took a deep breath.

For a moment, she pictured her shaky hand putting down the receiver that night, after hearing the worst news of her life, that her son had been in an accident.

She sighed and got up from the side of the bed and sauntered to the kitchen to take her insulin, humming under her breath. The rosary beads around her neck dangled from side-to-side as she shuffled on her swollen ankles.

As she passed through the living room, she stopped by the fireplace and scanned her collection of photographs on the mantel. She picked up the one of Beau and Deb on their wedding day. Her heart warmed, as she thought of Beau. He was always so happy. He was always making everyone feel comfortable. He took a real interest in those around him.

• • • •

September 30, 1989

"It's manageable," Beau said. He patted her knee and kept his eyes on the road. "People live with diabetes for a long time."

"If ya say so. I don know how I'm gonna keep up wit all da steps." She gazed out the window at the passing trees. The leaves were turning from green to orange. "Dr. Grayson talked so fast and I don know if I got it all."

"You'll get the hang of it. I'll help you," Beau said.

"You a good boy. Such a good boy." She smiled at him.

"Ya hungry?"

"I reckon I shuld."

Beau pulled the car into Mo's Diner. He dropped her off at the door.

From her booth, she watched as Beau spoke for a minute to the young kid—maybe thirteen or fourteen years old—hanging outside the door.

"I'm starving," Beau said as he slid across the leather bench.

"Once a growin' boy, always a growin' boy." She laughed.

When they were almost done with their meal, Beau looked outside to the parking lot. The young boy still there, bouncing an old tennis ball up and down on the sidewalk.

"Waiter." Beau motioned from across the room.

The waiter came by. "Add a burger and fries to go on the bill."

As they left the diner, Beau helped her into the car. "I'll be right back."

She watched, as he walked across the parking lot, finding the boy. She rolled down the window to hear.

"Lunch." Beau handed the boy the takeout box.

"Thanks." The pale-faced boy stared down, unable to look Beau in the eyes. He opened the container, took out a handful of fries, and gobbled them down.

"Why aren't you in school?"

The boy was quiet for a minute, wolfing down the food, but then stopped and looked into the distance. He saw her waiting in the car.

"I'm not gonna get you in trouble. I just wanna help." Beau leaned against the building.

The boy looked up and caught the welcoming gaze in Beau's eyes. "My dad...he got arrested yesterday...he's gonna be in jail for who know's how long this time.... I might not ever see him again...what's the point?"

Beau put his arm around the boy. "It's not your fault, son. I'm sorry about your dad, but he loves you, even if he isn't around. I'm a dad myself, and I know. I see quite a magnificent young man in front of me. Who is smart. Who knows he oughta go back to school." Beau winked and picked a fry out of the box.

"Thanks." The boy smiled back, and Beau trotted across the parking lot.

• • • •

Arletta sighed, exhaling the memories.

She studied Deb's face from the wedding photo. She put her finger on the glass right over Deb, hoping that somehow she could touch her heart and make it warm again, make it so she'd smile like the way she was smiling in the photo, the way she used to smile when Beau was around.

Chapter 5
The Art of War

~LINCOLN~

The Jefferson Junior High Art Show was not an event that Lincoln desired to attend, but this year was different. Last year as a sixth grader, he was new to junior high, had no artistic talent, and didn't enter. But as a seventh grader, Lizzy Robinson had a painting and a piece of pottery on display, so he submitted his drawing of the Chicago Cubs logo under the category "graphite sketching."

He noticed the soft vapor of his breath in the night air as he and his mom walked up the sidewalk. There was something special about going to the school building at night. Parents and teachers mingled, while the kids relished in the rare unsupervised moments when all the adults were distracted with each other.

He listened to the singular clicking of his mother's heels. He missed the melody. How his parents had walked in perfect step. The blend of dainty heel and rubber sole, like treble and bass. He wished he could walk in his father's footsteps. To give her what she needed.

But tonight he was focused on Lizzy.

· · · ·

~DEB~

"Why don't you show me your drawing?" she asked Lincoln, as they walked through the double doors of the school.

Plaster masks and paintings hung on the walls. Black-clothed tables lined the hallways displaying glazed pottery and beaded dreamcatchers. Judges walked around taking notes on their clipboards.

Lincoln pushed into the crowd.

She reached her arm out to grasp him, but he eluded her dancing fingertips. She tugged at the handbag on her shoulder as she sighed and tried to ward off the pang of rejection.

"Hello, Mrs. Peterson."

Although startled, she welcomed the warm voice. She turned. Principal Murphy stood towering over her. His stature reminded her of him.

"Oh please, call me Deb." She wanted to be friendly, but she also couldn't bear hearing the 'Mrs.' part of her name. The salutation like a dagger, reminding her of what no longer was.

"I'm so sorry...I didn't...I just thought..." Principal Murphy fumbled his words as she detected the red hue painting his cheeks.

"It's okay." She felt bad for him; he was trying to be nice.

She stared, unable to make eye contact. His tie, fastened with a tiny American flag pin, sloped off his strong chest, dangling in space a few centimeters from his torso. Something deep inside her ignited.

• • • •

~DAN~

He gulped hard. They stood in silence. He'd always wanted to talk to Deb, but she hadn't been at school much in the past year. Here was his chance, and he was blowing it.

"I'm so happy Lincoln entered the show this year." He broke the awkward silence in his high-pitched rehearsed voice, one he used to strike up conversations with parents he didn't know. He smiled, lamenting his regression, and caught Deb's eye. He could tell she agreed his tone was ill-timed.

"Yes, I was surprised he wanted to. He's much more interested in sports than art." The half-smile held on Deb's face.

"I was the same way when I was a kid." His cheeks still glowing.

Another silence.

He watched her fidget with her handbag. Time to pull out the big guns.

"I know it might not be my place. And I know I already got off on the wrong foot...but...Lincoln's a very special kid—smart and cares about his classmates. You should be really proud of him."

"Thanks." Deb blushed and tipped her head to the side.

"So I wanted to tell you about last week."

"Oh?" The smile dropped from her face.

"I don't want to worry you or anything. It's probably nothing."

"Well, what is it?" Her eyes widened.

"I found him in the hall. It was after the bell—"

"Oh, Principal Murphy, hello! I wanted to talk to you about my daughter." A parent wedged between him and Deb.

He bobbed his head to the side to find her.

"Deb, I'm so sorry. I'll catch up with you later. It was nice talking to you." He gave her a little wave, as the intruding parent corralled him across the hall. He should have known better than to try and approach her at a school event.

· · · ·

~LINCOLN~

"That's really good." He came up behind Lizzy and pointed at her painting. She had depicted a momma swan and three baby swans swimming behind in a perfect triangle on a lake that looked as still as glass, the water a thirsty blue.

"Oh, hi, Lincoln. I didn't know you were coming tonight. Did you enter something in the show?"

His eyes darted from her picture to her smile. He wasn't prepared for the beach ball of energy that she'd tossed him, but he caught it and played back to her.

"I did, but it's not any good. I just wanted to come see your stuff." His smile rolled up the right side of his face and squinted his eye. He caught himself in the moment, realizing he hadn't smiled like that in a long time. "I mean, I wanted to come see you."

"That's so sweet." Lizzy grinned. "Hey, why don't we go look at your entry?" She snatched his hand and pulled him down the hallway.

"I haven't seen it yet; I'm not sure where it is." He savored the warmth of her hand in his.

"What medium is it?"

"What?" He curled his nose.

"I mean, what kind of piece is it? A painting? Pottery?"

"Oh, it's just a drawing—that I did in pencil. Like I said, it's not any good."

"Okay, the graphite section is over here." She led the way. The little tug on his hand sent a shock through him. "Oh look, they started putting the ribbons up. Oh my gosh, look! You won third place!"

He couldn't believe his eyes—there was a tiny yellow ribbon hanging on his sketch.

"I could always tell you were a good drawer. I know you're always doodling during class. This time you finally put that to good use!" She laughed and leaned into him.

He caught her shoulder and smirked. "It's all Mr. Hudson's fault. His lessons are so boring. He just reads from the book. I already read the book, so there's nothing interesting to pay attention to."

"You gotta be careful with Mr. Hudson. He's always looking for someone to send to detention. It's like he's got a bug up his ass."

He chuckled at Lizzy's confident use of a swear word and nodded.

* * * *

~DEB~

Deb wandered the halls, studying the little name tag under each piece of art, trying to locate her son's project. She stopped at one painting that she thought was particularly well done for a junior high student. The watercolor was a vase of flowers and looked so lifelike, but yet like a dream. She lost herself in the wonder until she couldn't help but overhear two parents behind her having a very in-depth conversation in a hushed yell.

"I can't believe you even made us come here tonight, Ryan. This is exactly the kind of distraction that's going to keep her from getting into an Ivy League school. Math and science are so much more important, especially if she's going to go to medical school."

The harsh tone stung Deb's heart.

"Elizabeth, stop. This is not the time for this. We are here. Let's just have a good time. Lizzy knows this is just for fun and that she has to keep getting good grades in all subjects."

"Fun? How can you be so blasé? This is her future."

The male voice lowered his tone. "Ever since your mom died, you've been a bitch—to Lizzy and to me."

A pause.

"I'm sorry, I'm sorry." The male voice whispered. "That was unfair."

Deb swallowed hard and peeked a glance over her shoulder at the arguing couple. They'd never fought like that. Sure, they had disagreements, but they worked through them, with respect and in private.

Lizzy. She searched her memory banks. She'd never heard that name before. Maybe she was in another grade? She felt for her and at the same time thought about Lincoln. At least she didn't force him to do things he didn't want to do.

Sighing, she turned down the hall, spotting Lincoln. He was with a girl and they were giggling and pointing at a ribbon on the wall. Deb snaked herself through the stagnant crowd who paid more attention to the artwork than passersby.

"Is that yours?" she asked Lincoln, as she glanced at the third-place pencil sketch. She didn't know sports but recognized the Chicago logo from where she'd grown up. How nice that he'd remembered a little fact like that.

· · · ·

~LINCOLN~

"Yeah."

He didn't know what else to say; he felt trapped. His dad had always told him to fall back on his manners whenever he wasn't sure what to do. "Lizzy, this is my mom. And this is Lizzy."

Deb smiled and shook Lizzy's hand. "It's so nice to meet you."

"Yes, nice to meet you too. Did you see Lincoln won third place?"

He felt Lizzy tug on his shirt sleeve. He loved the spotlight she put him in, but at the same time he wanted to look humble.

"Oh, that's wonderful." His mom leaned in and studied the sketch. She looked back at him. "I didn't know you could draw like that."

He looked down and shook his head. "I draw all the time. And I only got third place." He popped his head up and placed his hand on the small of Lizzy's back. "Lizzy's the real artist."

"Oh? Why don't we go have a look at her stuff?" Deb suggested.

"Really?" Lizzy said. He loved the way her eyes perked up.

"Of course. Lead the way." His mom gestured.

"Look!" He ran up ahead. "You got first place!"

He pointed at a ceramic bowl, weaved with multiple layers that fanned out like rose petals.

"Oh my." Lizzy gasped and covered her mouth.

"It's so good!" He looked her right in the eye.

"Lizzy, what a magnificent bowl. I would love to have this on my dining room table as a centerpiece. You really have a natural talent." His mom bent over to whisper into Lizzy's ear.

He watched as jealousy gripped his throat. He wanted to lash out, but he couldn't move.

His mom winked at Lizzy and stood back up.

"Thank you." Lizzy smiled back.

"What did you say?" he clamored.

"Oh, nothing," his mom said.

He raised his eyebrows and turned his back to his mom.

"Why don't we look at some other pieces?" he suggested, taking Lizzy's hand.

"Sure." Lizzy obliged.

He waited until there was enough people and noise between him and his mom before asking, "What did she say?"

"Oh...," Lizzy said.

He could tell he'd made her uncomfortable. "I'm sorry." He looked down and got quiet.

"Hey." Lizzy settled her hand on his shoulder. "It was nothing—she just complimented me."

"What's the big deal then—why the secret whisper?"

"I think she was trying to be respectful. She must have run into my parents. My mom is not happy I'm here. She'd rather me be studying for the honor's algebra test I have next week. My dad and her fight about it all the time, ever since my grandma died. Your mom just said that even if my mom's not proud of me, she was."

"Wow..." He took a step back and squeezed his hands into tight fists. He shook his head and took a deep breath. "I'm sorry, I'm just surprised."

Lizzy looked back at him with soothing eyes. He was so impressed by her, never fazed by anything. He released his fists.

"She's proud of you too."

"What?" He stood up straight.

"I know what you're searching for. It's okay. She loves you. She's probably just having a hard time—you know, with your dad and everything..." Lizzy faded off but kept her soft eyes locked on him.

He didn't know what to say. She had said it all.

· · · ·

~DAN~

"Just who I was looking for." He offered Deb a glass of champagne. "Don't worry, it's in the teacher's lounge, off limits to students. But for special guests..." He beamed his incandescent white teeth and waited for her to take the glass.

"Oh, no thank you." Deb half-fluttered her fingers.

"Please, I insist. Have a few sips while we talk?"

"Okay, I guess for a minute. But you know the people in this town, how they talk." Deb accepted the champagne flute.

He nodded but couldn't take his eyes off the way she wrapped her delicate fingers around the stem of the glass.

"So, what was it you were saying about Lincoln?"

"Oh." He stumbled out of his stupor. "I know things have been really hard for him...and for you.... I'm just so happy to see him so lively tonight. I was getting a little worried about him."

Deb handed him the glass back. "Thank you for the concern. If you'll excuse me."

He held the returned flute in front of him, motionless and speechless, as he stood alone watching her walk away.

· · · ·

~DEB~

The nerve of the principal to try to parent her child *and* to hit on her. How unprofessional. She scoured the crowd.

"Oh, there you are honey. It's time to go." She gave Lincoln *the look*.

"Bye, Lizzy." Deb smiled and gave a little wave to her.

"Okay, see you tomorrow, Lizzy. And congrats again," Lincoln said.

She was pleased Lincoln obeyed her without protest.

"I'm not feeling so great. Can I go to the bathroom real quick?" Lincoln said, as he scrunched his forehead.

She noticed tiny beads of sweat seeping down from his hair line and next to his ear. "Okay. You sure you want to go now? You don't look so good, honey. Why don't we get you home so you can lay down?" She wiped his brow with a tissue she'd pulled out of her purse.

"It's okay. I want to go now." He left without allowing any more discussion.

· · · ·

~LINCOLN~

Lincoln darted down the empty hall. He passed the bathroom and went straight for the library. Inside, the room was dark except for the emergency exit lights. He'd never been in the library alone, especially at night, and felt a twinge of danger.

He walked up to the painting on the back wall of George Washington leading the Continental Army across the Delaware River. Washington had such a confident look on his face. He sensed fear in the soldiers' eyes but at the same time faith in their leader. Lincoln felt the same concoction of fear and faith. He wanted nothing more than to escape this night and be in that boat.

He fixated on the picture and drew in a large breath of air.

His eyelids dropped.

Gray faded to black.

Silence.

Only his heart beating.

His breath releasing.

The atmosphere fizzled.

The sun split through the fog. He sat in the boat, an oar in hand.

He looked down at his body—he was older and stronger and dressed in a blue coat, white vest, and tan breeches with a tricorne hat. Despite the heavy uniform, every inch of his body shivered. He let go of the oar and jammed his hands into his pockets. He felt an envelope. He slipped it out—there it was, the same blue dove seal. The card said *Dark*. He tried to remember the string of clues, but was startled.

"You there." He heard a commanding yet soft-spoken voice behind him. As he turned to look, it was the anchorman. "Keep rowing."

He slid the envelope into his pocket and gripped the oar, dipping it deep into the water. He pulled back, amazed at the strength he possessed, rowing in sync shoulder-to-shoulder with the other soldiers. The heavy boat full of supplies rocked side-to-side as it bounced through the treacherous waters. Splashes of icy cold water cascaded over the edge and into his lap. He shivered.

"Get ready, men, this is our best shot." Washington pointed ahead.

"This is going to be brilliant."

He heard a whisper between the two soldiers rowing in front of him.

"Yes, the Hessians haven't the faintest idea that we are coming from the west and on Christmas!"

"If all goes well, this will be a very Merry Christmas, indeed." The other solider winked back.

Lincoln's jaw dropped—they were headed into a surprise attack. A warm trickle ran down his leg. "Shit!" He reached down.

"Quiet!" Washington snapped.

He breathed—in and out, in and out.

All eyes were on him. His heart pounded faster and faster, the pain growing in his chest.

He wished with all his heart to be back at the library and closed his eyes, hoping that would transport him back. It didn't.

He sat in the boat, headed into war. In the distance a cannon fired and he saw a flash of the explosion.

Then, the weight of fatigue pulled at his insides.

His body unclenched.

The light of day faded.

Darkness turned to black.

Heat returned to his limbs.

He was back in the library. Patting his pocket, his fingers brushed over the wax seal as he shuffled down the hallway.

"Everything okay?" His mom asked.

"Yeah." He didn't know what else to say. He was upset from her telling secrets to Lizzy and his heart hadn't slowed to a resting pace after all the excitement on the Delaware.

"I was getting worried."

He gave a small nod. "Nothing to worry about." Did she really worry about him? How could he trust her?

"Okay. Let's go home then, Mr. Third Place Artiste." His mom smiled and wrapped her arm around his shoulder.

He laughed, despite his best efforts not to.

Chapter 6
Starving for Connection

~DEB~

As Deb glided up the three shallow steps to the Radisson entrance, the image of Principal Murphy handing her champagne with a boyish smile hung in her subconscious. Inside the bustling lobby she looked for signs of the networking conference.

She never thought she'd be so desperate for business. Driving two hours for some leads. These events made her tongue crawl to the back of her throat, but she painted on a happy face and blended in without suspicion, volleying empty small talk in exchange for a few business cards. Not many were interested in buying a house. It was a builder's market. Everyone wanted land to build their dream home.

On the way out, she stopped at the end of the long front desk. She put her purse on the marble countertop and searched for her keys.

"Excuse me, ma'am, are you and your husband checking in?" A bellman approached.

She pulled her purse against her chest, one hand deep inside.

"I'm sorry, no." She shook her head and looked down, her cheeks on fire.

The bellman stood silent.

"My husband died." The words rolled off her tongue, tasteless. There was an eeriness of ease. A simple fact.

The bellman paused. "Oh, I'm so sorry. How did he die?"

Her head snapped up. "Excuse me?" She flavored the words with heavy spice. Why would anyone, especially a stranger, have the right to ask how he died? What did it matter? Would knowing a cursory piece of information make his blundering line of questioning any more empathetic? Somehow forge a connection between two strangers that would make her feel better? No, never in a million years.

"I'm sorry." The bellman walked away.

She watched him with envy. Wouldn't it be nice to say sorry and move on?

· · · ·

~LINCOLN~

He had the house to himself since his mom was at the conference. He needed the space. He still didn't know how to handle the betrayal he felt with her whispers to Lizzy at the art show.

Time to think about Dad. He scrummaged through his dad's toolbox in the garage. Since the tools had a practical purpose, in case of a leaky faucet or tightening the electric outlet cover he'd bumped too hard while rough-housing with his friends, the toolbox wasn't sold at the auction.

He snatched the hammer, pulled it up to his heart, and rocked it like an infant. Having something to hold facilitated connection. He imagined his dad gripping the handle. Maybe someday he'd be able to pass the tools on to his own children.

He placed the hammer back with its family of other tools. He closed the lid and held his hand over the latch.

The quiet and emptiness of the garage subdued him. As he scanned the walls, his eyes stopped at his dad's poster of the Beatles' *Abbey Road* album—wouldn't that be cool, to meet the Beatles?

He put his feet shoulder width apart, square in front of the poster.

Breathe in.

Hold.

Breathe out.

His blinking slowed until his eyelids stuck together.

Gray, then black.

Softness in the silence.

Then the sun.

The cold cement of the garage floor changed to thick white stripes over steaming blacktop. He dodged to his left. The four of them headed right toward him. He was impeding their progress—or pro-gress as the British might say.

"Pardon me," said Paul McCartney.

"I'm sorry." Lincoln gulped, hoping to mask his boyish giddiness. His dad had told him all about the Beatles.

"Okay, let's shoot it again," he heard an accented voice cry out.

"Hey, son, could you please stand off to the side? We're trying to take a photograph."

He saw the man holding the camera and heeded his advice to move aside. Sitting down on the curb, he looked down and took note of his apparel. He wore plaid bell bottom pants and a tight, tucked-in denim collared shirt. In the front shirt pocket, he sensed another envelope.

He pulled out the notecard and read, *Eyes.*

Hmmm. What could this be? He put the envelope back into his pocket. His chest began pounding. Louder. Harder. He winced as a myriad of high-pitched shrieks emerged from the assembling crowd, as teenage girls swooned over the four young men strolling down the crosswalk.

"Why don't you sing something for us?" a voice in the crowd called out.

The four of them exchanged glances and made their way to the crowd. They hummed a chord and sang a cappella "All You Need Is Love."

The song normally would have calmed him, but his chest heaved. He closed his eyes, hoping for a safe return.

The song faded.

He held his breath.

Waiting.

Everything dark.

And then his eyes lifted.

He crouched in the garage in front of the poster, his chest slowly resuscitating.

Scrrreetch. The garage door folded and rose one section at a time. The grill of the Oldsmobile greeted him within a few inches.

"Mom? You're home already?"

"Oh my, I had no idea you were down there. You could have been hurt!" She gathered her briefcase from the front seat.

"I'm sorry." He slid the toolbox with his foot behind some other boxes on the floor and ran inside.

• • • •

~DEB~

She stood still, a blank stare stamped on her face, as she watched her son try to hide the toolbox and run away.

She'd skipped the social hour. All her posturing had been left in the main ballroom. She needed to be home. She needed to be alone.

Plopping her briefcase on the kitchen table took the load off her shoulder, but not the load off her mind. The cabinet sink door taunted her. She bent down and fished out her vodka. She took a gulp while kneeling on the floor. The liquid burned. She exhaled as she retreated to the living room, before she took another swig—and then another...

· · · ·

July 3, 1984

Beau's smooth, naked body cooled her clammy skin.

She'd wiggled around all night; the humidity and the kicks in her belly kept her up.

The rain pitter-pattered the leaves of the big oak tree in the backyard. The sun peaked through the clouds. A fresh morning breeze sifted through the screen of the cracked window.

"There must be a rainbow somewhere," Beau said, as he leaned over and kissed her belly.

She slid her hand next to him and he interlocked his fingers.

As he squeezed her hand, he whispered, "You are going to be the best mother."

· · · ·

She felt coarse yarn brush her cheek. Her eyes peeled back a smidge, enough to see Lincoln for a split second, then she closed them. He had covered her with his grandmother Helen's crotched blanket. She felt warm all over. After his back turned, she watched him tiptoe toward the stairs. He stopped and turned around after the first step, watching her rest.

The crisp sunrise burst through the windows and painted bright lines across the interior of the living room. She squinted as a ray of light welcomed her to a new day—and a pulsing headache. She moaned and scolded herself for overdrinking and falling asleep on the couch. As she pulled the heavy crocheted blanket aside and folded it, she longed for more caring moments from her son. Or anyone.

She trudged up the stairs to force herself into another day.

In the shower, the warm water sprayed against her back like a therapeutic massage. She wished she could stand there all day. She wished that he would walk in and start humming and brushing his teeth. He used to make even the mundane things in life seem a little bit more fun. With the water and hot steam all around her, she took a deep breath in, and tears rained down on the exhale. Something about the calming sound of the cascading water and the cleansing goal of a shower always made it a place she felt permission to cry, with no judgment to let it all go—plus Lincoln couldn't hear.

The droplets traced dribbly paths through the fog-steamed mirror before Deb wiped them away. What appeared in the blurry oval of glass was more than she could bear. Her pale, moist flesh amassed into the outline of her middle body. She brushed the tips of the fingers on her right hand on her shoulder and palmed her breast with her left hand. A cup she now had to hold. But her touch blunted in comparison with... She couldn't even say his name. The agonizing absence of his strong weathered hands. The physical connection no more.

Leaning closer to the ever-clearing mirror, her face coming into view, she ran her finger across the scar on her forehead. Her prodding produced little pain.

Bash it.

She swallowed the idea and stepped back from the mirror. More of her body was visible as the steam crept down toward the sink. She took her right nipple and twisted it as hard as she could. The message traveled through her body as expected, but she still felt empty. Would she ever melt into weightlessness or surrender into safety again?

She heard the doorbell as she rubbed the towel across her back.

"Lincoln? Lincoln, can you get the door?"

"I got it!"

"Why hello dere!" She heard Arletta's voice winding up the stairs.

"Grandma Arletta!" She heard Lincoln cry.

"Lincoln, who is it?" She called from the top of the stairs. She knew, but she wanted to pretend it wasn't true. She reached the bottom and saw Arletta, a fresh bouquet of flowers in hand.

"What do you want?" Deb's eyebrows turned down toward her nose and her cheeks flashed from pale to rouge.

"I've just come ta visit my grand-baby, the only blood relative I 'av left. Dat too much ta ask?"

"Are you ever gonna stop laying all that guilt on me? Do you think that's healthy? How am I supposed to be a good mother for Lincoln if you're constantly reminding me that he's not around?... Huh?... Answer me." She put her hand on her hip.

"Child, I think dat accident scrambled a few ah ya screws in ya brain up dere. I haven't the slightest idea what ya are talkin' 'bout, but what I do know is I wanna spend time with my grand-baby."

"He's got to get to school. You know it's a school day. Why would you come this morning of all mornings?"

"I'm sorry, dear. I was just missin' him." Arletta handed Lincoln the flowers. "Here, go find you a vase and put deese in some water."

Lincoln scampered away to find a vase in the kitchen.

"Not today." Deb started to close the front door.

"Why're ya makin' this so difficult?" Areletta frowned.

"Listen, I'm sorry that you miss him, but it's a school day. You call next time, and we can arrange a visit. Okay?"

Arletta nodded and stepped backward off the stoop and headed down the sidewalk to the driveway.

Deb watched as Arletta struggled to pull the heavy door shut. The car crept down the driveway, the gravel crunching under the slow-moving tires. She felt Lincoln come up behind her.

"Another day, okay?" She looked at him. "Go get ready for school." She brushed the hair away from his forehead. She was glad Arletta was gone. She didn't have the energy.

• • • •

~LINCOLN~

He slouched and went to get ready for school. He loved spending time with his grandmas and wished his mom would let them visit more.

He saw a lot of Arletta when his dad was alive. Arletta lived alone after Grandpa Peterson passed away from heart disease when he was a toddler, so Dad made it a point to visit her every week for Sunday lunch after church and brought him along.

His mom rarely came. He never wondered why his mother didn't come back then, but now he wished he knew because maybe he could construe some type of argument that would convince her that Arletta was fun to spend time with. Plus, she reminded him of his dad.

On his mom's side of the family, he didn't know his Grandma Helen very well. Helen's husband left her and they divorced before he was born so he had never met his grandpa on his mother's side either. The few times he and Grandma Helen had spent time together stuck out in his memory. The most recent occasion, at the funeral.

• • • •

April 14, 1995

"You're a brave little soldier." Grandma Helen pinched his cheek.

Lincoln turned away. His face burned.

"Oh, I'm sorry. Let's try that again." She dug out her hanky and wiped his cheek, as if she were erasing the pinch. "There, all gone." She laughed gently as if she were amusing herself.

He smiled back.

"I know you loved your dad very much."

He nodded and his palms turned sweaty.

"This is such a grave loss and so much to put on a young man's shoulders." She took a deep, hollowing breath as her lungs sounded clogged. "But I want you to know, you don't have to put it all on your shoulders. It's okay to feel sad and cry."

She pulled him in closer so she could whisper. "Your mom is strong and she's going to get through this, but this is going to be hard on her. And you are going to have to watch her go through it. But don't ever think that any of this is your fault or that you have to take care of her. You have a right to your own grief, whatever that might look like."

She paused and raised the hanky up to her eyes, poking at the budding tears. "I know she doesn't let me see you that much, but know that I'm always thinking about you and praying for you. And that I'll always be here for you. I love you." She planted a soft kiss on his forehead.

"Hey Prez, over here!" Lincoln detected Trent's muffled request above the roar of gossip and petty chatter circling the cafeteria.

He saw Trent with a group of his friends and hurried over to join.

"So how's the lady friend?" JJ asked in a high-pitched feminine voice.

He glared at JJ and looked down at the brown paper bag in front of him. "What?"

"C'mon, Prez, don't be stupid. We all saw you and Lizzy Robinson at the art show." JJ nudged Trent, seeking approval. "Yeah, did you guys do any K-I-S-S-I-N-G?" JJ sung the annoying tune.

Lincoln unwrapped his peanut butter sandwich and positioned a hand on each side, ready to devour it.

"You did kiss her, didn't you?" Trent assumed.

"Hey, put 'er here," JJ reached out to give him a high-five.

He dropped his sandwich and swatted JJ's hand away.

"Guys, I didn't kiss her. Can we please just eat?" He picked up his peanut butter sandwich again. He took a giant bite and washed it down with a big chug of chocolate milk.

"I dare you to go over there and ask her out." JJ raised his eyebrows, as if he was using them to point across the cafeteria at Lizzy.

Lincoln rolled his eyes and groaned.

"Hey look! She just sat down." JJ pointed to the table across the lunchroom.

Lincoln spotted Lizzy across the way. The sight of her made him feel all warm inside. Lizzy smiled back at him—and the smile was enough. He got up and walked to her table. He giggled on the inside—his friends underestimated him.

"Hey," he said.

"Hey." All of Lizzy's Student Council friends stared at her as she replied.

"You look nice today."

"Oh, thanks." Lizzy blushed and tucked a free-flying strand of hair behind her ear.

"So what are you doing after school?"

Lizzy remained silent. She turned her attention away from him and scanned the looks on her friends' faces.

"Wanna come over after school? We can study for tomorrow's science test."

"Okay—yeah, probably." Lizzy sat up in her chair. "Let me check with my mom after school."

He tipped his head and walked away as he heard Lizzy's friends snickering. He didn't look back; he could read the looks on his friends' faces ahead of him, indicating he had made the right moves.

He sat down next to Trent.

Trent leaned back and whispered to Lincoln. "Hey, man, that was pretty bomb."

"Thanks." He took the last bite of his peanut butter sandwich.

As the bell rang at the end of the lunch period, Trent grabbed his arm. "Hey, man, can I talk to you for a minute?" Trent waited for everyone else at the table to get up.

"Sure, man, what's up?"

"I think something's wrong with JJ. He won't give me any space." Trent quieted, as he gazed across the cafeteria.

He followed Trent's gaze and saw JJ.

JJ flipped them off and stomped away.

"Dude, I'm sorry. That's not cool," Lincoln said.

"It doesn't make any sense either. Every minute of the day he wants to be hanging out with me, and then the one second I want to talk to you alone, he flips me off? It's weird." Trent shrugged.

"I mean, didn't his parents just get divorced?"

"Uh, I don't know. He doesn't talk about that kind of stuff with me." Trent scratched his head.

"I think they did. I'm sure that's pretty hard."

"Yeah. Well, I'll just see how things go and maybe cut him a little bit of slack."

"Yeah, sounds like a good plan."

"Thanks, Prez." Trent slapped his back.

"No problem, man."

• • • •

~LIZZY~

"Are you seriously gonna go out with Lincoln Peterson?" Rachel asked. She crunched her last potato chip and crumbled the bag.

Lizzy twisted her thermos shut. "Yeah, why not?" She was so tired of all the judgment.

"I mean, he's damaged goods. He's been a little weird since his dad died." Rachel flipped her arm up, inviting the other girls to nod.

"He's no more damaged than anyone else. You're only eating potato chips for lunch."

"Let's go, girls." Rachel swirled around in her chair and the other girls paraded behind her.

Their loss, Lizzy thought to herself as she couldn't wait to see Lincoln after school.

• • • •

~DEB~

Deb snatched the phone up and punched at the keypad.

"Can you believe she had the nerve to just show up unannounced and expect to see him? It drives me crazy! And she *has* to remind me at every turn that Lincoln's her only blood relative. I don't know how she handles grief, but I'd prefer not to bring up his absence over and over again—it hurts—and—and I don't know what to do about it..." Her voice trailed off.

"Honey? Take a deep breath."

She heard Helen's soothing voice on the other end of the line. That's what she'd called for anyway, to unload her anger and be tamed.

"Everyone has their own way. She's just as upset as you. You can't hold that against her, now, can you?"

Helen's soft questions grated at her because she knew she was right. "I'm sorry, I just can't forgive her right now for how she's making me feel. What kind of person goes around trying to make a grieving widow feel guilty? I just don't understand and I don't care to find out. I don't want her around Lincoln."

"Do you think that's what Lincoln wants?"

"Right now, that's what's best for both of us." She slammed down the phone, hanging up on her own mother. There was a limit to how many questions Deb could handle. She had enough doubt about her parenting that any hint from someone else that she wasn't doing it right completely shut her down.

. . . .

~HELEN~

Helen dropped the receiver at her side and stared into space with an empty gaze.

Her daughter had never appreciated her or returned her love.

But she gave Deb a chance *every* time, thinking the next time would be different. She'd always answer her daughter's call or come to her aid when she was in need, even if Deb pushed her away, because that was what being a good mother meant to her. She couldn't help that Deb had been born an independent spirit.

She took a deep breath and leaned over to pick up her crotchet needle and proceeded to weave the yarn loop by loop. The rhythm predictable.

Chapter 7

Disparities of Love

~LINCOLN~

Lincoln barged through the door, sweaty and smelly after baseball practice, and raced to the shower. While usually he'd shower in the locker room with the team, he was too nervous he might miss Lizzy.

After he dressed, he pulled the aftershave from the top shelf of the medicine cabinet. The bottle was a gift from his dad at the last Christmas before he died. His dad said the scent would help him "be a man." Lincoln still wasn't sure what it meant to be a man and he wished his dad was still around to fill him in. He rationed and savored each spicy drop as he dabbed the cooling liquid on his skin.

As he waited, he busied himself with his Game Boy. He sat on the edge of his bed tapping his foot on the floor. When the doorbell rang, he dropped the game and hurried to the door.

"Hey," Lizzy said.

He was silent for a moment as he ushered her inside. She hugged her science book against her pale pink T-shirt. He took a deep breath, getting a whiff of the aftershave, which infused him with masculinity and confidence.

"Did you want something to drink?"

"No, I'm fine." She wandered over to the window. "You have a big backyard. Do you ever go down to the creek?"

"Oh yeah, all the time. You wanna go check it out?" He tried to seem calm, but his insides pleaded.

"Umm, we should probably do our homework first?" She twisted her legs around each other.

"It's gonna be dark soon, so we should go now."

He took the lead and didn't look back. He guided Lizzy down to the creek. She didn't protest.

The sun approached the horizon, and its yellow hue shifted to a deep orange. The leaves on the surrounding trees rustled as the wind picked up.

"You cold?" He stopped at the top of the hill before the dip in the field leading to the creek.

"I'm okay." Lizzy shivered.

"Here." He took off his hoodie and wrapped it around her shoulders.

"Thanks." She smiled back, pulling the sides of the hoodie snug around her body.

"I used to come down here a lot with my dad."

"Oh?" She looked at him with wide eyes.

He surprised himself. He hadn't opened up to anyone at school about his dad's death, but something about being in his own backyard and being with Lizzy felt right.

"Yeah, my dad and I would fish a lot." He looked down at his feet and closed his eyes for a second. He pictured the bright sunny day when he made his first catch—the one in the photograph. He sighed and gathered himself. "But now I like to come down here and just remember, I guess."

"Yeah, I'm sure that helps."

"A little." He looked down.

Lizzy kicked a rock, and his eyes followed as it tumbled off the dirt path into the higher grass.

He reached to his left and clutched Lizzy's hand. She squeezed back, as he led her down to the bank.

He crouched and rummaged among the pebbles and dirt. He pulled out a smooth, flat rock and hurled it over the water. The rock skipped across the surface a few times before disappearing, swallowed by the creek.

"You've got quite an arm."

"Ya think so?" He rolled his shoulder.

"Sure." Lizzy smiled and looked at him.

"Well, my coach says I need to work harder on my pitching and have more discipline if I wanna make the traveling team this summer."

"I'm sure you'll make it."

"Yeah, maybe."

Lizzy bent over and picked up her own rock. She flung it high into the air but it landed half as far as his rock with no skips, rather a singular ker-plunking splash.

"Not bad. What did you wish for?"

"Oh, I didn't know I had to make a wish. Can I throw another one?"

"Sure, go for it."

This time, he watched as Lizzy closed her eyes and cocked back. She burst them open as she lunged forward, the rock catapulting into the sky with a high arc.

"So what did you wish for?"

"I'm not going to tell you. If I tell you, it won't come true."

"Well, I wished..." He paused and pointed to himself in the chest. "...that a cute girl would arrive at my door tonight, and that's already come true, so no harm in saying it." He winked at her.

"You're sweet." She twirled a strand of hair between her fingers.

He nudged her hand aside and leaned in for a kiss. The instinct to intertwine their tongues was natural. He felt a strange sensation he wished to know more about but fear overrode his instincts. Unaware of how long a kiss should last, he pulled away and grabbed her hand again. He led her up the embankment and back to the house.

• • • •

~LIZZY~

"So how was it? Did you get a lot of studying done?" Lizzy's mom asked as she pulled out of Lincoln's driveway.

Lizzy closed her eyes for a second. She angled her body toward the car door. "It was nice."

"Nice. What's that supposed to mean? Can I have more than a one-word answer? Plus, you didn't tell me how much studying you got done." Her mom didn't yell, but her word choice deafened the mood.

"Enough."

"Excuse me, young lady?"

"Enough studying. We did enough studying."

"We'll see about that once you take the test."

That evening, as she lay in bed, she stared at the ceiling, replaying the kiss in her mind on a loop. The magical moment tickled in the pit of her stomach.

She was proud of herself for allowing it to even happen. All she heard was her mother's voice in her head. "Schoolwork *always* comes first." The commandment not up for debate. But that day she had chosen differently; life could be about more than homework.

And how he smelled. Ugh, so good. Like grown up confidence.

She thought about the wish she'd made. No kid deserved to lose a parent. She was so sad after losing her gran-mama. Even though her parents were tough, she couldn't imagine how it would feel to lose one. She wished for him to find some sense of peace and closure. He was the bravest, strongest person she knew, but it seemed like he was hiding something. She vowed to be there for him. She couldn't bring his dad back, but she could maybe help him feel less alone.

• • • •

~DAN~

He slid a few manilla folders into his briefcase and snapped the brass latches shut. "You still here?" he asked Linda as he strolled by her desk.

"Oh, yes, just finishing up the calendar for next month. It's been a mess trying to make it all fit."

"I'm sure you'll figure it out, you always do." He smiled and left.

He thought about his gratitude for Linda, his sweet sweater-vest-wearing, snow-haired secretary. She had worked at the school for thirty-five years and never complained. She always came to work with a smile on her face and she was great with the children, even without ever having any of her own. He wondered why for a minute and sighed, realizing it was none of his business. Nonetheless, he looked forward to seeing her every day.

He fired up his Mustang. The engine popcorned boom sounds in a roaring frenzy, announcing to everyone within a mile's distance he was around. He felt drained but dreaded going home to an empty house, so he took the long way home.

On his way, he passed The Brass Knuckle, a bar out in the middle of nowhere sitting at the intersection of two country roads with only enough traffic to warrant a four-way stop. He made a questionable rolling stop and drove past the bar. After a minute or two, he slammed on the brakes and made a three-point turn and headed back, guided by the neon red and white Budweiser sign outside the bar.

He stared at the hand of the speedometer resting motionless at 0, debating on whether to go in.

• • • •

September 2, 1990

The hand of the speedometer jumped as the Humvee bumped along the road outside of Baghdad. He tasted the sand in his teeth, and the hot air whipped across his face through the half-rolled-down window.

"Watch out up ahead, checkpoint! Divert! Divert!" he heard a command through his radio.

"Roger that," he squawked back. "Everybody hold on and gear up."

He twirled the steering wheel hard to the right. The Humvee swerved onto two wheels and everyone plopped down hard against the roll bars, helmets, and equipment clanging against each other.

"Jesus, Murphy, you gonna kill us!" one of the battalion members shouted.

"Hopefully not..."

• • • •

Dan rattled his head from side to side. His breath raced as he sat in his Mustang. The flashbacks exhausted him, frustrated him. He got out of the car and slammed the door.

As he entered the bar, he scanned the room. He'd never stopped there before, only driven past a bunch of times. He choked on the smell of fried food, sawdust, dirty bleach water, and cigarette smoke.

He took tabs—four people in the bar, plus the bartender. Two older men clung to the bar in overalls and Carhartt jackets, sipping tall draft beers served in frosty steins. A boy who looked not quite twenty-one played the Pac-Man arcade game in the back. The boy didn't even look up when Dan entered the bar, letting in a blinding stream of sun that spotlit the machine. The fourth patron, a woman, sat at the end of the bar with loose curls that bounced at the end of her long dark strands. She munched on peanuts, tossing the shells onto the floor as she stared into a book. The bartender, bald and muscular looked tired but nodded to welcome him.

"What'll ya have?"

He noticed the wings of the Air Force tattooed on the bartender's bulging forearm.

"You serve?" Dan asked.

"Yep, Desert Storm."

"Me too." He coughed, trying to hold back his excitement. Finally someone he could relate to.

"I'd rather not talk about it."

"Yeah, me either." He coughed, deeper that time. "Gimme a Jack and Coke."

The bartender walked away to make the drink and Dan glanced at the end of the bar where the woman sat, but she had disappeared.

"Here ya go—that's four bucks." The bartender slid the Jack and Coke in front of him.

He got out his wallet and left a five on the bar and felt a hand on his arm.

"I've never seen you in here before." The voice, smoky and low, belonged to the woman caressing his bicep.

"Oh, hi, you scared me. How did I miss you coming over here?"

"I'm good at what I do."

"Oh?"

"Don't sweat it, I'm a state trooper. I have the best hiding spots to catch the speeders. I wanted to be a cop, but my father said being a state trooper was less dangerous, so here I am. I like to hang out here and read. I know that probably sounds weird, but it's usually pretty quiet here, and I like meeting new people." She traced her fingertip up the curve of his bicep and tapped his shoulder.

His blood sped through his veins and he tried to change the subject to something less flirty. "Yeah, he's probably right. At least you didn't join the Army. That's the least safe…"

"Oh? You speaking from experience?"

"Yeah, unfortunately."

"Well, thank you for your service."

He nodded. She was standing close enough now that he felt her breasts against his shoulder. Although this beautiful woman was his for the taking, all he could think about was Deb; he couldn't get her image out of his mind. He took a big gulp of his drink and pushed the barstool back.

"But you haven't even finished your drink yet?" The woman pled for him to return but he was on his way to the door.

He jumped in the car and revved his engine. He peeled out of the stone parking lot, spewing a short wave of little pebbles in his midst.

When he got home, he ripped off his shirt, turned up the boombox, and started pushing reps on the bench press in his garage.

That night he tossed and turned, fighting off nightmare after nightmare of flashbacks. He wondered if he'd ever be able to be close to someone.

• • • •

~HELEN~

"Mom? You home?"

Helen heard a voice as she soaked in a warm bath. She clutched the grab bar Beau had been so kind to install on the shower wall and pulled herself up.

"Deb? Is that you?" She waited so she could hear the answer before wrapping a towel around her wet head.

"Yes, it's me."

"Oh, I didn't know you were coming by. How'd you get in?" She put on her robe.

"I used the hide-a-key. You know you should really hide it better. It was a piece of cake finding it. I worry about you living alone in this house. You should get a dog for some protection and company."

She dismissed her daughter's comment, appreciative for the visit. "To what do I owe this surprise?" She sat down on the sofa, smelling like fresh bar soap and flowery perfume.

"I'm sorry. I can come back later."

"It's quite all right, dear. What brings you by? Everything okay?" She wished she could freeze time whenever Deb came by.

"I don't know if things will ever be okay." Deb let out a big sigh and put both hands over her eyes for a moment and then slapped them down against her thighs.

She watched her daughter, as if Deb needed the physical motion to help get the words out.

"I just wanted to come by and...and well...apologize. I shouldn't have hung up on you the other day. I just got upset, but I shouldn't have taken it out on you."

She removed the towel from her head and took a slow, deep breath. "I accept your apology." She opened her arms and invited Deb to make contrition by accepting a hug. She longed for Deb to be more receptive of her physical affection. She waited for a few moments, enough for Deb to succumb at least out of obligation.

"Thanks, Mom." Deb wiggled out of the millisecond hug.

"So what else has been going on since we last spoke? Did Arletta cause the trouble you were expecting?" Sometimes the only way Helen felt she could get through to her daughter was by pushing her buttons.

"She's incomprehensible to me."

"Oh?"

"It was a school day. I don't know what she expected me to do."

"Did you ask?"

Deb was silent and rolled her eyes, accepting her point.

"How's Lincoln doing? I'd love to see him."

"Now you sound just like her." Deb grunted and crossed her arms. "I'm sorry." She pulled back her tone.

"What's troubling you, dear? You can tell me..." She sensed Deb held something inside, something other than the grief that she could read off her daughter's face oh so well.

Deb hung her head.

"What? What is it?"

Deb sighed.

She reached out and put her hand on Deb's shoulder.

"I did something stupid."

"What?" She remained calm. She knew Deb was over-critical.

"We were at the art show."

"Oh, that's so wonderful. He submitted something? It's good for him to have interests."

"Mom, can I?"

Helen went through the motions of zipping her lips, but it was hard to contain her excitement. Deb was so reluctant to tell her anything.

"I overheard some parents talking about their daughter. The mother disapproved of art and only cared about math and science. I couldn't imagine trying to limit Lincoln like that."

Helen nodded and her heart glowed.

"Well it turns out, the girl was Lincoln's friend, maybe even a girlfriend. We went and saw her pottery and it was stunning, I mean something I would use to stage houses. So when we were leaving, I whispered to her that I was proud of her."

"Nothing wrong with that."

"But Lincoln saw it. And he's pissed at me."

She leaned back. "Have you tried talking to him?"

"No." Deb looked away. "I don't know what to say. It's like I betrayed him and there's this elephant in the room."

"Listen, sweetie. I know this is hard, but being a mother is not always easy. You have to start the conversation. You're the parent. Don't make this something bigger than it is. You didn't mean any harm."

"You might be right."

"What?" She cupped her hand by her ear.

"Oh stop it." Deb smiled. "It's just so hard to get through to him. I think there's a lot he's going through that he's not saying."

"You want him to open up to you? You've got to show a little vulnerability yourself."

"I don't know if I can do that."

"Just be honest. Say that you are sad too. That it's okay to be sad. You both miss Beau. You have that in common...that can be what brings you together."

Deb stared at her. "Please don't say his name."

"Well, you let me know how it goes. I know this is hard."

"It's just how things are right now." Deb sprung up from the couch to leave.

"It doesn't have to be...you're going so soon?" Her voice dropped.

"I need to get home. It's been a long day."

"Okay. Thanks for dropping by. You are always welcome, anytime. I love you, honey—see you soon." She frowned as she watched the door shut, wishing Deb had said "I love you" back. She never had any luck with Deb. All her life trying to get through to her child and make a connection and now watching her daughter struggle with the same thing—it tore her up inside.

• • • •

May 4, 1975

Helen stared at the clock, as its slow ticks were the only movement and sound in the dark living room. The hour hand was hovering at the two. While she'd given Deb a rather gracious 11:30 p.m. curfew, Deb always pushed the limits. But this time Deb was going too far. What could a high school sophomore be doing out at two in the morning? Helen tried not to contemplate the answers.

Irrrk. The front door squeaked open.

Deb wobbled in. A trail of black tears crawled down her face from runny mascara. Deb's shirt was ripped.

"What happened?" Helen asked, reaching out to comfort her.

"Noth-ung." Through the slurred word, Deb pushed Helen away, escaping to her room and slamming the door.

Helen put on a kettle and waited for the hot water to whistle. With a mug in one hand, she knelt on the ground and cupped her free hand against the thick wooden door. Silence. Deb had at least stopped crying, so Helen tapped her knuckle on the door and eased it open.

Deb was curled up, shaking, her head buried under the pillow. She was fully clothed in her leather jacket and tight miniskirt. Deb didn't notice her presence. Helen sat on the edge of the bed and put the tea on the nightstand.

"Here, honey," she said, touching her shoulder. "I brought you some tea. It seems like you've had a really rough night."

Deb emerged from under the pillow, wheezing and with the look of unspoken pain all over her face.

"Do you want to talk about it?" Helen was calm, not forceful.

"Why do you care?" Deb snapped back. "You can't do anything to help me."

"Why don't you let me try? I love you..."

"Please go away and leave me alone."

And with that, she left.

Chapter 8

Rewriting Stories

~LINCOLN~

The whole class lined up along the curb in front of the science museum.

"Prez, what's up with you?" Trent elbowed him.

"Oh, nothing." He couldn't take his mind off the kiss with Lizzy.

"If you say so."

"How was your weekend?" Lincoln tried to change the subject.

"Boring. My dad was out of town again—this time Phoenix—so there wasn't that much to do," Trent said.

"I'm sorry, man. We should've hung out. How's it going with JJ?"

"Oh, it's —" Trent shrugged and then stopped as Mr. Hudson's voice boomed over the group.

"Quiet, everyone. Pipe down! I want everyone listening and staying with the group. You don't want to spoil the trip for the class next year, now do you?"

He bobbed his head up and down along with his classmates. The annual seventh grade trip to the science museum was better than being in class.

"Good—now let's get to it," said Mr. Hudson.

Lincoln followed the rest of the class from the main lobby to the first corridor, which revealed a huge dinosaur skeleton.

"Whoa!" He held his arm up next to the shinbone.

"What are you doing? Don't touch it. You might get into trouble." The high-pitched voice annoyed him.

"I'm not going to touch it." He spun around to find it was Lizzy. He smirked to himself. Since it was *her* bossiness, it turned him on.

As the class moved along to the next exhibit, he wandered off, mesmerized by the large murals on the walls. What if? A little bubble sprang in his stomach.

He stood in front of a huge mural of the solar system painted on the opposite wall. He wondered what would happen. Would it be safe to go into space? Would he float around? Would he survive without a spacesuit? He remembered Mr. Hudson telling his class there was no air or air pressure in space. Would he be able to breathe? Would it be cold? All these questions frightened him, but he pined to see what would happen and...if he could find another envelope.

He walked up to the mural and stood about six feet from the wall so he could see the whole work of art in his frame of vision. He checked if the coast was clear. The echoes of his classmates' voices bounced off the marble floor and vaulted ceilings and faded out as he stood immobile, feeling more and more alone. He pictured the group snaking through the other exhibits. Part of him wanted to be with them, walking next to Lizzy, learning about new stuff. But a bigger part of him wanted to be right where his feet were rooted. One step closer to what happened to his dad that night.

He stared at the mural.

He sucked in a deep breath.

Hold it.

His eyelids fell.

Blackness.

Silence.

He opened his eyes.

Through the glass bubble of his helmet, he saw a line of planets to his left, like drops of gold in the dark blackness. His body was numb, but he moved his arms and swam through the vastness, his doggie paddle effective as he picked up the pace. He couldn't judge his speed due to the lack of any vantage point but felt the atmosphere rush past him so fast he couldn't hear himself think. He came in hot and approached one of Saturn's moons. He braced for impact but landed unharmed, moon boots first.

He gazed across the icy surface. Jagged stalagmites dotted the golden landscape as far he could see. He hopped up and down a few times, testing the loose limits of the gravitational pull. This was better than the big trampoline he had begged for but his parents would never let him have because it was too dangerous.

As he bounced around, he came upon some rippled brown dunes. The granular substance wasn't sand; it looked like cocoa powder. A tiny liquid stream trickled through the curves of the powder. Was this water? He wished he could stay and explore but his heart started racing. The pain pulsed between his ribcage.

But, he hadn't found a clue yet. Where was the envelope? He burst out in sweat and his helmet fogged up. He spun his head around, scanning for any sign of an object. Nothing. He patted the outside of the astronaut suit, searching all the seams. There was a horizontal zipper pocket on the inside of his left arm. There it was!

He plucked the envelope from the sleeve but before he had a firm grip, it floated into the air. He snatched it and pressed it close to his body, praying it would make the trip home with him.

His eyes closed and he took a deep breath.

Blackness.

Quiet.

Peace.

When he opened his eyes he stood back at the mural, the envelope pressed to his chest.

"Wow, that was awesome. It was like Ms. Frizzle and the Magic School Bus."

He peeled open the envelope and found a card with the word *Deer*.

He already knew they swerved because of a deer. What else was there to know? The clues seemed to be teasing him.

• • • •

~TRENT~

"Hey, did you see Lincoln?" Lizzy tugged at his baggy Mets jersey. Despite being a head taller than most of the other boys in the seventh grade, the silk-screened heavy fabric hung to his knees. His dad had picked out the adult-size jersey from the airport gift shop after a trip to New York, with no time to find an age-appropriate size. At least he knew he liked baseball, so he wore it all the time.

He looked around. "I don't know where he is. Sorry."

"I hope he's okay. Mr. Hudson looks pissed. I hope he didn't get into trouble again," said Lizzy.

"Prez? He'll be fine. He's not a troublemaker."

"Oh?" Lizzy peered at him with an open invitation to rebut her argument.

"What?"

"You don't notice? I feel so bad...you know...about his dad..." Lizzy trailed off.

"Yeah, that sucked, but that was last year." He shrugged. Why was she stating the obvious and getting all in his business? "He's my best friend. I would know—he would tell me. He's cool."

"Did he ever talk about it with you? He seems like he hasn't. It's like he's a volcano going to explode at any time. Sorry, couldn't resist the urge. We *are* at the science museum."

"No, not really." He couldn't keep up with Lizzy's changing tone. Was she mad or joking around?

"Did you ever ask?"

The question hit him like a ton of bricks. He stood frozen.

Why hadn't he? What kind of friend was he? He hung his head and sighed.

He missed Beau too. He was like a second father to him—maybe even a first father as he remembered his dad was in Phoenix and wouldn't see him until next week.

"His dad was just a special guy..."

"Oh? Like how?" Lizzy leaned in.

"He cared...he like really cared.... I felt like he understood what it was like to be in our shoes. He would always come down to our level, never make us feel stupid, always make us feel special, like we mattered." He sniffled a bit, fighting back tears.

"I wish I could have known him too."

"Yeah, I guess I'm lucky to have got to spend so much time with him—more time than my real dad, it seems...but yeah, I feel bad for Prez. He's all alone now, and his mom can't handle it. He came by my house a few times and I could tell he probably needed to talk about it, but he didn't say much. I didn't really know—I don't know—how to talk to him. I wish I could help more...but I don't want to make him feel any worse."

"You don't make him feel worse. He needs someone to talk to. You being there—even if you don't know what to say—just listen."

"Let's keep moving to the next exhibit. Trent, keep up with the group." Mr. Hudson's voice interrupted their conversation.

Lizzy ducked to avoid Mr. Hudson's glare. "I'm gonna go find him," she mouthed to him.

Trent nodded and went on with the group.

• • • •

~LIZZY~

"There you are," she whispered.

Lincoln turned at the sound of her voice.

"What are you doing? You're gonna get in trouble." She waved at him to come over to her.

He looked disoriented, and she watched him slip something into his pocket. "Are you okay?" Her eyebrows were raised.

"Yeah, I'm okay." Lincoln smoothed his hair.

"Let's get back." She turned to lead him to the group when they were confronted by Mr. Hudson.

"Yes, you better get back. What're you doing wandering around?" Mr. Hudson stood with his legs spread and his hands on his hips, blocking their way.

Her throat clenched.

"I'm sorry, I got distracted by the mural of the planets." Lincoln spoke up first.

"What did I say before we started this morning?" Mr. Hudson didn't budge. He stared at Lincoln right between the eyes, like he was looking through him.

Lincoln stood there, his chest puffed out, but she could tell his heart was racing.

"Just tell him." She whispered as she pulled at Lincoln's arm.

Lincoln looked at her and back at Mr. Hudson. "We were supposed to stay with the group."

"Ah ha." Mr. Hudson shook his head. "If you took one second longer to give me that answer, you were going to be in the principal's office this afternoon. But instead, I'll just give you detention. The both of you."

The pit of her stomach dropped to the floor. She'd never gotten detention before—her parents were going to kill her!

"But Mr. Hudson, Lizzy didn't do anything. She came back to get me. She shouldn't have to get in trouble for that."

"Oh all right, you want to play the hero. Sure. Fine." Mr. Hudson chuckled to himself. "You have detention for two days now. One for yourself and one for covering for Ms. Henry."

"Okay, no problem," Lincoln agreed.

The air exhaled from her lungs. She couldn't believe what had happened.

"Now, get back up with the group." Mr. Hudson looked at them sternly. "Now."

She and Lincoln scurried ahead. They blended into the back of the group, looking at the remains of an ancient mummy.

"You didn't have to do that." She smiled at him. Deep down she loved that he did.

"I didn't have to...but I wanted to."

. . . .

~LINCOLN~

"Oh hello, Mr. Peterson." Mr. Hudson checked his name off the list, as he took a seat in the back for detention.

Several empty desks filled the room around the three kids who had detention that day. He was in the company of Heath, who never said a word to anybody but always got in trouble for smoking in the bathroom, and Misty, who had a strand of pink hair and a nose ring and didn't take shit from anybody—including the teachers she talked back to.

He took out his math book and laid it on the desk in front of him. He stared at his sloppy handwriting; the letters "M-A-T-H" scribbled in black Sharpie on the brown paper bag cover. When the school year started, he didn't care about the neatness of titling his schoolbooks. But things had changed. When he applied himself, like at the art fair, he'd won third place for his sketching. Lizzy made him want to care about things again—like before, when his dad was around. He smiled and opened his math book to do his homework.

· · · ·

~MR. HUDSON~

He told himself to stay focused on grading the quizzes, but he couldn't resist the urge to look up to scope out Lincoln. The tension in the room increased his blood pressure. He knew something was off about Lincoln. He couldn't put his finger on it yet, but curiosity lingered.

"Okay, that's it," he noted as the clock on the wall struck 4 p.m.

He watched Lincoln sling his backpack over one shoulder and head for the door. Heath and Misty were already gone.

"You know..." He snuck up behind Lincoln in the hallway.

Lincoln turned and looked him in the eye.

"I know something is going on. Catching you in the hallway without a hall pass the other day and now these shenanigans on the field trip. Your dad's been gone long enough. I'm not giving you any extra slack. You better not screw up again, or I will have to take this to Principal Murphy."

Lincoln slipped his backpack off his shoulder and squeezed it close to his chest.

"Okay," Lincoln said and shuffled away.

He watched Lincoln until he was out of sight, his head pounding with fear and guilt. How could this young man be so strong in the face of grief?

· · · ·

~DEB~

She heard the back door unlatch. "How was the field trip?"

"Okay." She heard Lincoln fling his bookbag onto the kitchen table and open the refrigerator.

"What did you see?" She sat among a sea of paperwork in the other room. She put her pen down and went to join him in the kitchen, the eagerness a welcomed bright spot in her day.

"A bunch of stuff." Lincoln hid behind the refrigerator door.

"What kind of stuff?"

"Just stuff." Lincoln snapped open a can of Mountain Dew as he went into the living room and turned on the TV.

She stood still for a minute as she took a deep breath, then walked into the living room, took the remote, and flipped off the TV.

"Hey..." Lincoln clenched his teeth. "I was watching that."

"What's going on?" She crossed her arms, still holding the remote.

"Nothing." Lincoln picked up a magazine from the end table.

"Lincoln, I'm not going to get upset." She pointed at him with the remote. "Now just tell me. What happened today?"

"Uggggh." Lincoln let out a low grumble as he slapped the magazine back on top of the stack in front of him. "I got a detention. Are you happy?"

She stepped back and raised her eyebrows. "A detention?"

"Yeah, that's what I said."

"You've never gotten a detention before?" She shook her head in disbelief.

"It's no big deal. I just did my homework."

She studied Lincoln's face, but it was stone cold. He wasn't letting on about anything. "Why did you get it?"

"Oh, I...Mr. Hudson gave it to me."

"But why?" She set the remote down and threaded her fingers through her hair.

"I can't talk about it."

"What's that supposed to mean?"

Lincoln gulped and guzzled a big swig of Mountain Dew. "You're just gonna have to trust me on this." He put the can down, got off the couch, and went upstairs to his room.

She stood speechless. Her arms hung at her sides, like weights anchoring her to the ground. She didn't blame him for not wanting to talk. It's not like she set any example of how to open up about having feelings. All she did was grill him; she didn't show any vulnerability like she promised she'd try.

She worried about him as she tried to sleep. He'd never gotten into any trouble before. What could be going on? She hoped it was nothing serious. She could ask his teacher or maybe even Principal Murphy? But if they thought she needed to know, they would have called, right?

As fatigue set in, her thoughts of Lincoln faded. She tossed and turned in the darkness as her body radiated with heat, kicking her legs across the mattress to find the cool spots in the sheets. The red lights on the clock read 2:34 a.m. She closed her eyes and imagined...

• • • •

April 5, 1995

"But honey, let's go out. I've worked two doubles this week, and I just want to have some time with you." Beau pleaded with his big blue eyes, holding her hand. "Let me take you to a nice place. I don't want you to have to cook tonight."

She dropped her hand from his. "But this rain. It's really coming down."

"I'd never let a little rain stop me from taking my beautiful wife out." He winked and wrapped his arm around her and kissed her neck.

"Are you sure you want to go out?" She laughed. His warm lips tickled her skin.

"You're quite the negotiator!" He laughed as he nibbled her ear.

"And what about Lincoln?" She pulled away.

"He'll be fine. He's eleven now. I think he can stay home for one evening alone."

"I don't know about this. Plus, it's Saturday and we don't have reservations."

Beau leapt across the kitchen and grabbed the phone book from the cupboard. "No problem—I'll get us a reservation." He flipped the pages and slid his finger down the column of restaurants. "Ah ha!" He picked up the phone and dialed.

A crack of thunder boomed and shook the house, followed by a flash of light.

"See? There's a thunderstorm warning. Can we do a raincheck?"

That was the point in the story that she always changed.

She grabbed Beau with her eyes and held him long enough so he could sense her fear.

"Well, maybe you are right, hon. I see folks every day in really bad shape who wish they might've chosen a different path." He put down the phone and pulled her into his chest.

She could smell his aftershave.

. . . .

She turned and looked at the clock again: 2:39 a.m. The bounce of her head against the pillow as she flipped nauseated her stomach. She clutched the plush comforter between her elbows and wished for sleep.

Chapter 9

Phantom Dad

"Lincoln, can you grab some more peanut butter?" She realized she'd missed that aisle and didn't want to retrace her steps.

She hated grocery shopping. But she had a system of walking down every aisle to register in her mind the items needed. She kept lists in her head, never writing them down. Maybe this habit came from her teenage and college days of waiting tables. She had been too cool to write orders down, but that didn't mean she wasn't taking stock in her head. After she'd made a point, he would tease her about what else she had on "her list." But ever since he died, her brain didn't seem to remember as well.

She watched as Lincoln scampered off to retrieve the peanut butter.

As she debated whether to get penne or farfalle, she noticed Principal Murphy turn his shopping cart into the pasta aisle. She lowered her head and shimmied her cart closer to the shelf so he could get by. Maybe he wouldn't recognize her?

"Deb, how are ya?" His eyebrows rose in unison with the appearance of his adorable dimples.

The pasta rattled as she tossed the box into her cart. "Oh, Principal Murphy. Hello." She'd frantically changed her mind to rigatoni.

"Hey? What did I say? Call me Dan." He reached across her cart to grab a box of spaghetti. His muscular tattooed forearm came close enough for her to smell his cologne.

"Dan. Sure. Sorry." Her face felt like fire. She felt like a teenager.

"Having pasta tonight?"

"Seems like it. I haven't been too much in the mood to cook. This is easy enough, though. Plus, Lincoln loves it."

"Ah, as any growing boy would." He moved down the aisle a few steps and picked up a jar of sauce and studied the ingredients on the label.

She pushed her cart and closed the gap so she could whisper. "You haven't heard anything about Lincoln, have you?"

"No." Dan shook his head and his forehead wrinkled. "Why?"

"It's just that he told me he got a detention." She sighed.

"Oh? That's nothing to worry about. Kids get them all the time. It's part of being in junior high."

"It's not for Lincoln. He's never had one before." She dropped her shoulders.

"I think you're okay." Dan's voice quieted, as Lincoln arrived with a big jar of Jiffy in his hand.

"Oh, hi, Principal Murphy." Lincoln dropped the Jiffy into her shopping cart.

"Lincoln, good to see you. You keeping a good eye on your mother?"

Lincoln nodded, and she caught a glimpse of his eye roll as he looked away.

"Well, it was nice to see you." Principal Murphy looked at Lincoln. "And it was nice to see you too." And then he winked at her.

"Bye, Dan," she said in a trance. She turned the cart around and headed out of the aisle.

• • • •

~DAN~

As he watched them leave, he wondered why Lincoln had gotten into trouble and who'd given him detention. He made a mental note to check on it the next day. Maybe he shouldn't have told Deb not to worry? But it had been a year now and they seemed to be doing ok, but what did he know?

A vision of last year's newspaper article in the *Brightonville Gazette* describing Lincoln's dad's car accident flashed in his head. When he first saw the article, he'd been surprised that a local newspaper would publish such a graphic photo of an accident. He couldn't make out any of the victims, but the gnarled skeleton of the car blackened from the fire was not anything he wanted to look at. It reminded him of his time in Iraq...

• • • •

September 2, 1990

He saw cement and rubble. A cloud of smoke billowed above his head. He put his finger in the warm pool of blood on his chest.

"Hang tight, Corporal. We're gonna get you out of here." The medic eased and then jarred him onto a stretcher.

He winced, as a shooting pain ran through his spine. He imagined his parents receiving his casket with the flag draped across.

. . . .

"Excuse me." An older woman warbled, as she tried to push her cart past him. He had stopped in the middle and blocked the aisle.

He flinched and reappeared from his waking nightmare.

"Sorry, ma'am." He shimmied to the side and slid both hands through his hair, reconnecting to his surroundings.

. . . .

~DEB~

"Go wash up," she instructed Lincoln, as she put away the groceries. She tried to extinguish Dan from her mind, but the tickle deep in her belly made it difficult.

"Are you okay?" Lincoln stood over the kitchen sink washing his hands.

"What?" She was in a fog.

Lincoln switched off the running water and the kitchen became silent.

"Why did Principal Murphy wink at you?"

She felt hot and pushed the sleeves up on her sweater. "Oh, he did?"

"C'mon. I saw it. Do you think this is some kind of joke?"

"What do you mean joke?" She felt the walls closing in on her.

"Never mind." Lincoln hurried up to his room.

She stood alone, speechless. She grabbed the counter for balance. She felt nauseous.

. . . .

~LINCOLN~

On his hands and knees, he slid out the orange shoebox from under his bed. He gazed at the collection of envelopes he'd assembled. A total of six. He removed the cards from the envelopes and spread them across the floor.

Dinner. Car. Rain. Dark. Eyes. Deer.

What was this message trying to say? He shuffled the cards around, rearranging the order again and again. He knew it was raining and they crashed while swerving to miss a deer. What else was there to know? And what or who was behind all this? All the questions made him anxious; he needed to blow off some steam.

He stacked the cards in a pile and placed them back in the shoebox on the right side, leaving the pile of envelopes empty on the left side. He closed his secret treasure and pushed it back under his bed. All the way against the wall. As far out of sight as he could.

He grabbed his coat and tiptoed downstairs. His mom lay slumped in a ball on the couch. He snuck past her and out the front door.

Five minutes later, he banged on Trent's front door, out of breath.

"Hey, Prez, what're ya doing?" Trent opened the door. "It's chilly outside. You walk here?" Trent peered outside, looking to see if his mom had dropped him off.

"No, I ran. I need your help with something."

"Yeah, man, come in."

"I gotta whiz first."

"Yeah, upstairs." Trent pointed.

Lincoln bolted upstairs and closed the door behind him. As he flipped on the light switch, he noticed the picture on the wall over the toilet. Oh great. He stared at the familiar black and white photo of *Lunch Atop a Skyscraper* depicting eleven men sitting on a steel support beam dangling eight hundred feet above the streets of Manhattan. Before he inhaled, he hesitated for a moment. He was afraid of heights. But, Dad.

He closed his eyes.

He took a big breath.

Held it.

He listened to his heartbeat.

Blackness.

Stillness.

Then his eyes parted.

The skyline appeared.

He felt the warmth of steel on his bottom and the whip of wind in his hair. The sun shined across a blue sky and the man sitting next to him popped a bright red cherry tomato into his mouth.

"Want one?" the man offered.

"Sure." He ate one and felt refreshed. "Thank you. Tastes wonderful."

"My wife grows 'em in our little rooftop garden. Not much to be thankful for these days, but I'm thankful we have these 'em tomatoes."

He wondered what year it was but guessed it was the Great Depression. He smiled back at the man, who was barely a man. He looked eighteen or nineteen years old.

The fear was real. But so was the temptation. He looked down.

The size of the drop equaled the size of the drop in his stomach. He couldn't make out much, not even people. They were smaller than ants. Little specks jig-sawing around. He pictured himself falling. He gasped. The beam wobbled.

"Steady, men!" another man at the opposite end of the beam yelled. "What's the problem down there?"

"Oh, nothing," the man with the tomato replied in his defense, as he put his hand behind his back to secure him. He looked around. No one wore a safety harness.

"Thanks," Lincoln whispered to the man. "How come no one has any ropes or anything?"

"We ain't got none. All's we got is a job, and that's worth more than my life." The man winked at him.

Lincoln turned his head so he could roll his eyes in terror. He wasn't sure how much longer he could stay suspended above the Earth. He checked his pockets. No envelope. He had to hold on for a little bit more.

"Ya wanna a smoke?"

"Oh, no thanks." His heart started pumping. The deep, painful throbs unsteadied him again.

A black crow appeared and landed on a beam across the way. Ah ha! The crow carried an envelope in its mouth. He cringed at the idea of trying to get the message when the target beam was twenty feet away. But then the crow hopped over to the end of the beam where they all sat.

"Hey look-y there! Somebody's girl send 'em a love letter?" One of the men joked and everyone else laughed.

He weened himself from a sitting position. His stomach laid flat on the beam. His heart pounded against the metal. He extended his right arm.

"Be careful, son," someone called out.

His motion startled the crow, and it took off. The envelope remained, teetering on the edge. The wind was bound to blow it away in a matter of seconds. He had to act fast. Sweat bubbled out of every pore of his body. His shoes felt full of sand and his feet tingled. He clawed the beam with clenched hands and legs, like a panda bear climbing a bamboo tree. He reached the envelope. He put it in his teeth and shimmied back to the men.

"Be careful, kid. Who knows what kind of disease that crow could've been carryin.'"

His eyes bulged at the thought. A huge yawn shuddered through his body.

He hung onto the beam.

The sun and the sky faded.

Gray.

Black.

Silence.

He waited.

His breath kept tabs.

Then his eyes glazed open.

As the sink and vanity came into view, he sat down on the closed toilet lid and took a deep breath. He studied his two feet secure on the ground, still tingling. He was grateful for another envelope and grateful he survived.

He peeled off the seal and removed the card. It read, *Guardrail.* So they hit the guardrail. What was the significance?

"Hey, Prez, you all right up there?" He heard Trent's voice from downstairs.

As he rushed out of the bathroom, he saw Trent's room out of the corner of his eye. He stopped for a moment, scanning the wall lined with trinkets and souvenirs from all the major U.S. cities—an empty Wrigley Field picture frame, a stuffed giraffe from the San Diego Zoo, a Coke bottle from the 1996 Olympic Games in Atlanta that summer, a giant tumbler with glitter floating inside clear walls that said "Fun in the Sun" from Miami.

He felt for Trent; an absent dad might feel worse than a dead one. He knew his dad was not coming back. At least he didn't have to tug the line of hoping and wondering about the next disappointment. He sighed and hurried downstairs.

• • • •

~TRENT~

"You okay, man?" As Lincoln appeared, Trent put down his Nintendo controller on the couch. Lizzy must have been right; he wasn't acting like himself.

"Yeah, I'm fine." Lincoln plopped down on the couch next to him.

"So what did you want my help with?" Trent asked.

"Oh..." Lincoln paused. "Do you mind if we play first?" Lincoln grabbed the second controller.

"Yeah, sure, whatever. You be Yoshi."

The two boys raced each other in *Super Mario Kart*, entranced in a world on screen.

Nearly an hour later, Trent's mom arrived home and asked if they were hungry. As they munched on mini pizza bagels, Trent tried Lincoln again. "So, man, you gonna tell me what's going on?"

"I just had to get out for a little while."

"Sure. You can come over whenever you want." He sensed Lincoln holding back.

They continued to play another game.

"It's getting late, boys. Lincoln, does your mom know you're over here?" Trent's mom asked as she picked up the empty plates on the coffee table in front of them.

"Just one more game?" Trent pleaded.

"Okay, one more and then we'll call it a night." His mom left juggling the plates on one arm like a pro.

After the next game started, Lincoln pressed pause.

"So, something weird happened today." Lincoln bent his knee and propped his leg up so he could turn toward him on the couch.

"Oh?" Trent put down his controller. Finally.

"Yeah. We were at the grocery store."

"Nothing weird about that?" He tried to counsel him. He didn't know what else to say.

"Ha, yeah, let me finish."

"Yeah, sure, man." Trent tried to calm down and listen.

"Principal Murphy was there."

"Oooh." Trent squiggled his face and then straightened up. "I mean the man's gotta eat."

"Yeah, but I saw him on my way to get some peanut butter and he was talking to my mom when I got back. They were really close, like whispering. And then they stopped right when they saw me."

"But you don't know what they were talking about. It could be nothing."

"Yeah, you could be right. But you know I got a detention? For going off on my own during the science field trip."

"Oh yeah. Sorry 'bout that. Did it go okay?"

"Yeah, it was no big deal. I just got my homework done. I have another one tomorrow. I covered for Lizzy."

"Geez, Prez, you must really like her."

Lincoln smiled. "I do."

Trent unpaused the game, thinking the conversation was over.

"But there's one more thing." Lincoln hit pause again.

"What?"

"They stopped talking when I showed up. And then when he said goodbye, he winked at her. I mean, what is that?" Lincoln raised his voice.

"I don't know. It's probably nothing. He was probably just being nice."

"Yeah, he was being nice all right. I don't like it. And you should have seen the way my mom looked back at him. I just wanted to die."

"I'm sorry, man. This seems like a lot. I know your dad..." Trent stopped mid-sentence.

Lincoln slumped his shoulders and put his forehead in his hands.

"Hey, I'm sorry..." Trent put his hand on Lincoln's back, trying to comfort him. He didn't know what else to do. Or say.

"It's okay." Lincoln mumbled through his hands. "I just miss him, I guess. And I don't know what to think about everything."

"Yeah, it's hard." Trent sat still for a few minutes.

"Boys? It sounds like the game is over." His mom called from the other room as she approached. "Oh, is everything okay?"

"Yeah." Lincoln lifted his head up and cracked a half smile.

"Okay. It's late, so I'll drive you home."

As Trent got ready for bed, he thought about Lincoln and couldn't imagine what he was going through.

· · · ·

October 15, 1994

"Get in there and show 'em what you got. You can do it!" Beau tapped Trent's shoulder pads, as he ran back to the huddle after getting the call for the next play.

Trent's peewee football team was down by three with ten seconds left, no timeouts remaining. He had to make the perfect pass to send his team to the playoffs.

He looked right and left, and up and down the line. Then his gaze averted into the stands. He located his mom holding up a big sign with his name on it while sitting among a sea of parents...more like a sea of other dads.

"Hut hut, hike!" He stepped back, planted his foot, cocked his arm, and launched a prayer into the end zone.

Everyone in the crowd gasped as the ball sailed through the air. It danced across several players' fingertips, landing on the ground.

The other team stormed the field and chanted, as they jumped up and down in a big huddle in the end zone.

He walked to the sidelines, his head slunk between his shoulders. Before he reached the bench to sit down and sulk, Beau's fingers were intertwined in his face mask, lifting his head. He looked him in the eye.

"No head hanging today. You did everything you could. You ran the play, you threw a great pass. I'm proud of you. That's just how this one turned out. Gotta keep showing up—the next one could turn out different."

Trent smiled, as the weight lifted off his shoulders.

. . . .

"Good night," Trent's dad appeared in his bedroom door and flipped off the light.

"Night, Dad."

Trent turned on his side, facing his back to the doorway, pulling the covers over his head.

"I'm leaving for Denver in the morning. Early. I wanted to let you know. I probably won't see you. Be good for your mother."

"Yeah, okay." His reply was muffled under the covers. He waited a second. Then he peeked out. Nothing but an empty doorway. He sighed and buried his head under the pillow.

Chapter 10
Unwelcome Advances

~DAN~

The moment he entered the teacher's lounge, coffee mugs hung mid-air, the refrigerator door froze half-open, pencils dropped, and all chatter silenced. While he worked hard to earn the respect of the veteran teaching staff, no one had given him the benefit of the doubt yet. The jury of his peers had already made up their mind.

He hadn't asked for the promotion to principal. The school board, full of Vietnam vets, jumped at the chance to persuade the superintendent to put him there without an official post of the open position. The teachers petitioned to re-open the position and let everyone apply, but the request was denied.

"Morning, everyone," Dan bellowed with a smile. He refused to acknowledge the cold shoulders sitting among the room. He poured himself a cup of coffee.

The low mumble of chatter returned after it was clear he didn't have any other announcements.

He crouched down next to Mr. Hudson. "Can I talk to you about a student?"

Mr. Hudson sat alone in an old armchair in the back of the lounge filling out the *Chicago Tribune* crossword. He folded the newspaper, latched one side of his glasses under his sweater, and looked him in the eye as he grumbled, "Okay. Which one?"

"Lincoln Peterson. You gave him a detention?"

"Yes. He served one and has another today."

"Oh. I didn't know he got two of them." He scratched his head. "What were they for?"

"He wandered off during the field trip. I found Elizabeth Henry with him too, but I believe she went looking for him, and he took the blame for her. I had no problem giving him both detentions."

"I see."

"Listen, I need to go so I can prep for today's lesson." Mr. Hudson slid the newspaper under his arm and got up without waiting for a reply.

"Okay, thank you." Dan plopped down in the vacated armchair.

Everyone in the room stared at him again.

"Have a great day, everyone. Let's build those young minds!" His enthusiasm flared through his nostrils with an inauthentic tone he knew would be met by eye rolls and smart-ass smirks. Most of the teachers left on cue.

• • • •

~DEB~

The shrill beep of the digital alarm clock rattled her mind from a deep sleep. As she picked up her head to silence it, the bright red hue of the flashing stick-figured numbers blinded her. She rolled back over. The quiet darkness of the room swallowed any motivation. The voice in her head shouted there was no point.

He's gone. You'll never be happy again. Your life will never be the same. You'll never find love again. You used it all up.

The dam of stockpiled emotions splintered. Her skin tingled, as raw pain surged through her body. Tears flooded her eyes and swamped through the crevices of her face. Of all the days she missed him, some were harder than others. She couldn't curtail the backlash after her cocktail of emotions had been simmering below the surface for too long.

As her mind twisted and turned to make sense of her feelings and her life, her body remained heavy and stagnant, too exhausted to move. She mustered the will to talk herself into getting up and going to the bathroom. Once she was on her feet, she made a few phone calls to cancel her day, took three sleeping pills, and returned to bed. Within minutes she passed out cold.

When she woke, it was four in the afternoon. Dazed, she rubbed her eyes. She looked over to her nightstand and visions of her failed morning flashed by, reminders of her grim reality.

The doorbell rang.

She groaned, and retrieved her robe, only to hear it ring again. "I'm coming. Hold your horses."

The ringing didn't subside until the sound of the deadbolt unlatching caught the unknown visitor's attention. She opened the door in a hurry, seeing Lincoln.

"What were you doing ringing so many times?"

"Sorry Mom. Tryouts were today for the summer travel team, so I couldn't take the bus home. I waited for you, but after a while everyone was gone. Principal Murphy was leaving and asked me if I needed a ride. When I got here, I realized I'd left my key in my locker."

"Principal Murphy dropped you off?" She looked around.

"Yeah, he's right there, making sure I get in okay." Lincoln waved to Principal Murphy who sat in his black Mustang in the driveway. Principal Murphy waved back.

"Get inside." She commanded and Lincoln rushed up to his room.

She went to the kitchen to pour herself a glass of wine, when she heard a knock on the door.

"What in the world is going on here?" She opened the door and found Dan.

"I'm sorry, Lincoln left his baseball mitt in my car." He held out the mitt.

She snatched it, but in the process her robe flashed open. She wasn't wearing anything underneath. A rush of cold air hit her skin. She caught Dan's eye intercepting the opening and getting a peek. She watched his face turn red. A flash of desire lit up her dormant parts as she wrapped the robe shut.

"Have a good evening." He blurted out and turned to go.

"Wait. Would you like to come in? I have a bottle of wine open." Her impulse surprised her, but she didn't fight it.

"I really shouldn't." The coy look in his eyes told her he didn't mean it.

"Suit yourself." She caressed her hand against the top of her robe that crisscrossed her chest. She had no idea where all this energy was coming from.

"Well, I guess just one glass couldn't hurt, right? Where are my manners?"

"That's more like it." She winked back. "Come, the kitchen is this way."

She grabbed a glass from the cupboard and gave him a healthy pour, sliding the glass across the table. "You like Merlot?"

"Oh, yes, thank you." He took a big gulp.

She watched, as he crossed and un-crossed his legs and fidgeted with his watch.

She topped off her glass and welcomed the warm liquid courage washing down her throat. The tension built in the room. She liked having his company, but was she going to let herself enjoy it?

"So, I found out about Lincoln." He slowed down and took a more respectable sip this time.

"Oh?" She leaned in and pushed Lincoln's mitt aside on the counter.

"Yes, about his detention. You asked me about it?"

"Of course, yes I remember. What happened?" She ran her fingers across the top of her glass. Somehow the only thing she could focus on was undressing the handsome man in front of her, but she knew she should be listening for the details about Lincoln.

"It happened on the field trip. He wandered away from the group."

"That's not like him." She tried her best to nod and follow Dan's words.

"Well, the other part is that he took detention for another girl. Shows what a good heart he has—what a good mother he has to raise him as such a gentleman."

Lincoln appeared in the doorway. "Oh, I'm sorry. I just wanted a Gatorade."

Her stomach dropped, as she saw Lincoln's pale face. "Go ahead," she urged, trying to play it cool. "You left your mitt in the car, so I invited Dan in to have a glass of wine. To thank him for his troubles."

Lincoln grabbed a bottle out of the refrigerator door. "I'm going to go over to Trent's."

"Sure, go on." She sighed and watched Lincoln flee the room. "Now, that we have the place to ourselves, what do you say Dan?" She reached across the table and put her hand over his.

Dan pulled back. "This is probably not a good idea, Deborah."

"That's because you've only had one glass of wine."

"It's probably better that way."

"Okay, sure, I guess you're right." She dropped her shoulders in surrender. What had gotten into her?

"I'd better be going now. Thank you for the wine." He headed for the door.

"Dan?"

"Yes?" He stopped and made eye contact with her.

"Can we try this again sometime?"

"Sure, I'd like that." He smiled and she regained a little bit of dignity.

"Okay." She nodded.

Dan returned the nod and left. She stood in her robe, holding her glass of wine. Alone again with her feelings. Terrified. But for a different reason.

. . . .

~DAN~

He raced to the car. His heart hammered so loudly it was hard to hear the engine start, as he turned the key in the ignition. All the impulses in his body he'd been restraining in front of Deb coursed through him. He stared at her through the windshield admiring every curve of her figure and fighting the urge to walk back inside.

He knew he could never get involved with a parent, it would ruin his already fragile reputation, he might even lose his job.

But on the other hand, he wanted her.

He'd have to just settle for holding those thoughts in his mind. Fantasizing about the possibilities. Enjoying the little high that shot through his veins at the thought of *what if.* Maybe one day those feelings could be real.

. . . .

~TRENT~

"Trent! Lincoln's here." Trent heard his mom call from the front door. He put down his math homework and rushed downstairs.

"Hey man," Lincoln said, as he stood in the doorway, clutching the strap of his bookbag.

"Hey, what's up?" Trent noticed Lincoln was out of breath.

"How about you boys go upstairs and finish your homework, and I'll start some dinner?" Trent's mom suggested.

"Okay, thanks mom." Trent rolled his eyes. "We don't really have to do our homework." He whispered to Lincoln as they climbed the stairs side by side.

He shoved his math homework into his bookbag and made space for Lincoln to sit down on his bed. "You okay?"

"I don't know," Lincoln said, his speech fast.

Trent watched Lincoln's eyes dart across the room. He waited in silence. There was something more. He could tell Lincoln wanted to open up.

"After tryouts...you were already gone, but my mom..." Lincoln paused and shook his head. "This is embarrassing."

"No, it's okay. Just tell me. Get if off your chest." He inched closer to Lincoln on the bed.

"She fucking forgot to pick me up. I was waiting, probably twenty minutes, alone. I went back inside. There I am, sitting in the empty cafeteria, and Principal Murphy walks up. He said he could take me home. I didn't want to go with him, but I didn't think I had a choice." Lincoln crossed his arms.

"That was nice of him."

"Yeah, sure, but that's not all."

"Oh?"

"Yeah, he dropped me off and stayed in the car. No big deal, but then like a dummy I left my mitt in his car. He came to the door to give it to my mom. Anyway, she invited him in! Can you believe that? I mean why?" Lincoln stomped around his bedroom.

"I don't know." Trent scratched the side of his neck and held his hand there, feeling his quickening pulse.

Lincoln stopped pacing. Silence filled the room.

He didn't know what to say, but he knew he needed to say something.

"Maybe she's lonely? I mean she's gonna move on sometime." Trent shrugged his shoulders.

Lincoln narrowed his eyes and studied Trent's face. Trent's stomach dropped, as Lincoln looked at him like a stranger.

"You have no right to say that." Lincoln ripped his bookbag off the bed, rumbled down the stairs, and slammed the front door on his way out.

Trent's mom appeared in the living room. "What was that all about?" She stared up at him as he stood atop the stairs.

"I screwed up."

"What do you mean?"

"I said the wrong thing. I was just trying to help."

"What happened? Come down here, tell me." She sat on the couch.

Trent slunk down the stairs and plopped next to her on the couch.

"Prez is just going through a lot."

"Yes, I know, baby." She nodded.

"I don't know what to say sometimes." He looked down and picked at his short, chewed fingernails in his lap.

"It's so hard to have to go through something like Lincoln is going through at your age. The impact of loss is great and it affects everyone differently. I know it's probably hard for you to relate. But you don't have to know everything. You can just be his friend. You can just listen."

"I was listening. And then I pissed him off."

"Tell me what happened. It's okay. You're not going to upset me." She grabbed his hand.

Trent looked up and grabbed his thigh with his other hand. "He thinks something's going on with his mom and Principal Murphy. I just told him that maybe it was okay and that his mom was lonely. Like maybe it could be a good thing for her?" He looked up to find his mom's eyes, searching for her approval.

"Aww, honey." Her eyes melted. "You just spoke from your heart and tried to suggest something positive. But I can see why he might've been upset. Adult relationships are complicated and Lincoln's probably caught up in trying to understand. He'll come around. But in his own time. You have to give him some space. I'm sorry, though. I know he's such a good friend to you and it's hard to see him in pain." She pulled him in and hugged him.

He took a deep breath in. His mom always knew how to make him feel better. He wished his dad had an ounce of the love and understanding that his mom had. But maybe a start would be just to be home.

• • • •

~LINCOLN~

Lincoln's legs were an extension of his anger. They churned as he raced on the berm of the country road. He didn't care that he was wearing jeans—he was flying. The upper part of his body commanded the lower part of his body. While the two parts worked in unison, his mind felt disconnected and driven by the angry fuel pumping from his heart.

After the adrenaline depleted, he trotted into a slow jog and stopped. As he caught his breath, he looked around. What was he doing? Maybe Trent *was* just trying to help? His mom deserved her happiness and independence just as much as he did. He turned around and ran back to Trent's house.

He banged on the door, out of breath.

"Prez?" Trent opened the door. His eyebrows popped up, etching lines across his forehead.

"Hey." Lincoln leaned over with his head between his knees to take a couple sips of the cool night air. "I'm sorry," he said, standing up.

"It's okay, man. You want to come in?"

"No. I should get home. I just wanted to say sorry. I overreacted. It's just tough dealing with everything. I never know how I'm going to feel. It's like I'm not in control."

"I'm sorry, dude. Are you sure you don't want to come in and get a drink? Or need a ride or something?"

"No, it's okay. I probably should talk to my mom. I'll just run home. It helps me think."

"Okay, see ya tomorrow at school." Trent waved.

Lincoln jogged down the driveway.

As he approached home, he let out a sigh of relief, noticing the empty driveway. No sign of Principal Murphy's car.

"Mom?" He snuck in the front door that he'd left open.

"In here."

He followed the soft voice coming from the kitchen. She sat at the kitchen table, her head resting on her sprawled-out arm and her other hand wrapped around the stem of the empty wine glass that sat a few inches from an empty bottle.

"Are you okay?"

"I'm fine." She sat up, clutching the side of the table for leverage.

He pulled up the chair next to her.

"I don't know how to ask you this."

"Oh honey, I'm sorry. This is not a good time." She rubbed her head. He saw the red lines in the whites of her eyes and the damp remnants of tears.

He nodded in defeat and walked out of the kitchen. How much more of this? When would she be ready to be his mom again?

Chapter 11

Roots

Her knees creaked as she bent down to pick up the morning paper. The toss that day had only reached the middle of the yard versus the usual positioning on the front porch. Must be a new paperboy.

Paperboy. The word bounced around her head and lit a smile on her face. She remembered Beau's first paper route. He'd begged and pleaded until she let him do it, which meant getting up at the butt-crack of dawn and driving him to the print warehouse to pick up his daily allotment. His father helped him attach a basket on the front and back of his bicycle so he could transport the full load and not have to return home to restock.

She winced, as the memory wandered into the dusty cobwebs of repressed pain from her late husband, Clark. He'd passed away a decade ago from heart disease. While she'd lost her son, her own flesh and blood, it seemed different than losing her husband. Losing her son hurt more. Beau was a part of her. She wanted to feel all that pain. She wanted to explore it. Live it. Honor it. She wanted to think about him. Remember him. All of him. She wanted Beau to live on forever in her heart.

But with her husband, the grief was different. She felt a sinking feeling. Nursing him through his final days and watching his fragile body surrender took a piece of her soul. She had sat at his bedside as he took his last breath. The thoughts swept a cold wind through her bones. A reminder of her own mortality.

But she pushed that old fear aside. She had to be there now for her grandson. She had to set an example of how to grieve. It's what Beau would have wanted.

Ah, Beau, her sweet little boy. She smiled and returned to the original memory, still standing in the front yard in her robe clutching the newspaper to her heart.

Beau never missed a day on his paper route. There were rainy days, snowy days—it didn't matter. His work ethic inspired her. He loved pedaling around alone in the early morning darkness, hurling the papers one by one. She worried about him, though, getting hit by a car, or worse.

Even though she'd lived in Brightonville for all her life among an all-white community, she never forgot her past.

Her great-great-grandmother, Charlotte, had been a slave deep in rural Georgia. She was raped by her plantation owner. She had a baby, Abigail. Abigail, also a slave, when grown, had a secret affair with a white bar owner. Their baby boy, Mack, was born into slavery, but went on to be freed.

Mack moved to Savannah during Reconstruction. He was a train porter on the Central of Georgia Railway. He had a secret relationship with a white woman and had Arletta's mother, Patrice. Patrice, a schoolteacher, married a white man and had Arletta.

Arletta had always passed for white. Growing up in the South her parents raised her to understand her heritage but also encouraged her to follow her dreams.

One day she met, Clark Peterson, a handsome, young white traveling salesman while waiting tables at the local diner. He left his telephone number on a napkin that said, "I hope you're as interested in me, as me in you."

She called. A year later they were married, and she moved north to move in.

Beau was the miracle of her life. After three miscarriages, she and Clark had given up. The grief sent her into a deep depression. But in the spring, when the ice melted from the gutters and the roses sprouted from their buds, life also sprang for the Petersons.

She told Beau about his slavery roots when he was about Lincoln's age. He was surprised but he was proud of who he was.

• • • •

Cummings/Peterson Family Tree

Charlotte Cummings—slave	Henry Phillip Jones—Birdsville Plantation owner
-	
Abigail Cummings—slave	Tom Wells—bar owner
-	
Mack Cummings—slave, freed	Catherine Watson—white schoolteacher
-	
Patrice (Cummings) York—biracial housewife	Herbert York—white carpenter
-	
Arletta (York) Peterson—biracial housewife	Clark Peterson—white salesman
-	
Beau Peterson—biracial paramedic	Deborah (Wyndall) Peterson—white real estate agent
-	
Lincoln Peterson	

· · · ·

"Morning Ms. Arletta!" The neighbor lday across the street waved. She was on her morning walk with her tiny little pooch, tail wagging.

Arletta waved back and went inside. As she slinked the rubber band off the newspaper, she felt dizzy. She reached out to balance herself against the wall. Her legs wobbled. A heavy pain. Shooting pain. Her chest. Her legs buckled.

Beau.

Lincoln.

Her husband.

They all flashed in front of her eyes. Then everything went dark.

· · · ·

~LINCOLN~

He couldn't concentrate. He kept thinking about the envelopes. When could he find out more?

He stared at his science test about the parts of a cell—cytoplasm, mitochondrion, ribosome—the words jumped all over the page. They moved so fast they looked like tiny black flies buzzing across a rectangular white sky. He closed his eyes to quiet his mind. As he took a big breath in, he felt Mr. Hudson standing over him.

"Why aren't you working?" Mr. Hudson asserted under his breath.

"I'm sorry. Can I use the hall pass? I need to go to the bathroom." He wiped his forearm across the desk, covering up his unanswered paper.

"We're in the middle of a test. Is this an emergency?" Mr. Hudson pressed.

"Yes."

"Go ahead then," Mr. Hudson scoffed. "You better be back in less than five minutes." Mr. Hudson pushed the timer on his Casio digital watch.

Lincoln felt safer in the hallway. When he was alone, he could focus on the constant thoughts running through his head. At that moment, all he could think about was obtaining another clue. On the way to the bathroom, he snuck into the library.

The librarian, Ms. Henderson, in a purple dress with an emerald broach of a stack of books, sat behind her computer—she was occupied by whatever she was working on—so he tiptoed right on by to the periodicals section.

He dug through the stack of *LIFE* magazines sitting on display. Wow, he thought, the library had a copy of the iconic "V-J Day in Times Square." He took a deep breath and held the magazine out in front of him.

He squinted his eyes.

His vision fuzzed.

Gray.

Black.

The dark silence.

A familiar comfort.

He exhaled.

As he opened his eyes, he found himself dressed as a sailor in a sea of people.

"Ain't it grand to be back among all the landlubbers?"

Lincoln felt a hearty hand on his shoulder.

"Sure is." Lincoln smiled.

He glanced up at the surrounding kingdom of skyscrapers. Neon lights flashed advertisements for Imperial whiskey, Pepsi-Cola, and Camel cigarettes. He saw the Hotel Astor and the Rialto Theater. Many in the crowd waved American flags. They held up the front pages of different newspapers, announcing the surrender of the Japanese and the complete end of World War II.

He stopped and took it all in. The air was electric. Everyone around him skipped and jumped and laughed. There was a true party in the street.

He noticed a woman dressed as a nurse. His gut told him she was the woman in the picture. He followed her. After a few minutes, a sailor approached her from behind. He whispered something to her. Then he bowed her backwards and kissed her so deep it was like he was breathing life back into her.

He couldn't take his eyes off the couple as there was something mesmerizing about their spontaneous embrace. The lightbulbs flashed around them as a few photographers captured the moment. When the sailor let go, the crowd cheered. The infamous pair giggled to each other and scattered back into the crowd. There was too much excitement. They wanted to move on to the next stranger they could celebrate with.

He looked down at the street littered with debris. He skipped over the train rail, being careful not to trip. His heart pumped louder.

He noticed a man with an apron pushing trash with a broom along the curb. As the man pushed the pile, he noticed a flash of blue.

"Wait!" He ran over and grabbed the broom handle from the man.

"Hey, stop that!" the man yelled back as the handle fell to the ground.

Lincoln ignored the man and bent over, sifting through the pile of newspapers and bottles. The pounding in his chest made him gasp.

"I got it!" He held up the envelope with the blue dove seal.

"Hey, what is that?"

Lincoln ran the other way.

"Hey, come back here!"

He kept running. Would his heart hold?

"Hey!"

The man's voice faded, as he got farther and farther from the curb and deeper and deeper into the crowd. He pulled himself into a phone booth and opened the envelope. Inside the card read, *Tree.*

His heart raced but the rest of his body felt like quicksand. We wanted to think about what a tree could mean, but his body had other ideas.

His eyelids slowed.

The phone booth disappeared.

Darkness.

Then light.

He opened his eyes and stood again in front of the stack of magazines in the library. The books behind him shifted as Ms. Henderson reshelved new ones. He hurried out into the hallway. As he speed-walked, he realized that he needed to pee after all, so he stopped at the restroom on his way back to class.

He slid into his seat, hoping to go unnoticed. He pulled out his notebook and put the envelope inside for safe keeping.

"Excuse me?" Mr. Hudson shouted across the room, breaking the silence. He checked his stopwatch.

He froze, realizing he was caught.

"I'm talking to *you.*" Mr. Hudson raised one eyebrow, identifying his misbehavior to the whole class.

He closed his notebook and squirmed in his seat, not knowing what to do next. All the eyes in the classroom sized him up and down. Well, all except Lizzy. He caught a glimpse of her from across the room, but knew he couldn't make eye contact. She pretended like the current spectacle was not happening. He smiled as he thought about her.

"Wipe that smile off your face. You're late from the bathroom, and there is a no-tolerance policy on cheating. No notebooks allowed during tests—you know the rules. That's another detention for you, Mr. Peterson."

Mr. Hudson wrote his name on the chalkboard, his face flush and two veins popping out of the side of his neck as he spoke.

· · · ·

~DEB~

She couldn't stop daydreaming. She'd been showing a retired couple around all morning but had trouble talking about the homes. Visions of her surprise night with Dan spun around her. She kept undressing him in her mind. Each button on his shirt revealed more of his chiseled chest and left her wondering how many tattoos he had.

She longed for connection. For intimacy. For anything. She knew getting involved with Lincoln's principal would be a terrible idea, but she couldn't get the idea out of her head.

Her lapse in concentration converted to clumsiness. She bumped the wall as she led the couple down the hallway. The minor imbalance went unnoticed.

As they passed through the kitchen, the phone rang.

"Yes, this is Deb Peterson. How may I help you?"

Her expression flashed from neutral to fear as she nodded.

"I understand. I'll be right there." She hung up. "I'm sorry, there is an emergency with my mother-in-law. I have to go."

The couple understood and offered her their best wishes as she raced out the door.

"Arletta?" She rushed up the driveway past the parked ambulance with the lights silently flashing. The red and yellow beams reminded her of the accident, but she held her breath and kept going. She walked through the open front door. Arletta sat propped up in her burgundy recliner, the EMTs laughing with her and packing up their supplies.

"Debra, dear. Bless yur heart. The boys were just finishin' and they say I'm gonna be just fine. Isn't dat right, Jake?"

She looked at Jake like she'd seen a ghost. She pictured Jake standing in her backyard with a beer in hand. He had often invited a few of his EMT buddies to grill burgers and corn. Her knees buckled. She tried to hide it by continuing downward, landing on the sofa across the room.

"Are you okay?" Jake put his arm out, as if he could catch her, even though he was six feet away.

She shook her head yes and rustled around in her purse so she didn't have to make eye contact. "I'm fine. The question is—Arletta, are you okay?"

"Oh, hon, I'm still chuggin' along like a steam engine. Just a minor issue." Arletta patted her chest with pride.

"Minor issue?" She looked at Jake for answers.

"Her blood sugar was low and she passed out. She didn't have enough at dinner and hadn't had breakfast yet. She knows better." Jake gave Arletta a stern glare and then lifted the corners of his mouth in a gentle smile.

"All's fine now, dear. I know I gotta be watchin' my numbers. I got distracted."

"Okay, well, I'm glad everything's all right. Thanks for calling me, Jake." She stood up to leave.

"Wait!" Arletta called out. "Can ya send Lincoln over after school? It'd make me feel better."

She thought about it for a few seconds. "Okay."

"Bless yur heart." Arletta called after her as she walked out the door.

• • • •

~LINCOLN~

"Where are your baseball clothes?" his mom asked as he climbed into the car.

"I got another detention." He didn't have the energy to concoct some elaborate story.

She remained silent.

He sighed and appreciated not having to explain further. "Where are we going? Aren't we going home?"

She looked at him as she pulled up to the stoplight, her left blinker on. Their house was right. "Your grandmother wants to see you."

"Grandma Arletta?"

"Yes."

"How come?" He knew she was hiding something.

"I didn't want to worry you, and I don't want you making a big deal out of it when you get there either, do you hear?"

"Okay. But about what?"

"She passed out and fell this morning. Her blood sugar was low. But she's going to be fine." She reached over and put her hand on his leg, her eyes still facing the road.

Her hand was cold, and he nodded, as he processed the information. He remembered overhearing his dad talk about all the different kinds of medical issues, but it felt different hearing it about someone he knew. His grandma fainting scared him. He couldn't lose her.

"Are you okay?" She wiggled his knee.

"It's just a surprise." He looked away, out the passenger side window. He removed her hand.

"Lincoln?"

He didn't move.

"Listen. I'm sorry about last night. You wanted to ask me something?"

His stomach knotted, and he pulled on the seatbelt.

"You can ask me now if you want." Her voice faded at the end of her sentence.

"I just want to think about Grandma right now."

"Okay." She gripped both hands on the wheel. "Okay then. That's probably a good idea." He noticed a small tear rolling down her cheek.

He hopped out the moment the car came to a stop. Closing the door without a word, he ran up the driveway. He didn't turn around to wave goodbye.

"My boy!" Arletta cried out as he walked in the door.

"Hi, Grandma. How ya doing?" The thought of her surrounded by the EMTs made his insides twist. He slung his bookbag onto the couch.

"Oh, I'm all right, child. Just a lil low blood sugar. The boys fixed me up good. You don't need-be worryin' now. How was school?"

He grimaced at her question and went to the kitchen. "Do you want something to drink?" He peered into the refrigerator, not seeing much.

"It's okay, baby. I got my water cup rite 'ere. Why doncha come 'ere and tell me 'bout what's goin' on wit ya."

He had no idea where to start. Or if he could even start at all.

He skipped around the room, stopping at the fireplace on his tiptoes to explore the collection of framed family photos. He noticed one in the back he'd never seen before. He picked it up. Dust covered the glass and he smudged his finger to clear it. "What's this one?"

Arletta closed her eyes for a moment as she bowed her head. She snapped up and held her rosary as she said, "Dat's my grae gran-ma Ab'gail, so guess dat would make her yur—geez, I dunno, maybe four times grae gran-ma."

"But she's—"

"Yeah baby, she was a slave. Come sit 'ere. You wan me ta tell ya 'bout her?" She dropped the rosary and pointed to the couch.

He sat down with the photo on his lap. He couldn't take his eyes off it. Even though the paper was weathered and yellowed, torn and faded, he could make out the tattered white dress, her tightly wrapped hair and the pain in her eyes.

"She worked on da Birdsville plantation in Georgia. She—"

"Why didn't you tell me?" He cut her off.

"Baby—I'm sorry. I was just tryin' ta protect ya. It's a burden I don't wan ya ta carry."

He looked deep into Arletta's eye. "Something bad happened, didn't it?"

Arletta's eyes welled up. She nodded and blotted her forehead with the wet rag from the end table next to her. "Yes. It did." She took a deep breath and held the cross at the end of the rosary around her neck between her index finger and thumb. "She was raped. And we both light cuz each generation after her gone procreated wit a white. It was survival."

He held still, only feeling the pounding of his heartbeat in his chest. He looked at the picture and then looked at the skin on his arm. A deep wave rolled inside him, but he didn't know what to feel. He didn't know what to think.

"It's okay, baby. I love ya." Arletta reached her arms out and invited him in for a hug.

"Were you ever going to tell me?" He remained on the couch, head still bent over the picture.

"Oh, my sweet baby." Arletta put both hands on her heart and gasped for air.

"Are you okay?" He jerked from despair to worry.

Arletta gasped again and then took a long, smooth breath. "Yeah. I'm okay."

They sat in silence; only the clock could be heard. *Tick. Tick. Tick.*

"Baby, I know 'dis is all a lot. But it was up to your dad. We decided it would be his decision on when to tell ya."

The blood boiled in his veins, speeding away from his heart. "I hate my family!" He bolted out the front door.

• • • •

~ARLETTA~

"My child, I'm so sorry," she whispered, but Lincoln was gone.

She hobbled across the room and retrieved the photo from the couch. Weeping, she picked up the picture frame and put it back on the shelf, this time in the front, right next to a picture of baby Beau.

The moment Lincoln reached toward the back, she had known the exact photo he picked up without even looking. She felt the sting of Lincoln's innocence fading away as her chest tightened again. She hoped she hadn't let Beau down.

Chapter 12

Secrets in Love

He convinced his mom that spending his Saturday hanging out at the public library was better than tagging along on her open house. How could she keep such a big secret from him? He wanted to stay angry for a while.

When she dropped him off, he slammed the door shut and didn't look back. As he neared the entrance, the automatic sliding door, which had been put in by the most recent city council to help make the building more handicap accessible, whooshed open and welcomed him inside with the smell of worn carpet and old books. He breathed in the heritage scent.

The encyclopedia section was his favorite. They didn't have a collection at home so this was a place he could explore anything he wanted. The breadth and depth of information arranged in alphabetical order was like an ocean of knowledge, waiting to be swum in.

The Civil War was the latest topic in his social studies class and he wanted to know more, not to mention the relevance to the photo Arletta had divulged.

He scanned the shelves and found "Volume No. 3, BE-CU" printed in gold against the navy-blue leather binding and pulled it down. With the book under his arm, he walked across the main lobby under an arched atrium ceiling to nab the open brown leather chair, his favorite seat in the library. Flipping through the pages to find the Civil War, he got distracted by other articles. He stopped and read about Billy the Kid, botulism, and Cleopatra.

"Hey." He heard a whisper and a finger appeared in the middle of the page.

His eyes traced up the arm and saw Lizzy. He smiled and whispered back. "Hey."

"How come you're in the library? It's Saturday." She twisted the hair between her fingers.

"Oh, it was either this or showing houses with my mom. So yeah, this wins every time." He laughed.

"What were you reading about?" Her eyes scanned the page.

He slammed the encyclopedia shut. "Oh, just some stuff. I like to skip around. How come you're here?"

"Oh me? I have a book report to write for extra credit on *The Call of the Wild*. Sometimes I just need a break from my mom always checking on me. She will ask to read it as soon as I'm done here. If I was at home, though, she would be looking over my shoulder the whole time. It's hard to concentrate."

"I see." He tried to empathize with her, but had no idea what that might feel like. His mom never even looked at his report card let alone reviewed his work before he turned it in. He guessed she trusted him to do well in school, which had always been the case, even when his dad was around.

"Do you want to sit with me?" she asked, pulling the heavy, wooden-framed chair out from the wooden table a few feet away from him.

"Sure." He got up from his beloved leather throne and helped her adjust the bulky wood chair. He took a seat at their shared table, her belongings scattered across. He noticed a picture of her grandma sticking out of the top of her wallet. If memory served him right, she had told him at his dad's funeral that she'd lost her gran-mama. He splayed open the encyclopedia, but instead of reading the articles, he watched her scrawl notes.

"Are you gonna just stare at me?" She moved her eyes to look at him, but her head remained crooked over her notebook.

He blushed, not realizing she'd been paying attention to his glance. He felt the playfulness of her gesture, but shame boiled up inside him. His raw heart, exposed and vulnerable, throbbed and pleaded to be heard.

"Is everything all right?" she asked.

He leaned back and put his hands over each open page of the encyclopedia. When he looked down and saw his hands, he blinked his eyes. He wanted to tell her everything. "I'm just tired."

"That's all?"

"Yeah. Sorry. I'm distracting you more than your mom from that book report." He chuckled.

She giggled but kept her head down. Her pencil looped beautiful cursive handwriting across the wide-ruled page.

He squirmed in his seat. The pressure was too much. He went to explore.

He turned down the last aisle in the library, as far away from Lizzy as possible. At the end of the aisle, he saw the Last Supper painting hanging on the wall. Would he really try something like that? He made the sign of the cross and took a deep breath as he felt his eyelids fading.

He stood still.

Eyes closed.

Waiting.

Darkness.

Then light.

When he opened his eyes, he felt the warmth of the sandstone floor underneath his thin sandaled feet. To his surprise, he sat at the table, three chairs over from the Son of God. He listened to the conversation, overhearing Jesus share that someone sitting at that very table would betray him. Everyone murmured and glanced around the room, reassuring themselves it surely wouldn't be them. He got a funny feeling in his stomach, thinking it could be him. He pushed back from the table, but Jesus noticed him leaving.

"Please...stay." Jesus outstretched his arm from the head of the table.

"Yes, of course." Lincoln resumed his seat.

"Now, I take this cup," Jesus went on.

The man next to him in a rusty orange cloak passed him a chalice filled with wine. He didn't know whether to take a sip. He wasn't old enough to drink. Staring into the chalice, he decided to go for it and tipped the cup backward. He winced at the sourness, choking a bit. The liquid burned his throat and he excused himself from the table, coughing all the way into the next room. He clutched his throbbing heart. A hand tapped his shoulder.

"I know your pain, my brother, but you will survive. Love will guide you," said Jesus.

He stared back into Jesus's eyes. Hypnotized. Surrounded by a cloud of love.

"Here, take this. It will bring you closer."

He took the envelope from Jesus's outstretched hand.

"And remember, you have the strength. It is inside of you."

"Thank you." He watched Jesus return to the table. The card in the envelope read, *Glass.*

He paused, feeling like his heart might explode. There would be glass at a car accident...

Then sleepiness washed over him. He closed his eyes.

The dark silence.

Black.

Gray.

Then light.

The library reappeared. Alone between the bookshelves, he let out a big sigh and tried to catch his breath. He wondered whether his body could continue to withstand the toll of the experience. He didn't want to have a heart attack. What is worth the risk to keep finding clues? They didn't seem to be leading anywhere? But still...

He staggered back and sat down across from Lizzy, non-consciously putting the envelope on the table.

"What's that?" Lizzy's head snapped up when he sat down.

The back of his throat seized. He snatched the envelope and thrust it into his bookbag all in one swipe. "Oh, nothing."

Lizzy gave him a death stare.

"Okay. It's a note." He scrambled to make up something. "It's from another girl in class." He breathed heavy. "I didn't want you to see it. It doesn't mean anything." Wiping his brow, he said, "I mean, we are together. And that's all that matters." He flashed a half smile toward her, hoping for the best.

Silence. She was thinking, but he had no idea what.

"It's okay if you don't want to tell me right now." Lizzy paused. "But if we are going to be together, like you say, then you will have to tell me eventually." She started writing again and then picked up her pencil. "And I do want to be together." She smiled at him and then turned back to her notebook.

. . . .

~LIZZY~

"Let me see it."

Lizzy unzipped her backpack and pulled out her notebook. Her mother wasn't leaving the parking lot until she read her book report. Her mother riffled through the pages.

"It's at the back." Lizzy tilted her head against the headrest and closed her eyes. She'd never seen Lincoln in the public library before on a weekend. The run-in was nice.

"You've got the symbolism of Buck all wrong. What were you doing in there?" Her mother shut the notebook and pressed it on her lap.

Lizzy's chest tightened. She bent over and slid her notebook into her backpack.

Her mother put the car into drive. "We'll discuss this when we get home."

Lizzy looked out the window. She knew what she'd written was good. There was more than one way to interpret Buck's death. She tried not to dwell on the negative. What she really wanted to know was, what was Lincoln hiding? That envelope wasn't a note. He didn't seem like a liar. What would make him lie? And where'd he get that strange envelope?

· · · ·

~DEB~

Deb's stomach growled as she heaved the "Open House" sign into the trunk of the Oldsmobile. She trotted back toward the house. The chorus of multiple key rings jingled in her purse as she stood on the front porch and fiddled to find the right key.

"Got it!" she said out loud to herself. Turning the key, she ran inside and grabbed the phone off the wall. Lincoln would be excited with the pizza she'd ordered.

"Order for Peterson," she called out, walking up to the counter.

The pizza parlor was empty except for two teenagers at a booth in the back with a tower of rumpled napkins on grease-spotted paper plates and an elderly man alone by the window hunched over spaghetti. She unbuttoned her coat and wiped her forehead with a hanky from her purse.

"Peterson?" The lanky teenager in a red polo shirt with a jagged stitched-on emblem for "Little Tony's" behind the counter repeated.

She nodded.

The teen searched the boxes stuffed with receipts like little white tongues. "Sorry, not ready yet."

She grunted under her breath and put a $10 bill on the counter. "Okay, I'll wait outside. The pizza oven is too much for me."

The lanky teenager stared back at her without moving a muscle in his face. She hoped Lincoln would have better manners once he got his first job.

Pushing open the door, a rush of cool air hit the few areas of her damp exposed skin. Her face, her ears, her hands, the slit on her chest from the plunging neckline of her blouse. She breathed deep and welcomed the cold pang, probably the last cold spell of the spring.

"Deb? What are you doing outside?"

She jumped.

Dan stood in front of her. "Sorry, I didn't mean to sneak up on you." He laughed and put his hand on her shoulder, his keys dangling.

"Nice keychain," she joked, noticing the a bobble-eyed cat medallion among his noisy collection of keys.

"I don't like to be too serious. Plus, it's something students always get a kick out of if I happen to run into them."

"You have cats?"

"No."

She giggled. "That makes it even funnier."

"Want to go inside?" He opened the door and held it, waiting for her to go inside. "This April chill is crazy."

"Hopefully my pizza's ready." She stepped inside and went straight for the counter.

"Sorry, still not ready," the lanky teenager shouted as he saw her.

"Geez, what's taking so long?" She mumbled under her breath.

"Murphy, hey!" The teenager wiped his hands on his apron and came to the side of the counter to give Dan a high-five. "Yours is ready." He handed him a box and rang him up.

"Hey, let's sit down and you can have some of mine while you wait?" Dan put his hand behind her back, ushering her to the empty booth.

She didn't think; she let him guide her. She landed on the bouncy green leather bench and peeled off her coat to get some reprieve from the thick tomato-smelling heat.

Dan smiled and opened the box, revealing a pizza piled high with every topping imaginable.

She grimaced. "What kind of pizza is this?"

"It's the Murphy special." He laughed. "I never got pizza while I was on tour and I just love it so much. I can never decide what toppings, so I just ask them to throw everything on. I pay extra for it."

"How long did you serve?"

"Five years." His smile melted, and he shoveled a big bite into his mouth.

She paused and picked the anchovies off her slice. "I'm sorry if you don't want to talk about it."

He swallowed and gazed toward the ceiling.

She waited. Was he going to say something?

His eyes shifted back and forth, but his body remained still.

"Dan?" Her panic meter started going off. "Are you okay?"

• • • •

~DAN~

He didn't hear a word. The ceiling of Tony's crumbled.

• • • •

September 2, 1990

He steered the Humvee right and left, evading incoming artillery fire. The bullets pelted and pierced the sides of the Humvee.

"Murphy, get us the fuck out of here!" The commands came from the chorus of voices in his vehicle.

He swerved and struggled to steer as the windshield cracked and obstructed his view.

"Fuck!" he screamed, as a bullet whizzed by his head through the driver's side window.

• • • •

"Are you okay?" He felt Deb's hand on his forearm.

"Yeah," he muttered and put his other hand on top of hers. "I've never told anybody this, but..."

"It's okay..." Deb softened her eyes.

"I think something is wrong with me." He shook his head and fought off the emotions, but he could feel all his usual guards disintegrating.

"Dan." She looked him square in the eye. "Nothing's wrong with you."

"I get these visions. Like hallucinations."

She looked at him funny.

"No, it's not drugs. It's memories. The war was five years ago, but I can't get away from it. Every time I close my eyes I wonder if I'm going to relive my nightmares. I was responsible for men who died." He looked up and noticed a tear dripping down Deb's face. "Deb?" He squeezed her hand.

She pulled her hand away. "I'm sorry," she said and rose from the booth, snatching her coat in a messy bundle and heading toward the door. "Thank you for the pizza, but I have to go."

"Wait! Yours is ready!" The lanky teenager held up a pizza box, a caricature of Little Tony etched on top. She took it and left without looking back.

He sat stunned in the booth, as a fly buzzed over and landed on top of his pizza.

• • • •

~DEB~

She slogged through the back door, her eyes tired and blank, pizza in hand.

"Pizza!" Lincoln's face lit up, but she looked away.

She set the box on the table and kept walking out of the kitchen. Heaving herself onto the couch, she covered her face with her arms.

What had just happened? She couldn't believe how she'd acted. Yes, she'd thought about him when Dan brought up how his memories haunted him. She was haunted every day too. She wanted to feel for Dan, but instead she felt jealousy. *She* was the one in pain. She wanted *him* to comfort *her*. Ugh, she hated herself for feeling that way. All she could think to do was run away. But how far could she run? He was the principal at her son's school.

"Mom? Are you okay?"

She returned her arms to her sides. "Yeah, honey. Just a long day."

"I saved you a few pieces." Lincoln handed her a plate.

"Thanks." She took a bite. The pizza was still warm. She needed some warmth.

Chapter 13

Lincoln's Fan Club

~DAN~

"Here are those permission slip forms you needed," said Linda, his secretary.

He smelled the fresh toner and Linda's vanilla and jasmine perfume, as she dropped the stack on his desk.

He didn't look up, so she hovered.

"Are you okay?"

"Oh, sorry, what?" He looked up and noticed Linda had removed her reading glasses. They rested on her chest, hanging on a multi-colored braided cord.

"I said, are you okay? You haven't come out of your office all day. Did something happen?"

He knew he couldn't lie to Linda—she was too sharp. Her age had yet to slow her down, and she reminded him of that fact every day. But he didn't even know what to say. He'd gone after a woman, even opened up to her about his inner demons, and she literally got up and ran. How much clearer were the signs? He was meant to be alone. He was meant to pay for his sins. He wished he'd died in Iraq.

Linda pulled out the chair in front of his desk and sat down. She squinted and studied him. He tried to uncrinkle his forehead. She sighed. He felt the room open up. There was a warm, fuzzy feeling about Linda. She reminded him of his mom.

He missed his mom. She was all the way across the country taking care of his grandfather, who suffered from dementia and needed constant supervision. There had been an incident. His grandfather went missing. Despite his return accompanied by a police officer, after that day, his mom never let his grandfather out of her sight. The situation was heartbreaking and he hated how parasitic it was to his mom's positive energy and warmth. Wasn't it enough she had to worry about her son being away at war for five years? Now she had to worry about her dad and watch his mind regress and deteriorate in front of her. Would she ever get a break from being a parent?

"It's so many things." He looked up at Linda, searching for permission to let it all go.

Linda just nodded and looked back at him with gentle eyes. "Go on."

"Well, I guess I could boil it down to one thing." He ran his fingers through his hair and leaned over the desk. "I'm broken."

Linda paused before saying, "Son, we are all broken."

"Not like me. I got some crazy thoughts. Haunting thoughts. They won't ever stop. That goddamn war. Fucked me up." He pounded his fist on the desk. "Excuse my language."

"I can't imagine what kind of things you've seen. It must've been horrible. I'm very sorry you're struggling, but you're not alone. Have you ever talked about this with another soldier?"

"It's not much use. Most guys don't want to talk about anything. They think it's too sensitive to talk about that kind of stuff. Anyway, I tried to talk to Deb about it, and she literally ran away. It was humiliating."

"Deb?"

"Yeah, Lincoln Peterson's mom, I know it's probably not great ethically. But I think it might be over before it ever really started."

Linda reached across the desk and grabbed his hand. "Dear, she's lost her husband. She doesn't know what she's doing yet. If you really like her, you got to give her another chance."

"You're probably right."

"You gotta keep trying. You deserve love and you deserve peace. But they are not always gonna fall in your lap. You should think about seeing someone to talk through what you're still holding from the war. You're a hero, and you should think that way about yourself. And you better give Deb a call." Linda winked as she got up and walked out.

He sighed and felt a sense of release circulate through his body.

• • • •

~DEB~

She tossed a bag of carrots into her shopping cart as she walked like a zombie through the produce section. She didn't even think about what she was buying. That would have been too taxing. Her mind couldn't focus. She did her best to make sure Lincoln had what he needed. She trudged along and picked up a carton of eggs. As she peeked inside to inspect the eggs for cracks, she remembered the trip to Turtle Lake.

• • • •

August 8, 1982

He rented a cottage on the lake to celebrate their first anniversary. When they arrived, it was like walking into a children's storybook. The cottage had a curled orange ceramic tile roof, whitewashed siding, and flowerbeds sprouted with daisies attached along the bottom of the royal blue framed windows.

They woke up to chickens clucking and discovered a small coop behind the tall oak trees in the backyard. He opened the door and went inside.

"Isn't this a special treat? We can have a farm country breakfast!" His eyes lit up as he gathered a half dozen fresh brown eggs in the front of his outstretched flannel pajama top.

"That sounds great, honey."

She gazed at him through the door, standing outside in the dew-kissed grass. Her slippers were soggy around the edges and her toes were cold, but she couldn't stop watching him. She admired and wanted to have his innocence and pure joy for life. Could she ever get that excited over an egg?

• • • •

"Excuse me."

Deb heard a faint voice.

"Excuse me, dear." She heard it again, louder this time.

"Oh, I'm sorry." Deb stepped aside to let the elderly woman grab a carton of eggs from the cooler.

The elderly woman examined each egg, turning each with a gentle flick of her wrist. Deb stood still, staring into the cooler. She felt stuck.

"Honey, you all right?"

She felt the elderly woman's hand on her arm. She blinked and then focused on the woman. "Oh, yes. It's just lack of sleep."

"I sure get my fair share. You will too someday." The woman snickered and pushed off from her arm to walk away.

• • • •

~LINCOLN~

He heard the garage open and ran to the back door. His mom pulled in, turned off the engine, and popped the trunk.

"There are groceries in the back." She walked inside without looking back.

"Okay, I got it." He made a face.

He lugged in two heavy brown paper bags of groceries, worrying they were so full they might break, but he made it and slid them on the counter.

"Thanks." She pulled at the top of one of the bags and unloaded.

He watched her, transferring items onto random shelves in the fridge as the door hung wide open. She stopped when she got to the eggs. She stood there motionless.

"Mom, you okay?"

She didn't reply. He thought she was tired from a long day.

"Don't forget I have my first baseball game tomorrow."

She nodded, placed the eggs on the shelf, and closed the refrigerator.

He was looking forward to his mom watching him play. He thought it might be a good thing for her to sit by a baseball diamond again. His dad used to coach him, and while being at the field might be hard for her, he hoped those hard things would become happy memories she wished to remember rather than push away.

• • • •

~JJ~

"Look who it is! Mr. Detention!" JJ shouted for everyone to hear, as he walked down the hallway.

JJ watched Lincoln open his locker to hide his face.

"What're ya hiding from?" JJ grabbed the locker door and wrestled it from Lincoln.

"Nothing." Lincoln appeared unfazed.

JJ's blood boiled. He was tired of Lincoln being so perfect and getting all the attention.

Trent grabbed the locker door from JJ. "Mr. Hudson is just being tough on him. He's always out to get someone—all those detentions must've sucked."

"It wasn't so bad. Just did my homework," Lincoln said.

"You ready for the game tonight? We need you to hit," Trent said to Lincoln and then looked at him. "JJ can't hit a ball for shit right now."

"Whatever, you'll see after school." JJ blushed and felt nauseous and rushed away so Trent and Lincoln couldn't see his face.

JJ prayed his batting slump would turn around. At the scrimmage last week, he'd struck out three times in a row. After the third strikeout, he heard a knock on the back of the dugout in the middle of the inning. He knew the sound was his dad's knock. When he went around back, his dad grabbed him by the arm, pushed him against the fence, and soft-shouted in his face so the crowd wouldn't notice.

When they got home, his dad grabbed him by the arm again and threw him against the wall in the garage before coming into the house.

He wanted to tell Lincoln. Maybe he would understand? He seemed smart in that way. But he couldn't find a way. He was too ashamed.

. . . .

~LINCOLN~

"Oh hey." He caught Lizzy's eye as she walked by with her friends.

She winked back and a chill shot down his spine. He wanted her to stop so they could talk, but he was scared she would ask him about the envelope from the library.

He turned and put the last book in his backpack and zipped it shut in one big swoop from right to left.

"Hey." Lizzy tapped him on the shoulder.

"Hey!" he shook a bit, startled. "I thought you were with your friends?"

"I was, but I wanted to ask you about something." She crouched to the side and swung her backpack around to the front so she could reach inside.

"Oh?" He swallowed hard, bracing for her to mention the envelope.

"I need a second opinion. I'm freaking out about this essay we had to write for English. I got a B+, and I've never got a B before. I don't know how I'm going to explain this to my mom if she finds out. She is going to be so angry.... I might even get grounded."

He let out a big sigh and leaned over to look.

She flashed the three-ring paper with neat cursive pencil covering the page in front of him. Right at the top a big fat B+ in red ink. As he took the paper, Lizzy put her fingers in her mouth, biting at her nails.

"Well geez, Lizzy, a B+ is not that bad. I only got a B on this paper. I think Ms. Williamson was being a really tough grader—maybe one of her cats got loose and she was having a bad night and took it out on her students." He laughed, trying to make light of the situation.

"It's not funny—this is serious. You don't understand—your parents are not that hard on you for grades."

His face dropped.

"I'm sorry." Lizzy stepped back.

He handed the paper back to her. "You're a really good writer, Lizzy," he said and walked away.

"Wait!"

He heard her plea but kept walking.

• • • •

~ARLETTA~

"Way to go, Prez!" The bench stood and cheered.

Arletta watched the events unfold from the bleachers. Lincoln's bat had cracked a good one. The ball sailed over the third baseman's head and bounced into the outfield. He rounded first and slid safely into second, beaming with pride as his double put his team in a favorable position in a one-out scoreless game in the bottom of the ninth. He signaled thumbs-up to his cheering team in the dugout across the diamond as he brushed the dirt off his pants.

"Great job, baby! Dat's my gran-baby out dere!" she remarked to the woman next to her. The woman nodded back, smiling but subdued.

The next batter was JJ. He swung and whiffed at the first pitch. The crowd let out a collective sigh.

"Don't screw this up!" JJ's dad yelled, leaning against the fence behind home plate.

She watched poor JJ glance back at his dad and choke up on the bat.

Arletta shot her gaze across the infield and caught Lincoln's scanning eye as he took a small lead off second base. Another game looking for his mom, only to be disappointed.

"C'mon, Jaybirds! Hit 'em home, JJ!" she cheered. She'd shown up to support her grandson despite Deb's constant negligence in sharing the team schedule with her.

As the next pitch whistled in, the bat cracked, and the ball flew toward the outfield. The right fielder ran backward, tracking the fly ball with his mitt and shielding his eyes from the sun with his free hand. Lincoln waited to see if he'd make the catch, and when the ball bounced off his mitt, Lincoln took off. He rounded third, pumping his arms.

She bit her lip and held her breath.

There was going to be a play at home. The right fielder cocked his arm to make a heroic throw. Lincoln outstretched his arms and dove face first toward the plate, plunging beneath the catcher's crouch.

"Safe!" the umpire declared.

As the cloud of dust dissipated, Lincoln emerged with a bloody lip and a smile. The rest of the team surrounded him, and the crowd cheered. Lincoln gave JJ a big pat on the back.

"'Bout time you got an RBI!" JJ's dad yelled across the field.

"Isn't JJ da best?" Arletta said loud enough for everyone around her to hear. "And that's my gran-baby right dere wit him." She smiled.

"Yes."

"Sc'use me?" Arletta turned.

"You asked if he was the best. I said yes, he's the best. I'm Lizzy." Lizzy reached out her hand to introduce herself. "I'm Lincoln's girlfriend. Nice to meet you."

"Darlin', aren't ya da sweetest thang?" She returned the handshake. "I didn't know there were other members of the Lincoln fan club." She laughed, as Lizzy giggled.

"Yeah..." Lizzy's cheeks glowed, and she leaned over so she could cover up her face, one hand on each cheek.

"My child! Don't be hidin' dat beautiful smile!"

Lizzy took her hands away.

"Dat's betta." She smiled.

They sat in silence for a few minutes as the bleachers began to empty before Lizzy whispered, "I don't know how to say this..."

"What's wrong?" She read the scared look on Lizzy's face. A look she knew all too well.

"Well...I'm worried...about Lincoln..."

"Oh?"

"Yeah...he seems really...well...overwhelmed. I'm not sure if that's the right word..."

"Dat's so kind of you, Lizzy. You seem like a real good friend. Lincoln needs people like yurself in his life."

"Yeah, I'm there for him, of course.... I kinda messed things up after school, though. I told him his parents weren't that hard on him about grades. I could tell it upset him, like I was dismissing what happened to his dad. But it was an accident, and I didn't mean to say it. I apologized right away, but I still feel terrible."

"Mistakes happen, my child. Lord knows I made my share."

Lizzy shook her head, but she was not convinced.

"But yur here. Ya came ta support. Dat's a big deal."

"I wish I knew more about how I could help him. I don't really know what to say sometimes."

She picked up her purse on the bleachers and invited Lizzy to move down a row. She put her hand on Lizzy's knee. "I know how hard dat is, honey. Dear Lord do I ever know...but...it's people like yourself who got the courage to say somethin' or even ask da question dat make it betta. Honey, there's no right way or no right words. Ya just gotta try."

Lizzy's eyes opened wider.

"My son, Lincoln's pop...he was my heart 'n' soul...my only child. He brought so much light and love ta dis here world. He looked ya in da eye and had dis magic abili-tay to just know what ya needed. Can I tell ya a story?"

Lizzy nodded and inched closer.

"When Beau was a youngin'—prolly 'bout yur age—he collapsed while playin' soccer. One minute he's runnin' round like a healthy lil' boy and da next he's layin' on da grass, not movin'. Of course, I was scared ta death. I thought I'd lost my boy, but da good Lord had other plans for 'em. It's just one of those things. Turns out he had a heart defect. He had ta have a very risky surgery, but he survived. All the doctors and nurses were so impressed with 'im—high-fivin' and telling him how brave he was. From dat day on, he always wanted ta be a doctor, he wanted ta help people. He wanted ta be wit 'em in da scariest time. He had dat special calmness 'bout 'im. Ya always knew ya were safe when ya were wit 'em." She sighed and clasped both hands around the rosary dangling from her neck.

"He sounds so special..." Lizzy put her hand on Arletta's knee.

She reached down and embraced Lizzy's hand. "Yes...he really was." A small tear puddled in her eye and slid down her puffy rouged cheek.

"Lincoln has that in him too, I can tell," Lizzy said.

"He sure does." She shook her head. "He sure does."

She and Lizzy looked toward the field as loud cheers of laughter erupted from the Jaybirds' dugout. The head coach failed to elude the celebratory Gatorade bath. His crisp white uniform with a big "C" on the back was now doused in bright orange liquid.

"Well, I should be going," Lizzy said. "Thank you for talking with me."

"Anytime, m'dear, anytime!" She waved and watched Lizzy scurry off with her friends. She smiled knowing Lincoln had a friend he could confide in and one who was looking out for him.

· · · ·

~LINCOLN~

"Baby, you were fantastic out dere. Let me take ya home and make sure ya get some ice on dat lip." He followed Arletta into the parking lot.

"Thanks." He picked at the dried blood.

"Hey, what's wrong? You were da star of da game."

"It's nothing."

"You think I'm buyin' that? No way, young man. And ya got ta show off yur big win in front of yur girlfriend, Lizzy! She's a sweet gurl. Ya should be on cloud nine right 'bout now. You're gonna tell me what's goin' on?"

He couldn't respond. He got into the car and closed the door. He saw Arletta standing still in the parking lot, her right hand on her dropped right hip. She stayed like that for a few minutes before getting in the car.

"Are we gonna go?"

"Are we? I'm not sure. We not goin' anywhere until ya tell me what's wrong. I promise I won't bite. I'll just listen," she smiled.

He chuckled.

"Okay, so what is it?"

His mind raced. He still hadn't forgiven her for keeping his history a secret from him, but Arletta's calm, open presence enticed him to surrender. The pressure built inside him. How could he hold a grudge if he had his own secret? Maybe Arletta was the right person to tell? But he knew that once he said something, there was no taking it back.

He sighed. "This is really hard."

"I know. But I promise if anyone can do somethin' hard, it's you, Lincoln Peterson. Yur da strongest boy I know."

Somehow, the look in her eyes was enough to unlock.

"Well, something strange has been happening to me."

"Oh? What kinda strange?"

His stomach twisted so hard he thought he was going to throw up. "Lizzy, she found a note I had. It was from another girl."

"Boy, dat's not strange. You an attractive yun man, gurls prolly all around ya. But ya gotta decide who ya gonna be wit. Dat Lizzy seems awful sweet. Ya be missing out if ya pass 'er by in my opinin."

He gulped down the residual fear. He'd survived the temptation to tell her about his big secret. Hopefully he could keep finding clues until he learned what he was supposed to know.

Chapter 14

Unspoken Blame

~LINCOLN~

"Look at that lip. Man! How ya gonna kiss your girlfriend?" JJ said, as he set his lunch tray on the table.

Lincoln saw the sneer across JJ's face.

Trent patted Lincoln's back. "Whatever, JJ. He sacrificed his body for the win so you could get your walk-off RBI. You should be happy, not cutting him down. What kind of teammate are you?"

Lincoln watched JJ's eyes follow Trent's hand across his shoulder blades.

"How's your lip anyway?" Trent asked him.

"It's fine." He touched his scraped mouth and confirmed no pain. The pain came from the pressure building in his chest. He'd almost gave up his secret to Grandma.

"Is Coach gonna let you pitch again on Friday?" JJ asked Trent.

Lincoln noticed JJ's eyes drop. JJ couldn't look Trent in the eye. What was going on? JJ never backed down from his signature taunting.

"Yeah, I think so." Trent wound up his arm, testing it out. Trent seemed unfazed at JJ's change of demeanor, but Lincoln couldn't help but wonder.

"Good, we're gonna need you. The Bombers are really good this year, I hear. But not as good as us. Right, Prez?" JJ nudged him.

Lincoln looked back at JJ, eyebrows raised. "Right. Listen, I've gotta check on something. I need something back at my locker."

He left the lunch table. As he walked the empty hallway, Principal Murphy approached.

"Hello, Lincoln," Principal Murphy nodded. Then he noticed his lip. "You oughta get that checked out. Do you need a nurse's pass?"

"No, thanks. I'm fine. Just getting my history book so I can study for my test this afternoon." He scurried away.

As the afternoon classes progressed, his anxiety built. He felt as if his head might explode.

"Hey, Lincoln. You okay?" Lizzy whispered while they were supposed to be reading.

He didn't want to get into trouble again. He passed a note back with, "I'm fine," scribbled in broken cursive.

She returned a note with, "You don't look fine. How's your lip from yesterday?" written in perfect looping letters between the light blue lined paper.

He stopped the note trading. He couldn't deal.

When the bell rang at the end of the day, he sprinted toward the door.

"Hey, you wanna study together tonight?" Lizzy flagged at him, but he whizzed by.

"Can't...have practice...sorry..." He made a conscious effort to avoid eye contact. Lizzy was smart enough to know something was wrong. He didn't have the energy to make up a story or the stamina to hold another lie. He wanted to get away as soon as possible.

After practice, he busted through the double doors. There was Arletta sitting in her old but well-maintained basil green station wagon. He hesitated, but then she put up both hands in a big, encouraging wave.

"How was school, baby?" she asked.

"Excruciating."

"My? Dat's a big word—maybe a vocabulary word this week?" She laughed.

He looked back at her, his face blank and white.

"Lincoln, honey. I'm sorry, baby."

She reached her hand toward his shoulder, but he shifted away.

"Okay. I've been thinkin'..." She paused and took a big gulp of air.

"About?" He shrugged back, his eyes softened.

"I wanna take ya some place and show ya somethin'."

"Okay." He nodded and repositioned himself in the middle of the seat. On accident, he kicked Arletta's purse sitting on the floor.

"I'm sorry, Grandma."

"It's o-kay baby." Arletta kept her eyes on the road, but heard him rummaging around to clean up the mess. "It's okay, baby—ya just leave dat mess, I'll git it later."

Before she could stop him, he noticed the blood test strips. They reminded him of the day when she fainted. He couldn't lose his grandma too. He sat back in his seat and took a deep breath, focusing on the passing trees.

In a few minutes, they pulled off the side of the road. When the car stopped, his heart sunk to the bottom of his stomach. His gaze fixed down at his worn Converses, as he stared at the small hole starting to form on the outside of his right shoe.

Arletta turned off the engine and looked over to him. She put her hand on his shoulder.

"Lincoln, I'm sorry if I'm oversteppin' my bounds 'ere, but I thought dis might help ya. Do ya know where we are?"

He raised his head and saw a crumpled guardrail with streaks of rust and black paint outside. He was so close to it, if he rolled down the window, he could reach out and touch it. Every muscle in his body froze.

Arletta waited and left her hand on his shoulder.

He summoned his courage to break the silence. "This is the place...isn't it?"

Arletta nodded and pulled him close. His face pressed against the rosary beads around her neck. He wept with her for a minute. He was sad, but it felt different. His sadness was accepted.

"It must be hard to lose a son." He wiped his tears and stopped crying.

"You're so brave." She looked at him, then looked away to bat her stained eyes, and then looked back at him. "You're my boy's son." She smiled through the tears.

He smiled back. "Do you know what happened that night?"

"Oh, honey, I'm 'fraid not. Nobody knows. Well, no one cept yur mama. The only thing I know is he was hurt real bad—they spun and hit on the driver's side."

"I wonder if he got to say goodbye."

"I hope so..."

"Grandma?"

"Yes, baby?"

"Thanks for bringing me here. It helps to talk about it. Mom won't talk about anything, but she has to sometime. I wish I could do something, but I don't know how to help. I think the sight of me makes things worse."

"Oh, my boy." She touched her heart and closed her eyes. Then she opened them and pointed right at him. "He's inside you. He's inside me. He's even inside your mama...but it ain't your job ta help her. It's her job ta help *you*. But before she can, she's gotta figure this out herself. She's gotta stop blamin' herself. I don't know what horrible things she saw dat night, but she's gotta find a way ta move on."

Arletta's tears re-ignited. "Oh, it's so hard ta miss someone, but our time on dis here Earth's limited. No one gets a pass. You've gotta live each day wit yur whole heart. Yur dad did that, didn't he?"

She cracked a smile, and he nodded with his own baby smile. "Yur mom'll come 'round. She'll find dat fire again. It's okay ta miss him, baby. It's okay ta cry sometimes. But ya can't let it consume ya. His life will always be a part of ya—don'tcha ever forget dat—but ya can't stop living yur own life. Yur dad would've never stood for that, now would he?"

"No," he sighed. "No way."

· · · ·

~ARLETTA~

Arletta's chest tightened as she pulled back onto the road. With the fading daylight, she wanted to get Lincoln home. She'd been to the cemetery and the crash site countless times, but never with anybody else.

She'd go there to cry, but the tears always eluded her. Her body numb. Her mind empty. All the memories gone, at least for the duration of the visit. After a while, she went because of the numbness; the emptiness gave her peace.

But something was different. She saw the fear in Lincoln's eyes after school and wanted to give him some peace. But what had she really done? She still wasn't sure. She felt closer to Lincoln, but she sensed that even after crying and talking about his dad, there was something deeper going on.

"You okay, baby?" She reached her right arm toward his leg and kept her left on the wheel.

"Yeah." He stared out the window.

"Ya know ya can talk ta me 'bout anything. 'Bout stuff dat isn't 'bout yur dad."

She waited for him to reply, but only the whoosh and rattle of the road filled the space. *He'll come 'round,* she thought.

. . . .

~DEB~

She gripped the wheel. She had had one hell of a day. The will had been officially executed and probate closed. There was some life insurance money, but a lot had gone to cover debts. She thought the end of the paperwork would give her closure, but all she felt was regret and a cold that felt like it was turning into pneumonia.

Tears welled and blurred her vision. Her lungs burned. She found herself panting and driving to her mom's.

She needed someone. Anyone. The emptiness filled her with pain. She couldn't stop thinking about Dan and how much she wanted a connection but also how much she was afraid of it. She couldn't stop thinking about Lincoln and how she had failed him time and time again in his life. All this pain was too much. She was always doing something wrong...

. . . .

February 11, 1985

She'd filled the bath with warm water. At first it was too hot, so she waited to put baby Lincoln into the water. She held him on one hip. He cried from the cold air and the booming sound of the water, rushing from the tub faucet, imploding into the rising bath water.

She kept testing the temperature with her finger. Dipping a finger in and brushing the wetness over the back of her hand. When it was the perfect temperature, she turned off the faucet and sat him upright in the tub. Lincoln's soft legs submerged, the water not deep enough to reach his belly button.

He stopped crying when he felt the warm water.

She reached to get the baby shampoo under the sink. Somehow it had moved all the way to the back of the cabinet. The path to reach the bottle was obstructed. Trapped behind tall stacks of toilet paper and a jumble of other half-open products. She put her head under the frame of the cabinet door. She strained her outstretched arm, her fingers clawing in the dark.

Brrring! Brrring!

The phone startled her. She bumped her head. Instant pain.

"Shit!"

She never got the shampoo.

The next thing she remembered was her husband crouched behind her. His body pushed and squeezed her against the cabinet door. The corner of the wood door pressed into chest. She struggled to close the cabinet door. She needed to breathe.

She turned.

He was giving Lincoln CPR on the bathroom floor.

• • • •

Deb tapped on the front door.

"Who is it?"

Deb heard a distant call from inside the door, but was too weak and dazed to reply.

The door opened. Helen stood inside. "Why Deb, what a pleasant surprise!"

Deb hung her head and stood still outside the door.

"What's going on, honey? Come in, let's talk."

She walked inside and plopped down on the floral printed sofa in her childhood home. She held her head in her hands. Not a single word came out before she cried.

"Honey..." Helen wrapped her arm around her.

"I'm so close," she spurted through her tears.

"So close to what, honey?"

"I'm so close to losing it."

"You can't put that pressure on yourself. It's going to be okay. I felt like my whole world ended when your father left me, but eventually I pulled myself out of it. You can too. You've got the strength. You have to give yourself a chance. You can't keep everything holed up inside. We've all got to lean on each other."

Her cries softened, but she couldn't bring herself to look at her mother yet.

"I'm proud of you for coming over. I'm proud of you raising my beautiful grandson. I'm proud of you for fighting so long. And I'm proud of you for realizing you don't need to fight anymore."

"I thought about the accident today..."

Helen paused and asked for clarification with her eyes.

"Yes...the accident from a long time ago..." Her sulking accelerated to heaving cries. She gasped for breath.

"Honey, it's okay. Take a deep breath." Helen stroked her back.

"Why?" She shouted through the tears. "Why?"

"That question is impossible to answer, sweetheart." Helen looked her in the eye.

"I have to know! I have to. I can't keep messing things up. I put everyone around me in danger."

"Honey, that's not true. You can't blame yourself. You have to let go of these things. It's in the past...and none of these things were your fault. You have to forgive yourself."

"I don't know if I'm ready.... How will I know?"

"I think you already know. I can see it in your eyes. You want to move on. You have to give yourself permission to move on. You have to leave the comfort of this pain. You have to find new and exciting experiences and fill your life with joy. You have to be there for Lincoln. He's right there waiting for you. He will receive you with open arms. You're his mother. He will love you no matter what and he'll always be your son—a beautiful life that you created—and I know you won't give yourself any credit, but you raised him and taught him so many things. You have a light inside of you—I gave that to you—you are *my* child. I know you can do this."

She sniffled and reached for her coat. "I'm sorry...I don't think I can."

Helen attempted to grab her arm as she got off the sofa.

. . . .

~HELEN~

Helen stared at Deb's back and the door closing.

She went to the window and watched Deb back down the driveway.

She didn't understand the strange magnetic forcefield that was their relationship. Deb could shut her out of her life and run away for real. But instead, she kept coming back. And right when they might have a connection, she would run away again. Repelled by any sense of her compassion and empathy. This push and pull exhausted her.

She wished. She hoped. But she was always left standing alone. Watching Deb walk away.

. . . .

~DEB~

As Deb sped down the road, she tried to think of anything to block out the pain. Sifting through memories, she envisioned the morning before her real estate license test.

. . . .

May 21, 1990

He had the day off, but got up early to make her a stack of pancakes. They were piled high and dripping with melted butter and warmed maple syrup they had brought back from their vacation to Vermont the winter before Lincoln was born.

"Pancakes aren't going to make me pass this test," she giggled.

"Of course not; you would ace this without any help. You are my beautiful and smart wife." He planted a delicate kiss on her cheek as she shimmied past him between the sink and the kitchen table. "And when you come home, you will be a real estate agent."

"I wish I was as sure of myself as you are of me."

"You have it in there—you just need to tap into it. You are the most confident woman I know." He tapped his heart and then hers.

"Oh? You know other women?" She flipped her hand up with a smirk on her face.

He grabbed her, putting one hand on each hip, and pulled her in close. "I only *know* one woman."

"You only know one real estate agent...well, in a few hours that will be true."

"Now that's the spirit—there you go!" His face lit up. He grabbed the last pancake from the pan, folded it in half, and held it out for her.

She leaned in and took a bite. "Delicious." She smiled.

Chapter 15
New Possibilities

~LINCOLN~

The time was late, after ten o'clock. Lincoln peered into his mom's bedroom. She sat Indian-style on the bed in her red silk pajama shorts and button-up top, sorting through a bunch of papers. She looked different. Calm. Most of the time, she'd be riffling through the papers, like they had done something to her—walked up and got themselves out of order. She'd be cursing under her breath and acting annoyed at everything.

But in that moment, she seemed subdued and peaceful. Her relaxed demeanor gave him the extra confidence he needed.

"Mom?"

She looked up and noticed him in the doorway. Pushing a few papers aside to clear a place on the bed, she motioned for him to come sit down.

He slid in through the doorway and sat on the edge of the bed, leaving a free leg on the floor.

"It's past your bedtime. What's on your mind?" Her words were strict, but her voice gentle.

He understood his mom's code and continued. "It's important."

"Go on..."

"I know this is hard...and I don't want to upset you...but it will help me..."

"It's okay. What is it?"

"...I went out on Cotton Highway...Grandma and I did...we talked about what happened..." He prepared for the wrath, but she sat motionless, absorbing his words one at a time. "It helped a little bit, but I have some questions..."

"Oh?"

"...Did you get to say goodbye?"

She paused and a single tear emerged before she said, "...in a way...yes..."

He gave his mom a minute, waiting for more explanation. But he watched her body clench up.

"I'm sorry, Mom." He reached out to hold her hand, but she didn't notice. She folded her arms around her stomach, hunching over.

"No, don't be sorry, honey," she muttered into her knees. "It's me that needs to be sorry…"

He didn't know what to say. Dropping his head, he went back to his room and slipped under the covers. He stared at the ceiling, wondering what would come next.

• • • •

~DEB~

When Deb looked up, Lincoln was gone.

She slumped her head into her lap and took several deep breaths. The pain was everywhere. In her bones, in her heart, in her mind. And it was in her son.

Everything she couldn't face was in her son. His pre-adolescent heart that was bigger than hers. A heart that had the courage to ask such a profound question. And she had to stop letting the answer haunt her.

• • • •

~LINCOLN~

As he tossed and turned in his bed, he looked at his alarm clock, which read 2:17 a.m. His frustration with the sleeplessness came to a breaking point and he got out of bed.

He tiptoed around the house, trying to make sense of everything. He wondered how his mom had said goodbye to his dad. What did she say? What did his dad look like? How might he have responded? He thought how hard that must have been. Watching someone take their last breath. Watching their eyes go still. A scene that would be heart-wrenching in any situation but heightened if it was your husband.

He sat on the couch in silence. The corner of the living room drew his eye, as that's where they put the Christmas tree. They hadn't gotten one that past year after Dad died.

He loved how much his dad loved Christmas and how fun it was decorating the tree. His dad would lift him up and let him put the star on top of the tree. On Christmas morning, his dad would make pancakes in the shape of snowmen and stockings. Everyone's stomach would be full and happy before the present opening commenced. He was thankful for all those Christmases, the feeling of pure joy, when he still believed in Santa and everything felt magical.

He took a big breath in, remembering and loving the past, while fearing the loss of it at the same time.

Wandering into the kitchen, he pulled out his mom's hidden vodka bottle. He twisted open the cap and smelled it. A rush of guilt and danger washed over him. On impulse, he put his lips on the bottle and knocked it back. The liquid burned and tasted like rubbing alcohol, but he closed his eyes and swallowed. He put the cap back on and slid it under the sink. Back on the couch, he stared at the Christmas tree corner as the warmth coated his insides.

He remembered how happy his mom had been during those Christmases. Those were the times she seemed to be stress-free. Having fun with the rest of us.

• • • •

December 25, 1989

"Hold that up. Let me see what Santa got you." She pointed across the room, the floor littered with scraps of wrapping paper.

"Look, Mom! Santa got me what I always wanted! It's a Transformer!"

"Wow, look at that. The car turns into a robot. How did Santa know you wanted that?" She bulldozed the blue and white snowflake paper into a pile and crouched next to him.

"Well, I made a list. And he brought it!" He held the car in the air.

"You must have been a good boy this year, huh?" She pinched his bunny foot pajamas.

He nodded and whooshed the car across the open spot on the floor she'd cleared. "I'm going to make it a robot now." He pulled the car close to his body and struggled to pull the sections apart.

"Here, let me help." She used her nails to pull out the first part, then twisted and turned a few other pieces. "Voila! You better watch out, he's going to eat you!"

He laughed and grabbed the robot. "Mom, robots don't eat people."

"What do you have going on over there?" She asked his dad.

"I'm working on Link's racetrack. Almost done."

"Wow, nice work. Santa really challenged you with that fifty-piece construction."

"Santa knows I can handle it." His dad winked at her.

• • • •

Talking about Santa seemed to be a way for her to let loose, Lincoln thought. A way to forget about the errands and scheduling.

But she seemed so different now. He felt the pain she carried; it infiltrated the house. The moment she walked in the door everything got heavy, and the moment she left everything lightened.

He wished she could find peace and be happy.

For the first time, he felt scared, wondering if she'd ever get better.

• • • •

~LIZZY~

Lizzy hid her yawn behind her hand. She enjoyed Mr. Hudson's lesson—symbiotic relationships made perfect sense—but she'd been up late writing another book report for extra credit to balance out the B+ she'd gotten on her previous English paper. She'd forgotten the extra credit deadline, which was not like her. She never left things until the last minute. The stress and the late night hung heavy in her chest.

Mr. Hudson switched the lights off and shuffled in his folder of transparency sheets, prepping the appropriate batch to slide onto the overhead projector. She put her pencil down to give her wrist a break from notetaking.

She spotted Lincoln across the room letting out a big yawn but doing nothing to hide it. Mr. Hudson was a stickler for yawning and would wrap on your desk if he caught you doing it. Lucky for Lincoln, Mr. Hudson didn't look up from the overhead projector.

"Hey, you looked tired in class. Are you okay?" She tracked Lincoln down in the hallway. She worried their symbiotic relationship might become parasitic if she didn't find out why he was avoiding her.

Lincoln sighed.

"Is there something I did? I said I was sorry about what I said about your parents."

Lincoln walked away.

She ran after him and caught his arm. "Listen, I care about you. I can tell there is something and instead of just running away from me, why don't you talk to me?"

Lincoln stared back at her, frozen.

"What do you have to lose?" She raised her right eyebrow.

"I guess I already lost enough, huh?" Lincoln half-smiled.

She smiled back and squeezed his arm. The tension melted.

"I just have a lot on my mind. I'm sorry I haven't wanted to talk about it. I'm just not sure what to say." He hung his head.

"Well, that's okay. That's all you have to say. You can talk to me when you are ready. But just don't ignore me. That's not fair."

"I got it. You're right. Sorry."

She started to walk away and then turned around. "You got quite the grandma. How come you never told me about her?"

"Oh, yeah, she's her own kind of special." Lincoln laughed. "I was saving her for later, but I guess you got an early preview."

She snickered and hugged her books as she headed down the hallway. Their symbiosis was back on.

. . . .

~LINCOLN~

"Just who I was looking for." Principal Murphy tapped him on the shoulder with an envelope.

Lincoln turned and smiled. The contagious big, bright, white smile on Principal Murphy's face was too strong to avoid.

"I normally wouldn't ask you to do something like this, but would you give this to your mother?" He handed him an envelope.

Lincoln studied the small but neat handwriting on the front that read, "Deb." He felt weird seeing his mom's first name. It made him feel even more distant from her.

"Lincoln, I'm sorry if me being around your mom is uncomfortable for you. Is there anything I can do better? I want you to know that I care about you too, not just her."

He just stared. He wanted to trust him. So much that he wanted to throw his arms around him and hug him and tell him he needed someone to care about him. Lincoln could tell he didn't mean any harm and that he was a warm, genuine guy—just like his dad.

But he also wanted to hate this man. He was intruding and changing their lives. He couldn't take any more change.

"Thanks, I don't really want to talk about it right now." He shoved the envelope in his backpack. "But I'll give it to her."

· · · ·

~DEB~

Deb tried to focus. She needed to close a deal. She hadn't sold a house in over a month. Her continuous daze had taken a toll on her work.

"Remember, it has those hardwood floors you love, all original. I think this could be a really smart investment for you." She mustered up a smile and some enthusiasm.

"I'm not sure. It's a little out of our budget." The Pachinskys were indecisive, as to be expected with any first-time homebuyers, she reminded herself. They were newly married and looking for a place to put down some roots.

"Well, you can at least make an offer, right? There haven't been a lot made to date. The seller might consider a low offer. What have you got to lose?"

All she could think to herself was what *she* had to lose. She'd lost too much already. She wasn't ready to witness her own career collapse as well.

Mrs. Pachinsky looked at her husband.

Deb could tell Mrs. Pachinsky wanted the house, but it was Mr. Pachinsky who was being chintzy.

"If you're worried about the money, it might be comforting to tell you that I've had a lot of first-time buyers go through these very same thoughts. It's a lot to commit yourself to. It's the most important purchase you'll ever make. You don't want to make any mistakes. But I'm here to tell you that nothing's going to work out perfect. You could put an offer on a house you love and it can be turned down or be taken off the market. It's all in the timing. And I think the timing is right on this one. If you go in at your budget, even though it's 10 percent below their asking price, I still think we can get it. You have to trust me." She kept her eyes locked on Mrs. Pachinsky, assuring her she meant well.

Mr. Pachinsky glanced at Mrs. Pachinsky to assess their answer. He looked down and shook his head in defeat. "Well, I guess it's worth a shot," he said.

Mrs. Pachinsky smiled and jumped up and down in place while rubbing her husband's back.

"Oh, that's wonderful! I'll call it in right now."

She left to make the call, her heart pounding a mile a minute. They had given it a shot, but it really was a long shot. She needed this deal to go through. She prayed the seller didn't laugh her off the phone line.

"Joe?"

"Yes, is this Deb?" The groggy voice on the other end of the phone cracked. Joe had moved into a retirement community six months ago and entrusted her as his real estate agent.

"Yes, Joe, it's me, Deb. I have some news for you." She kept her voice patient.

"Oh you do? I was just hoping you'd be calling me soon. I'm getting a little nervous over here. You know I ain't gonna be around forever." He laughed.

"I think this is the kind of news you'll want to hear."

"Okay, well then just tell it to me."

"I have an offer for you."

"Oh my good lord, finally. How much?"

"One twenty-five."

Joe didn't respond.

"I know it's under your asking, but I think you should consider it. I think this is a good buyer and this is a hard sell because of the location being a solid twenty minutes outside of town. I don't know when the next offer is gonna come around."

"I guess I don't have much of a choice. You think there'll be any more offers anytime soon?" He coughed, the kind of deep, wicked cough with fluid rising from the bottom of the lungs.

"Joe, you okay?"

"Yes—" He coughed again, but only half as bad as the first one.

"I'm sorry?"

"It's this god-damned emphysema..." He wheezed to catch his breath. "I don't normally talk this much."

"I'm so sorry, Joe. Do you need some time to think over the offer? Maybe you need to rest?"

"I'll take it," he said without a cough or wheeze.

"Okay." The acceptance surprised her.

"Okay!" Joe bellowed back. "You got it, honey. Let's finish this off." He coughed again.

"Sounds great, Joe. I will let the buyers know, and we'll get the home inspection scheduled. You take care, okay?" She felt giddy inside, a feeling so foreign to her that it frightened her.

"Okay, I have some news..." She rejoined the Pachinskys in the kitchen.

"What? What is it?" Mrs. Pachinsky shouted.

"He accepted the offer! Congratulations!"

"I can't believe it, honey!" Mrs. Pachinsky cried, as Mr. Pachinsky dipped her backwards and gave her a big kiss.

More relieved than ever, Deb took a deep breath. She thought of Lincoln and him...and even Dan.

· · · ·

~LINCOLN~

Lincoln finished his homework and shimmied his books into his backpack, but as he pulled on the zipper, it stuck. The envelope from Principal Murphy was caught. He snatched it away from the zipper teeth and sighed as he stared at it. What would Principal Murphy need to tell her? He turned it over. Ugh—sealed shut. He didn't trust his skills to open it undetected.

"Mom!" he shouted from his room. "Could you come here?"

He heard footsteps coming up the stairs. "What on earth are you screaming about?" She appeared in the doorway.

"Here." He threw the envelope across the room, but the lightweight paper didn't make it very far.

She bent over and picked up the envelope, reading her name on the front. "What's this?"

"It's from Principal Murphy."

"Oh?" She put her opposite hand on her chest. "He gave this to you at school?"

"Yeah, after school."

"Did he say anything else?"

"No." He clammed up. He wanted his mother to leave.

• • • •

~DEB~

"Okay." She took the envelope and went to her bedroom, closing the door behind her.

Inside was a handwritten note...

Deb, I'm sorry about the other night. I shouldn't have opened up to you so fast about the war. I didn't mean to scare you off like that. I really care about you and want to give this another chance. Will you forgive me?

~ Dan

She folded the paper and held it against her heart. Tears welled in her eyes. The excitement of selling Joe's house earlier had worn off. She felt ashamed for running away like a coward. Dan was doing everything right, and she could feel herself falling for him. She wanted to know about his time in the war and what he was going through. He was brave for opening up, and she wasn't being fair.

• • • •

~LINCOLN~

After his mom disappeared into her bedroom, Lincoln took advantage of some alone time in front of the TV. He wanted to get his mind off of what might be in that letter.

He sunk on the couch and flipped channels until he came to a rerun of *Saved by the Bell*. As he zoned out, he felt his eyelids droop a bit. No? Could he try jumping into a moving picture? The tiny hairs on his forearms stood up, waiting in anticipation.

He stared at the screen, holding his breath.

Gravity pulled his eyelids.

Darkness.

Sounds faded.

All still.

Then the light.

As he regained his sight, he found himself standing at the top of the stair steps by the lockers at Bayside High. Zach and Screech sauntered by and stopped at Zach's locker. They looked as if they were up to something. Then Kelly, in a purple tank top and white jean skirt, brushed his shoulder as she walked down the steps.

"Sorry," she said full of cheer.

He froze. That was Kelly!

Breathing in, he disciplined himself to focus on the objective. There had to be an envelope for him somewhere, but it was hard to resist the lure of talking to one of them. He watched Zach take a phone out of his over-sized green and blue bomber jacket pocket and extend the antennae. Zach saw him and made eye contact. Zach motioned for him to come down to his locker.

Me? He pointed his finger inward at his own chest.

Zach nodded.

He took in a big deep breath and walked over. His pounding heart had kicked in.

Zach handed the phone to Screech so he could reach into his light-washed Levi's.

"Exchange this for a hall pass?" Zach held out an envelope with a blue seal.

Lincoln's eyes widened and shoulders hunched.

"C'mon. It's a one-time offer."

Riiiing.

Everyone scattered.

Lincoln swiped the envelope and ducked behind a trash can. He heard the faint sound of an orchestra playing the theme song to the commercial, "Beef, it's what's for dinner."

The halls darkened.

His eyes shut.

Sounds faded.

Black.

Then gray.

He opened his eyes. The TV flashed in front of him. He was back on his living room couch. The beef commercial played on TV. How cool, he thought.

He ran up to his room and grabbed his box of clues. Dumping all of the cards on the floor, he tore open the new envelope. *Blood.*

Chapter 16
Playland

"Mom!?" he yelled, bursting through the front door.

"What? What's all the fuss?" His mom jerked her head from the pile of paperwork in front of her.

"I missed the bus. Will you take me to school?" He huffed and puffed. His attempt to chase the bus down was unsuccessful. Despite all his screaming and arm waving, Ms. Lohusky never saw him.

"Ugh. Get your things. We'll leave in a minute. I'm not very happy about this, young man. This had better not happen again. You know you've got to be out there five minutes ahead of time just in case the driver's early. You don't always get a second chance."

"Okay, whatever. Let's go."

He watched as she stood still, her eyes glazed over as if in deep thought.

"Mom, c'mon." He stomped his foot.

She shook her head. "Right, let's go."

They loaded into the car. She flipped the windshield wipers to clear the drops of dew cascading from the folding garage door as they passed under.

"Lincoln?"

"What?" He looked up as he buckled his seatbelt.

"I just got a crazy idea..."

"Oh?"

She grabbed the back of the seat and turned around to look him in the eye. "What do ya say we skip school and work today and drive to Playland? It's been a while since we romped around for a day? Too long, I say."

His eyes widened. He wanted to go, desperately even. He was so taken off guard by his mom's gesture, he couldn't respond.

"Well, I can tell by the look on your face, it's not a bad idea at least. So that's enough for me." She backed down the driveway and turned onto the road, heading the opposite direction of school.

After about five minutes of silence and the familiar scene of one open field after another overtaking his line of sight, he relaxed a little. He realized his mom *was* being serious, and a small flutter of excitement built in his core. There was no other explanation for where they were driving. But what had gotten into her? Breaking the rules was something he'd done with Dad.

· · · ·

May 13, 1994

"Peterson!" The coach stormed across the field.

Lincoln adjusted his batting helmet while standing upright at second base. He had just missed a collision with his teammate, Wilson, playing shortstop in their practice scrimmage.

"Hold the ball!" The coach pointed at Trent, who was standing on the mound.

The team stood like statues throughout the grass and infield, watching Coach's every move.

"Why the hell didn't you slide? You could've knocked heads! You have a helmet on, but Wilson doesn't. I ought to bench your ass!"

"Hey bud, what's up?" his dad asked as he closed the car door.

"What do you mean?" He crossed his arms over his equipment bag and looked down.

They spoke at the same time, talking over one another.

"Did something happen at practice?" / "Something happened at practice."

They both looked at each other and smiled.

"Want to go get some ice cream and talk about it?" his dad asked.

"But I have homework."

"It can wait." His dad winked and put the car in drive.

"Okay, can I get two scoops then?"

"Oh no, is this a two-scoop problem?"

They both laughed.

· · · ·

~DEB~

"Mom?"

"Yes, Lincoln?" She didn't turn around. She kept her hands square on the wheel. Her glance on the road. "Is everything all right?"

"I don't know. You seem..."

"Seem what?"

"...you seem like, well...I don't know..."

"Oh, c'mon. You must mean something?"

"...you just don't seem like yourself.... Is everything okay?"

"I know one thing..."

"What's that?"

"That everything *will* be okay." She leaned over and paused the Air Supply tape. "But it's going to take some time. It's going to take *me* some time. I think I'm finally ready to move on. I'm sorry that I was stuck in a bad place for so long. I know that hurt you. I'm sorry, honey. I can't promise everything will be perfect, but I am committed to making things better for us. I have to do that."

He stretched his lips to hide his smile, as he said, "Okay, Mom. I'd like that."

"Good." She glanced over to him. "Now—let's go have some fun for a change? We both deserve a little break, huh?"

He shook his head, no longer able to hide his smile.

• • • •

~LINCOLN~

The Playland sign emerged from behind the strip malls and fast food restaurants that bordered the street. Flags lined the top of the sign, one at the top of each letter, each a different color of the rainbow. The sign stood at the beginning of a grand parkway with a tree-filled median, welcoming guests to a day of excitement and fantasy.

Butterflies circled in his tummy, nerves that were more about exhilaration than anxiety for a change.

"What about school?" he said. "I don't want to get in trouble again."

"Don't worry about that. I'll call Principal Murphy once we park. It'll be fine."

He relaxed and the closer they got, the more he could scope out. The tops of the rollercoaster hills, the spokes of the Ferris wheel, and the people-mover buckets hanging down from the thick cable stretching from the front to the back of the amusement park.

They pulled into a parking spot, as directed by the parking attendant with the bright yellow flag.

As they approached the front gate, his mom bought tickets and headed to a line of payphones near the restrooms.

She dropped a dime into the payphone and dialed. "Yes, can I have Principal Murphy, please?... Okay.... Hi, Dan. I wanted to let you know Lincoln's going to be absent today.... Yes.... He's come down with something.... Yes of course...I will.... Wait, one more thing. About the other night at Little Tony's. I'm sorry, I shouldn't have run out like that.... Okay.... Let's talk again soon.... Okay, bye."

He cocked his head.

"See—that's settled." She hung up the phone with a smile.

"I guess so. What about Little Tony's?" He couldn't stand being left out. He knew something was going on.

"Oh, I ran into Dan at Little Tony's; remember I brought home the pizza?"

"Yeah." He nodded, not yet satisfied with her answer. "But why did you apologize? What do you mean, you 'ran out'?"

"Oh, I was just in a hurry, and it was rude of me. I barely even said hello."

"Yeah, you can be rude sometimes." He smirked and walked toward the entrance. He wanted to forget about it all and have some fun.

"What?" She ran to catch up with him. "What did you say to me?"

The concern dropped off her face as soon as he cast her a smile.

"C'mon, I'm just kidding. Let's just go inside. You were the one with this idea," Lincoln said.

"You're right. Let's go have some fun."

He couldn't believe his mom. After four roller coasters and countless other spinning, twisting, bumpy rides, she was still standing. The day was nearing 7 p.m., the park closing time, when they reached the back of the park. The sky glowed orange, as the spring sun descended, nearing sunset.

"Mom, can we go on Dragon's Flight? Everyone at school said it's the coolest roller coaster in the park. It has five different drops, it goes upside down, it goes over a lagoon for part of it, and it goes backwards at the end. Please, Mom, please?" He hoped she'd saved some energy for this last wicked ride.

She glanced over as a car whizzed by them on the track of Dragon's Flight with passengers screaming for their life. "I don't know. It's been a pretty long day. My head is starting to ache from all the excitement and motion." Her voice trailed off as she rubbed her forehead.

He sighed. A small frown materialized on his face. His eyes dropped. He turned and walked toward the park exit.

"Well, let's check out the line and see if we can even get on before the park closes," she whispered.

He turned around as she glanced down at her watch. "Oh yeah!" He jumped off the ground, pumping his fist.

They raced over to the entrance of Dragon's Flight, and the sign said, "45-minute wait."

"It'll be close, but let's give it a shot," she said, leading the way into the queue.

They snaked through the labyrinth of silver railings.

"Are you excited?" she asked.

"Yeah, of course. This ride's awesome! Are you?"

"Well I don't know if *excited* is the right word."

"Oh, c'mon. You're not scared, are ya?"

"Don't be silly. I'm not scared. I'm just preparing my stomach for the tumbling it's about to take." She laughed, rubbing her midsection.

"You'll be fine, Mom. You've made it all day. What's one more ride?"

She nodded her head accompanied by a slight eye roll.

His mind wandered. The wait was the longest one they'd had all day. They walked through an indoor tunnel in the queue lined with pictures of fiery dragons and knights trying to tame them. He felt tempted to stop and stare. To take a journey for another envelope, but realized that could never work. Not with the line moving and not with his mom right there. He sighed and realized he hadn't thought about his gift or stressed out about it once all day. It felt nice.

After about forty-five minutes, they reached the top of the loading platform. He sprinted toward the front car.

"Okay," she resigned and shook her head with a slight smirk.

They buckled up and pulled the harness over their heads. He giggled with excitement. Then with a whoosh, they were on their way, feet dangling above a green lagoon.

He watched his mom as they inched up the first big hill, the creaking gears pulling them straight into the sky.

"Open your eyes," he said.

"I can't." She crinkled her nose to try and force her eyes shut tighter.

"You don't want to be surprised, do you?"

"Just tell me when it's over."

"That's not gonna be for a few min–itzzzz…" His voice turned into a scream. "Whooo! Yeahhh!"

They plunged down the hill and whipped around turns, flipping upside down with no mercy.

"Isn't this fun?" he screamed but couldn't tell if she'd heard him. Her eyes were still closed. Her head volleyed back and forth between the rubber harness.

The car paused for a moment.

"Is that it?" she asked, her eyes still glued shut.

"Nope!" he screamed, as they whooshed backward for one final whip around the corkscrew turn, the signature ending that teased riders into thinking it was over.

As the car came to its true final stop, he said, "Okay, it's over, Mom. You can look now."

She opened her eyes as they sat stationary, waiting for the car in front of them to leave the platform so they could disembark.

"Phew, that was quite a ride…" She flicked the stray hairs out of her eyes.

"How would you know? You had your eyes closed the whole time." He laughed.

"Does that not count or something?"

"No, maybe it doesn't. Seems like we need to ride it again?"

"Very funny, mister." She glared back at him with a smile.

They walked down the exit ramp and checked out their picture.

"Photo evidence!" He blurted out as he pointed up to the screen, having located their photo. Plain as day, her eyes were closed.

"Oh dear, that's a terrible photo of me," she laughed.

He chuckled with his mom. "You missed seeing everything. They have another ride that takes you in the dark. We could have went on that if I knew."

She kept laughing. "What's the number on our photo? Let's get some evidence of this day and how much fun we had?" She handed him a twenty-dollar bill.

"Sure." He took it and ran to the cash register. He was surprised how much fun he had. He forgot what it was like to have a family.

· · · ·

~DEB~

As the glowing orange-pink sun danced its final steps with the horizon, Deb pulled the car door shut. After a day of screams, nausea, and foil-wrapped hot dogs, she sunk into the comfort of the leather seat. She leaned against the steering wheel, and her stomach twisted into that familiar pretzel. But this time was different—she felt some hope.

The thought finally hit her—she *had* gotten a second chance. Since the accident, she had never stopped to think and appreciate how blessed she was for what she had. Her life. Her son. She had been focused on what she lost and how much pain it brought. But that day, she had had so much fun with her son. She had let her guard down. She had lived.

At first, she worried the grand gesture of skipping school and an extravagant trip to Playland would seem like she was trying too hard. Like she could buy her way out of the emotional desert in which she had abandoned her son. Sure, she'd confused him at first—this was all out of the blue—but it freed them both. Despite feeling sick after the first spin on the giant octopus scrambler, she felt like a kid again. Every time Lincoln laughed, a full-hearted innocent child laugh, she laughed with him. His giggle was contagious, just like his dad's. And when Lincoln begged to go on one last coaster and ride in the first car, she forced her aching body to take one more pounding because she didn't want the day to end.

"That was great, Mom, thanks," Lincoln said as he buckled up.

"It sure was," she said with a smile. She plopped her purse on the floor, and the picture from Dragon's Flight fell out. She picked the photo up and studied her crinkled face. For the first time, she didn't care what she looked like. She only cared about the memory. The day she started living again.

• • • •

~TRENT~

"Hey, Prez. Where were you yesterday? You missed a really great game," Trent asked, as the boys walked up the stairs to the cafeteria.

Trent was worried. Lincoln had gotten in so much trouble at school lately. He wasn't acting like himself. He seemed worse than right after Beau died. He missed his friend.

"Yeah, where were you? Playing hooky?" JJ's voice rose and cracked.

"I told you. I was sick."

"What were you sick with?" JJ pressed.

"I had a cold, okay? So who's pitching on Friday?" Lincoln sat down with his packed lunch and chocolate milk carton.

"I'm pitching. Now where were you yesterday, seriously? We all know you weren't sick." Trent swiped Lincoln's milk from across the table.

"What does it matter? Why don't you guys leave me alone?" Lincoln grabbed the milk back from Trent and moved to an empty table across the cafeteria. Trent followed and behind him, JJ.

"Prez, why are you being such a dick about this? Why don't you just tell us?" Trent didn't like being shut out by his friend and he hated that he didn't know why.

"Screw you guys," Lincoln said under his breath as he popped up and headed toward the cafeteria exit.

"What was that?" JJ asked. "Trent, I think he just told us to screw off."

"Whatever!" Lincoln called back, not even bothering to turn around.

"See, I knew it!" JJ proclaimed. "F off!" JJ flipped the bird to Lincoln's back.

"Why?" Trent turned to JJ. "Why are you such a little bitch? Prez is my best friend and you treat him like crap. I was handling it."

"Sorry, didn't know you had a crush on him," JJ hissed as he scurried away.

"What?" Trent said as he watched JJ punch a locker on his way down the hallway.

Trent didn't understand anything. Why was his best friend giving him the cold shoulder? Why was JJ acting so weird? He didn't know what to think. He wished he could talk to someone about it. His dad was still out of town, and the one person he told everything to, Lincoln, was not talking to him.

· · · ·

~LINCOLN~

Lincoln escaped to the library to avoid his annoying friends. He picked up an encyclopedia. Flipping around, he stopped on the history section and the story of the *Titanic*. He'd always been so curious about what had happened. There was a full page of photos—the gigantic steel skeleton being built in the shipyard, the four steam stacks puffing white clouds into the blue sky as the ship pushed away from the Southampton pier, a portrait of Captain Ismay, a child and his father playing with a top on the deck, the bow sticking straight up in its last moments, the front railing resting under the sea covered in rusticles.

He looked away for a minute. Curiosity and danger danced on his chest. He remembered all the scenes he'd been in so far and survived. A war. Outer space. But his heart worried him. Would the throbbing pain intensify? Could his body withstand whatever was happening? *No*, none of that mattered. He sat up straight. This was happening for a reason and he needed to know where it was all leading. He took a deep breath and focused on the picture of the grand staircase.

His eyelids dropped.

He squeezed the edges of the book.

Gray.

Then black.

Everything numb.

Until the light.

Slow rays poked through dark.

He opened his eyes.

He stood at the bottom of the grand staircase. Above his head was the beautiful atrium, letting in the fleeting sunlight. The smell of warm bread and garlic circulated. He heard the light sound of violins. Dinner must be soon. He looked at the majestic clock perched at the middle landing of the stairs: 6:55 p.m.

He moved aside as a steady stream of first-class passengers dressed in ballgowns and formal suits made their way down the stairs and into the dining area. He couldn't help but feel eerie, knowing most were going to meet a terrifying, icy death.

"Excuse me," he asked a gentleman in a top hat and coattails passing by. "Can you remind me of today's date?"

He pulled out his pocket watch on a gold chain and flipped it open. "It's the 14th."

"Thank you." He swallowed hard. In a matter of hours, the ship would be at the bottom of the Atlantic Ocean.

He followed the crowd into the extravagant white, wood-paneled dining room carved with delicate patterns and goddess heads that stretched from the front to the back of the ship, the only room on the ship that did so. He wore a suit with satin peak lapels, a white bow tie, and a jacket with coattails, which helped him fit right in. Cigar smoke and the hum of gossip circled around him. He felt dizzy. Maybe he was seasick?

He seated himself and glanced at the menu—ten courses! Surely a meal fit for royalty with oysters, filet mignon, salmon, chicken, lamb, duck, foie gras, and a palate-cleansing ice, flavored orange and drenched in champagne called "Punch Romaine."

"Shall we have a drink?" He felt a tap on his shoulder. In front of him was the same gentleman from the stair landing who had told him the date.

"Yes, of course." He chose the most formal words he could think of. Even though most passengers spoke English, there were words sprinkled in he didn't recognize.

"This way, please join me at my table. I'm traveling solo, returning from business in Antwerp, and have reveled in acquainting with various fellows aboard."

He followed in silence. His stomach churned. The drumming of his heart started. He felt heaviness shoot down his legs.

"We'll have two Tom Collinses," the man ordered for them as they sat down. "Forgive me, let me introduce myself. I'm Jakob Birnbaum. I failed to inquire of you, sir. Please tell me your name."

"Oh." He froze. He managed to say, "Mr. Peterson."

"Of the Petersons from New York? New oil money?"

"Yes, of course." He didn't hesitate with his answer this time, but he shifted in his seat. The waiter placed the cocktails on the linen table cloth and Lincoln took a drink in haste. He felt the room enclosing around him.

"Oil is the new gold. I'm in the diamond business myself, but oil sure seems very promising."

"Ah, yes, indeed." He took a big gulp. The liquid burned his throat. He tried not to cough.

"So, I noticed the absence of a wedding ring. You are not married I presume?"

"No."

"Any lady friends?"

"No."

"Do you want to go on the make tonight? We can walk along the boat deck later and find some company for you."

"Sorry to interrupt, gentleman. I have a telegram for Mr. Peterson." The messenger handed him an envelope. Lincoln hid it under the table and turned it over in his lap, observing the blue waxed dove seal. He let out an anxious sigh.

"Excuse me, I'll be right back." Lincoln edged out of his seat, forcing his lead legs into a swift walk across the dining room. Sweat beaded on his forehead. Peeling open the envelope between steps, he pulled out the notecard, reading, *Seatbelt.*

His heart banged in his chest and his stomach tightened. Was his dad not wearing his seatbelt? That was not like him. He was always safety first.

Lincoln returned to the foot of the staircase and closed his eyes, hoping it would return him to the present.

He gripped his chest and gasped, and everything went black.

The scent of the cold sea faded.

Silence.

Darkness.

Then a flicker of light.

He opened his eyes.

He sat in between the bookshelves in the library.

"Excuse me?" JJ scowled in a sarcastic tone. "What do you think you're doing in here?"

"I don't have to tell you." Lincoln stood up, slammed the encyclopedia shut, and shoved it next to the other books.

"I'm going to report you to the principal for skipping lunch."

"Oh really? You're going to report me for that? How will that sound, JJ? 'Principal Murphy, Lincoln decided to skip lunch and study in the library. You should punish him.' Not too bright, huh?" He shimmied by JJ, who tried to block him from leaving.

"You better watch your back."

"I'll be fine," Lincoln said without turning around.

• • • •

~LIZZY~

"Hey." She wandered into the library, hearing the commotion from the hallway. "What was that all about? You okay?"

She watched Lincoln duck behind the bookshelf.

"I know you're there." She shook her head like an annoyed mother.

"It's nothing." Lincoln came out from behind the shelf and shoved something into his back pocket. "JJ's just being JJ."

"Oh, okay." She wanted to stay but didn't know what else to say. She promised Lincoln she wouldn't push him to talk about stuff before he was ready, but it was a hard promise to keep. This was more than just about JJ. She had noticed the small, strange-looking envelope that looked just like the one she saw him with at the public library. What was he hiding and would he ever open up?

"Listen, I gotta get to class. I don't want to get another detention." He gave her a little half smile.

She twinkled her eyes back at him. There was still a little hope.

Chapter 17

Facing the Pressure

~DEB~

Deb heard the back door open and shut.

"How was school today, honey?"

"Fine." He walked right past her.

"Did you have a lot of schoolwork to make up from yesterday?"

"Yeah, but I already got it all done."

"That's good. What do you want for dinner? Are you hungry yet?"

"No. I'll eat later." He bounded up the stairs and out of sight.

She dropped her hand from her hip and sighed. Of course making amends with her son would take more than a day at Playland. She thought back to him coaching Lincoln's little league teams and his peewee football team. All the boys looked up to him. They all wanted to be around him. She wished she could ask him what to do.

She leaned under the sink and gripped her fist around the neck of the vodka bottle. The deepest, darkest part of her coerced her to pull it out.

But she couldn't. Instead, she wept. Severe but soft, the tears edged their way out. Dormant after a few days of her renewed focus. She hated herself for feeling bad again and breaking the momentum. She let go of the bottle and slumped her head against the cabinet.

. . . .

~LINCOLN~

Lincoln swung open his bedroom door and dove onto the floor. Tickling his fingers under his bed, he located and grabbed the orange Nike shoebox. He spread out the words in the order he had received them.

Dinner. Car. Rain. Dark. Eyes. Deer. Guardrail. Tree. Glass. Blood. Seatbelt.

"Lincoln?"

His heart jumped. His mom was at the door.

"What are you working on? I thought you were done with your homework?"

She came in without waiting for his reply.

"Mom!"

He plunged across the floor. His outstretched arms covered the cards. His face blushed. "What are you doing?"

"I'm sorry." She backpedaled out of the doorway toward the hall.

He collected the cards, put them in the box, and shoved the box under his bed. He sighed and shirked his shoulders back.

"It's okay." He called into the hallway, hoping she had not left.

As she appeared in the doorway, he hopped onto the bed, patting the quilt next to him.

She came and sat next to him. Her eyes damp.

"I didn't mean to interrupt, but thought you might want to go down to Little Tony's for pizza and maybe we can stop and rent a video on the way home? *Jumanji* just came out."

"Sure, I can finish this stuff up later." He leaped off the bed and grabbed his sweatshirt from the back of his desk chair.

The offer shocked him. She wanted to sit and eat with him? She always ordered takeout. What would they talk about? He had never gone to Little Tony's with her.

Dad always took him for a slice and a root beer after his little league games. Covered in dust, they would sit and discuss the game, his dad reminding him that base running and sliding were overlooked skills. He always tried to steal or make the game-winning slide into home. He also always wound up with the dirtiest uniform at the end of the game.

"What stuff? You mean your homework?" she asked.

"Yeah, homework. I'm almost done. I was working ahead anyway. We can go to Little Tony's still?"

"Of course. Let's go."

"Is that good?" she asked, as he stretched a piece of cheese from the tip of the slice all the way to his mouth.

He pinched the string of cheese, wound it around his finger, and slipped it into his mouth. "Mmmm." He smiled after he swallowed.

"I'll take that as a yes?"

He nodded as he went for another bite. If he was eating, he didn't have to say anything

"So, tell me about those cards. Anything you want to tell me? Is everything okay?"

His heart stopped. "Yeah, it's nothing. Just an assignment for English." He sighed.

She looked up and questioned him with her eyes.

"Well, I...I didn't want you to see...it's a special assignment where we have to tell a story about something that we don't understand and how we are trying to find out more."

"Oh, I see. Like a research project." She looked down. "That must be hard."

The lie weighed on him, but not as much as his secret. He didn't know enough to say anything, he convinced himself. There were still clues to collect. There was still a message to complete. He was afraid if he told her, the clues might stop. He knew he must tell her eventually, but not yet. Not until he'd solved the puzzle.

· · · ·

~DEB~

Deb looked at the front door of Little Tony's, half hoping Dan would come in and half remembering her terrible behavior the last time they sat in that booth.

She shifted her focus back at Lincoln. She knew something wasn't right with him. He had a similar look on his face that she'd seen on herself in the dressing room mirror a few days before the funeral.

· · · ·

April 13, 1995

Lincoln was at home with Arletta, so she could go on a shopping trip. She hadn't slept after the hospital. No emotions or reality had registered. Everything was numb and void.

She wanted to wear something special. Something he would like. He still felt alive to her. She still felt close to him.

She didn't want to lose that feeling. But as she looked in the dressing room mirror at her reflection, an unfamiliar feeling washed over her...the bags under her eyes, the stitches and cuts on her face, and the paleness of her skin. She'd been lying to herself. The truth came crashing down. She'd been through her own hell with the accident.

She burst out of the door, expecting him to be standing there. He'd nod his head and smile. He'd shower her with compliments and put his fingers up, insisting she give him a little twirl. But there was just an empty changing room sofa.

She dashed out of the Ann Taylor. The ink tag on the dress set off the alarm.

She didn't stop, rushing through the main pavilion and into the mall restroom. She hunched on the dirty floor of the last stall. The tears came so violently she could barely breathe. She clung to the toilet bowl.

• • • •

~LINCOLN~

"Hey, Lincoln." A sweet voice whispered in his ear.

He closed his locker and turned around to find Lizzy. "Oh hey, Lizzy."

"What're ya doing after school today?"

"Uh, I dunno."

"My parents are taking me bowling tonight. You wanna come?"

"Yeah, that sounds fun."

"Cool. We'll pick you up at 5:30." She squeezed her books to her chest with a smile and walked away.

"Wait!"

She turned.

"You any good? 'Cause I can throw a bowling ball almost as good as I can throw a baseball. You might be sorry you invited me." He winked as he rotated his arm.

"Oh, I'm pretty good. You'll just have to see." She flipped her hair over her shoulder and strutted down the hallway.

All day long he couldn't stop fantasizing about the bowling alley. He went through the motions in his head. First, he would offer to carry her ball to the lane. Then he would enter his name as Prez into the monitor and tell her about how his dad named him. She would slide closer to him as they bent over putting on their bowling shoes. During the game, he would get strike after strike with no effort, and she'd be so impressed. And after he'd buy her a Cherry Coke and they'd play Pac-Man in the arcade. When her parents called to leave, he'd pull her behind the game console and kiss her.

"Lincoln?"

His head dropped as he pulled his hand out from under his chin.

"I asked you a question," Mr. Hudson said.

"I'm sorry. What was the question?" His tone bordered on sarcasm.

"Watch it, Mr. Peterson." Mr. Hudson crossed his arms and stood right next to his desk. "I said name the steps of the scientific method...all of them."

"Umm, okay. First you ask a question, then background research, then make a hypothesis, conduct the experiment, draw your conclusion, and present your findings. That's pretty much it."

"You're lucky." Mr. Hudson squinted at him. The bell rang.

"That was close. Mr. Hudson has it out for you, huh, Prez?" Trent nudged him from behind in the hallway after class.

"Yeah."

"Hey, are things okay? I'm sorry about the other day when JJ and I were ganging up on you. I'm just worried about you. You keep missing school and getting in trouble."

"Yeah, I'm sorry too." Lincoln hung his head and his cheeks turned hot. "I shouldn't have just run away."

"Is it your dad still?"

He paused. He wanted to cry at the mention of his dad but fought back the tears.

"Hey, man, I'm sorry. We all really miss him." Trent patted him on the back. "If it makes you feel any better, my dad is in China right now, and I don't even remember when he's coming back."

"Sorry, that's hard too." He closed his locker and looked up to meet Trent's concerned glance. "I just get confused a lot and need time to think, I guess."

"Yeah, I can see that."

"Lizzy invited me to go bowling tonight," he said, raising his tone a half octave.

"Hey, that's great, man. I knew there was something goin' on with you two. She's nice." Trent nodded.

"Yeah, she's really great. So great, I don't think I deserve her." He shrugged his shoulders.

"What? Are you kidding me? Of course you deserve her. Plus, it seems like she picked you, which is even better."

"Maybe you're right."

After school, Lincoln glanced out the window as he and the Robinson family pulled into the parking lot of the bowling alley. He'd been resting his hand on his knee the whole car ride, mustering the courage and waiting for the right moment to embrace Lizzy's hand. The car stopped. Sighing, he surrendered his hand into his pocket.

"This one looks good." Lizzy bobbled a bright pink ball in her arm.

"I can help you." He cupped the ball with one hand and wedged it inside the crease of his elbow.

"Aren't you so strong?" Lizzy giggled.

"Oh yeah? Watch this." He reached on the top rack and rolled a second ball inside his other elbow crease. His hands stretched around but didn't reach the front of the balls.

"That blue one is fourteen pounds. Isn't that heavy?"

"Not for me." Lincoln clutched the balls and walked to their lane, but his hands were sweaty. He didn't have a good grip. He tried to kiss the two balls together to adjust, but the heavy blue ball slipped and landed on his shoeless foot.

"Shit!"

"Oh my gosh, are you okay?" she cried. "I'm gonna get my dad!"

"I'm okay." He tried to hop but the movement made the pain worse and he crumbled to the floor. Lizzy had disappeared. He wished he could disappear. "Stupid idiot," he said to himself as he slapped the ball. He waited, immobile and embarrassed.

"He hurt his foot...," Lizzy said to her dad.

They stood over him and stared.

"What happened?" Lizzy's dad asked.

"It was stupid. I tried to..." He felt fuzzy. His foot was numb.

"Just relax, son." Lizzy's dad patted him on the back. "Let me take a look. Can I pull your sock off?" Her dad crouched next to him.

"Sure." He nodded.

"Does this hurt?" Lizzy's dad tapped the top of his foot and then pulled off his sock. His skin had a big circular blue mark.

"I can't feel my foot," he said, his heart racing.

"It'll probably take a little while to regain the blood flow. You should probably get X-rays to make sure nothing is broken. Lizzy, go ask at the counter for some ice. Let's call your parents and have them meet us at the emergency room."

"Emergency room?" He frowned.

"Yes." Lizzy's dad was firm, but kind, indicating there was no room for negotiation.

"Wait here, and I'll be back after I call your parents. What's their number?"

Lincoln paused. Lizzy's dad didn't remember he didn't have parents. He had *a* parent.

"My mom should be home. You can call her here."

Lincoln slid his mom's Realtor card out of his wallet. His breath shortened for a moment as he looked at his wallet, the wallet his dad had given him for his last birthday.

"You need something to keep your emergency information close," his dad had told him.

"Okay, great. Now just sit tight. I'll be right back," Lizzy's dad said as he walked away.

Lizzy came back with a bag full of ice and lowered it onto his foot.

"Ooh, that's cold."

"Sorry." She layered his sock between the ice bag and his skin. "That better?"

He nodded.

Lizzy snickered under her breath.

"Hey, what are you laughing about?" Lincoln asked.

Then the two of them stared at one another and busted up laughing together.

"This sure will be a night we remember, huh?" Lizzy asked.

"You got that right."

• • • •

~DEB~

Deb jumped in the car and raced to the ER. She cranked up the volume on the tape deck. The doors of the car rattled from the vibrating bass, as she attempted to overpower the thudding coming from the center of her chest.

She hadn't been to the hospital since the accident. The doctors examined and prodded at her face, arms, and legs, trying to stop the bleeding from the glass chards and identify the deeper cuts. But she didn't feel any physical pain. All she wanted was to stay at the scene. With the car. With him.

She parked and tried to shake the memories.

The automatic doors parted ways and whooshed her into the waiting room. The room buzzed with nurses holding clipboards, parents attending to their crying children, and the smell of disinfectant. She remembered the sounds and the smells. They hit her like a wave. She remembered the agonizing wait. She knew he wasn't coming, but after she got her stitches, she sat in the waiting room. Waiting for the next stretcher to burst through the sliding automatic doors. Hoping it was him.

She took a deep breath and marched up to the receiving desk.

"My son, Lincoln Peterson, is here. Is he okay?"

"Ma'am, take a seat, and we'll call you when we're ready for you."

Her hands shook, as she pulled out her insurance card and put it on the counter in front of the window. "No, I won't sit down until you tell me what's going on with my son. I'm his mother."

The nurse slid the window shut.

She banged on the frosted plexiglass. "What the hell?!"

"Give me a minute," came a muffled reply.

She growled and glared at the closed window.

"He's in room 5A," the nurse said, as the window slid open again.

"Was that so hard?" She flipped her hair and turned to find room 5A. In the next instant, she regretted her poor behavior.

"It's not broken, but he has a subperiosteal hematoma." The doctor pointed to the X-ray.

"That sounds serious. What can we do for that?" Deb said while rubbing Lincoln's knee.

Lincoln wiggled, as if to get her to stop touching him.

"Lincoln's got himself some blood pooling right below the bone. It's going to be painful for a while, so a lot of ice and heat for these first couple of days to reduce the swelling. Keep it elevated. Stay off of it as much as possible." The doctor faced her and then turned to Lincoln to look him square in the eye. "No sports, no running, just resting."

Lincoln rolled his eyes. "Okay."

"Lincoln, you heard the doctor. No running and lots of rest. You have to do that or you won't get better. You have to give your body the time it needs to heal."

"Okay, I heard," he stammered in forced agreement.

"Okay then, can we get going?" she asked.

"Yes, you're free to go."

"Thank you so much," she said to Mr. Robinson.

"Of course. I'm glad I was there to help, and I'm glad it wasn't a break."

• • • •

~LINCOLN~

On crutches, Lincoln hobbled across the lobby. He was glad Lizzy's dad dropped her at home while they waited. He looked out the window at the pouring rain that commenced while he was X-rayed, hoping he wouldn't slip with his new walking arrangement.

His mom pulled up the car and leaned across the front seat to pop open the passenger side door. He made a run for it and catapulted himself to the car, taking three giant bounds with the crutches. The trouble was crouching down into the car and getting the crutches inside. He managed to sit down, but the crutches were upright and standing perpendicular to the concrete. He struggled to turn them, eventually angling them and pulling them into the car.

He laughed. "So much for trying to keep dry."

She sighed. "Let's get you home so you can dry off and warm up."

After a few minutes of driving, he broke the silence. "I can't believe I was so stupid."

"What do you mean, honey?"

"I was trying to impress Lizzy, and instead I end up embarrassing myself." His head slouched.

"I'm sure she doesn't think any less of you. You...like this girl?"

"Aww, Mom." He blushed.

"It's good for you...to have a crush." She grinned.

"It's not a crush."

"Oh? What is it then?"

"Well, I guess she's my girlfriend." His cheeks lit up. "Or at least I hope she'll still be my girlfriend after all of this."

"That's great, honey. Lizzy's a very nice girl, and I'm sure this is nothing that's going to stop her from seeing what a great boy you are."

"Thanks, Mom." He couldn't help but feel warm inside knowing his mom approved.

Chapter 18

Clutched Reality

~LINCOLN~

"Hey, Prez." Trent tapped him on the shoulder as he leaned on his crutches at his locker. "Need help carrying your books to English?"

"Nah, I got it." He closed the locker door with the paperback *Where the Red Fern Grows* under his chin. Slinging his bookbag around his stomach, he slipped the book inside.

"Hey, bowling foot!" a passing eighth-grader yelled across the hallway.

"Haha, yeah and look at those giraffe arms!" his buddy added, laughing, as the two of them doled out insults without a care in the world.

"Hey, what did you say?" Trent pointed at the two culprits. "Come over here and say that again. I dare ya!"

"Hey, it's fine." Lincoln leaned on his left crutch and tugged with his right hand at Trent's outstretched arm but couldn't pull it down.

"We ain't got no problem, and we ain't comin' over there either." The two of them scurried down the hallway and around the corner.

"Pricks," Trent whispered under his breath.

Lincoln turned so Trent couldn't see his red-hot cheeks, but he couldn't help but crack a smile. Trent stepping up for him was nice.

"Sooo, aside from the ankle, how's it going with Lizzy?"

He wiped the smile from his face and turned back to Trent. "It's okay, I guess. I mean it's so embarrassing. I don't know what she thinks of me now. I wouldn't blame her if she dumped me."

"Hey, man, don't let this..." Trent circled his finger around pointing to his crutches. "...scare you from going with her. She's a really nice girl, Prez."

"Yeah, thanks."

Trent lowered his voice. "I mean, what do you think your dad would say?"

He paused for a minute. He knew Trent had good intentions, so he indulged in the question and pictured his dad holding a camera. He and Lizzy standing at their front door all dressed up for the school dance. There he was, forcing them to smile and get in close for the photo. His first real girlfriend, he could hear his dad boasting.

The corner of his lip rose up. "I think he'd say the same thing. I think he'd make me feel like a million bucks.... He was good at that, wasn't he?" He looked to Trent, who nodded in agreement.

"Take it easy, man. And let me know if you need help with those books later." Trent winked as he sauntered off down the hallway.

His concentration and interest level in Mr. Hudson's lesson on the periodic table dwindled. He doodled scales running up the back of a fire-breathing dragon in his notebook.

"Lincoln, I think you can answer this one." Mr. Hudson singled him out. "Please name the six noble gases."

He shifted in his seat but didn't hesitate. "Helium, neon, argon, krypton, xenon, radon."

Mr. Hudson rolled his eyes in protest of defeat. "Okay, now who knows the six alkali metals? Agnes?" Mr. Hudson proceeded with the lesson but kept throwing jeering glances his way.

The tension in the room didn't go unnoticed by his classmates. His cheeks turned red hot. This was the worst possible time for more attention. He had a bum foot and had Mr. Hudson on his back again.

He got out his science book and turned to the chapter on the elements to follow along with the class. Mr. Hudson witnessed his book open and tapped his desk with the tops of his knuckles in dutiful approval, as he marched by like a commander keeping his army in check. Science class was not a war, he thought to himself.

The bell rang for lunch, freeing him from Mr. Hudson's wrath. Or so he thought.

"Mr. Peterson."

He stopped dead in his tracks, his foot dangling midair.

"I'd like to see you before you go to lunch," Mr. Hudson ordered.

"Okay." His voice was quiet yet firm. He knew Mr. Hudson would pounce on any sign of weakness.

"Did I see you doodling during my lesson?"

He froze.

"C'mon. I saw you."

"Why...I was...drawing the table from memory. It's my way of taking notes."

"Okay, if that's true, let me see your drawing."

He knew he was cooked. "I erased it."

"Huh, well that's where I got ya." Mr. Hudson chuckled to himself.

Lincoln cocked his head to the side.

"Why don't you show me your pencil in your bookbag?"

"Okay." He held his breath and opened his bookbag. He only had pens. No pencils, no erasers.

"Well, let's see." Mr. Hudson peered into his bookbag atop his desk.

Lincoln stood still. His arms wobbled as he held up the crutches.

"I want to make sure I'm not missing anything." Mr. Hudson smirked and dumped open his whole bookbag. Sheets of paper, books butterflied open, and his calculator now with a broken screen lay strewn across the floor. Mr. Hudson got on his hands and knees and rummaged through the debris. "I don't see any pencils in here. I don't see any erasers either." Mr. Hudson chuckled with an evil grin.

The pit of his stomach sunk to the ground. He stared at the picture of Marie Curie receiving the Nobel Peace Prize from his science book lying open on the floor.

"What do you have to say for yourself?"

Lincoln squinted as hard as he could at the picture in the book and clenched his fists around the crutches. He felt the blood pulse through his veins.

"I said look at me..." Mr. Hudson's voice faded away.

His eyelids grew heavy.

He blinked them shut.

Darkness.

Quiet.

The black brightened to gray.

Streaks of light.

Inviting him.

His eyes cracked open.

He sat in the Hall of Mirrors at the Grand Hotel at the Nobel Banquet in Stockholm. He wore a suit, like the rest of the male-dominated crowd. A bowl of soup sat on the table in front of him. He read the tiny, printed menu next to his water glass. First course: Consommé Doria.

There was an announcement. "And now, Madam Marie Curie."

Everyone rose from their seats to give her a hearty standing ovation. She glided between the maze of tables, making her way to the stage. Behind the microphone, she explained in scientific terms her discovery of radium and separating it to study its therapeutic properties. Her voice was humble and precise, pronouncing the power of science and the role it could play in solving the world's problems. She talked about the power of the unknown and how harnessing the unknown led to the discovery of things no one thought imaginable. With his eyes wide, he stood up to applaud as she finished.

After the ceremony, he followed the dispersing crowd into the main lobby. His chest tightened. From behind, he felt a tap on his elbow.

"Excuse me, son." He heard a gentle, female voice.

He turned and there she was. Small and delicate. Her hair pulled back in a tight, twisted bun. Her eyes were warm and kind.

"Yes, what?" The thudding of his chest rushed his speech.

"I believe this is for you." She offered him an envelope.

He saw the blue wax emblem on the back. Phew, he had to get out—the vice grip on his chest was closing in.

"You take good care of that. And remember what I said about the unknown. You just keep chasing that and you will get where you need to go." She winked at him.

"Thank you." He bowed his head halfway and grasped at his chest.

He opened the envelope and found a card that said *Smoke*.

The chatter of the crowded lobby faded.

The lights dimmed.

Then died.

Alone in the dark.

He held his breath.

The company of his heartbeat.

Then the distant sound of hollering.

"Mr. Peterson?!"

He heard the faint call of his name.

He opened his eyes.

Mr. Hudson stood next to him. Within inches of his face. The mess of books surrounded them.

"What's going on in here?" Principal Murphy appeared in the doorway. "Is something wrong?" He observed the mess on the floor.

"It was an accident. I'm just helping him. He was having trouble with his crutches and knocked his bag over." Mr. Hudson bent over, picked up a book, and put it in his backpack.

"Ok—ay," Principal Murphy said, studying Mr. Hudson's face. "Then why were you yelling at him?"

"Oh, it just happened all of a sudden, and it startled me." Mr. Hudson leaned against the desk. "Really, it's all okay."

"*Is it* all okay?" Principal Murphy looked at Lincoln, his brows slanted toward his nose.

"Yeah." Lincoln swallowed the dry ball of fear in his throat. "Yeah, it's fine. I was just being clumsy like Mr. Hudson said."

"All right then." Principal Murphy straightened his tie and left.

Lincoln didn't know what to do, so he remained frozen.

"Don't just stand there. Here—take this and get to lunch. Not a word to anybody." Mr. Hudson handed him his backpack and shooed him out the door.

Lincoln hobbled into the cafeteria. The lunch period was in full swing. Empty wrappers and Ziplocs with only crumbs surrounded the packers, and the buyers' line only had a few kids left to get their trays. He took a seat alone at a table in the back.

As he bit into his peanut butter sandwich, Lizzy approached. "Hey, is everything okay? Why did Mr. Hudson talk to you after science?"

"It was nothing." He waited to see if she would buy his lame excuse.

"He kept you after class for nothing? What do you think I am, a dummy? It wasn't just nothing. Now spill."

He rolled his eyes—because he didn't want to tell her and because he was turned on by her bossiness.

"I'm the dummy." He laughed. "I'm lucky he didn't give me another detention, though."

"Why, what happened?"

"It was stupid, I was drawing in my notebook during class. Stupid dragons and stuff like that. I was bored. He asked me what I was drawing, and I told him the periodic table." He laughed at himself and how silly everything sounded. "He went crazy, though—you should have seen it. I told him I erased the drawing, and then he dumped out my bookbag and everything went flying so he could look for an eraser, which he did not find, as I didn't have one."

"Wow, that is crazy and you're lucky!" She put her hand on the bend in his elbow.

He glanced down at her hand. She just wouldn't give up on him, no matter how much he screwed up. If she knew how big of a secret he was keeping, she would run the other way.

"Hey, Prez, what're ya doing over there?" JJ hollered from across the cafeteria.

He waved JJ off. "He's so annoying. I'm sorry about him," he said to Lizzy.

"Oh, you don't have to apologize. I think he just wants attention." Lizzy didn't even turn to look at JJ.

"Ugh. And he goes about it in the most obnoxious way." Lincoln sighed.

The bell rang and the clatter of lunch trays returning to the kitchen and the buzz of the students clouded his judgment. As he got up, the envelope fell out of his back pocket and tumbled to the sticky floor.

"Oh, let me get that for you." Lizzy bent over to pick it up.

He gasped. Fire burned in the back of his throat. He held his breath, watching the envelope in her hand.

"What's this?"

Her question was fair, but he had no idea how to answer. The longer he waited, the more awkward the silence became and the tighter his stomach twisted into a knot.

"Here." She handed him the envelope as the warning bell rang and they were the only two left in the cafeteria. "I don't want you to be late to class and get another detention." She smiled and walked away.

He stood shell-shocked, the familiar blue wax seal in the palm of his hand. Visions of all his past picture jumps rushed through his memory. He couldn't lose the trail. He hurried to his locker to store the envelope.

"Hey, Lincoln, how ya doing?" Principal Murphy waved as he approached from the opposite side of the hallway.

Lincoln stopped at his locker and propped his crutches against the blue metal door.

"How's the foot doing?" Principal Murphy looked down at his bandaged appendage.

"It's all right. No more swelling. I should be off these things soon." He buried his face in his locker like he was searching for a lost pencil behind all the books.

"Listen, is everything all right? It seemed a little off earlier today with Mr. Hudson. Are you sure everything is okay?" Principal Murphy pried the locker door back, searching for his face.

Lincoln caught his glance. He looked his principal straight in the eye, as best he could to get him off his back. "Yeah. It's all good."

"Okay, you just let me know if that changes. I'm here for ya." Principal Murphy gave him a slight pat on the shoulder and walked away.

Lincoln couldn't understand him. Why was he so nosy? He didn't want his help and didn't need a new dad. He wanted his old dad back.

• • • •

~DAN~

He rubbed his forehead as he said hello to a few other students on his way back to his office. He knew he had to tread lightly with Lincoln, but he also couldn't stay away from him. Lincoln represented an unyielding magnetic pull that was one part his protector instincts in overdrive and probably three parts his attraction to Deb. Just being around Lincoln made him think about Deb and give him more things he could bring up if he ran into her.

As he rounded the corner, he heard gunfire. He ducked over into a crouch position. His armpits filled with sweat.

• • • •

September 2, 1990

The desert expanded around him as far as he could see. His heart raced. He struggled for air. The heat suffocated him. He felt like he was breathing fire into a brown paper bag. The sand blew in his face, stinging his parched, salty skin.

Dusty figures moved near him in disarray, their voices and commands masked by the dull pounding from the back of his head. Shell casings rained all around him.

He tried to get up. He couldn't move his neck. The unflinching hot sun reflected off the pool of blood on his chest.

A sharp pain shot down his spine, all the way to his feet. At least he could feel something, he thought.

"Get down!" The urgency of the outcry cut through his haze. "Incoming!"

He crouched his body as much as his limbs would allow him to move.

"No!" he shouted.

· · · ·

~LINDA~

"Are you okay?" She tapped Principal Murphy's shoulder.

"Oh, Linda." He shook his head and scratched his fingers through his hair. He was on the floor, leaning against a locker with his head sinking between his knees.

"What're you doing down there?" she asked.

He stood and straightened his tie. He took a giant gulp of air and looked at her with a blank stare.

She heard sounds coming from down the hallway. He flinched and raised his arm to shield his face.

"Wait here." She reached out her soft, wrinkled, cool hand and touched his warm, muscular forearm. Then she hustled down the hallway as best she could.

She followed the sound. As she got closer, she saw the janitor vacuuming. "Oh, Mr. Garcia. What happened?"

· · · ·

~MR. GARCIA~

Mr. Garcia saw Linda, but he didn't hear a word she said. He switched off the vacuum.

He had a thick black mustache to match his thick black hair and a mouthful of yellowing crooked teeth, which scared most of the students. His job ashamed him, but it put food on the table for his family of six with another on the way. He hadn't finished high school. His janitor position was a way to pay the bills, but he'd wanted to be in the Army, like Principal Murphy. The only time he wasn't ashamed of his job was when he was around Linda. She treated him like every other staff member.

"Someone broke some glass and left it here. Probably didn't wanna get in trouble." He stood with the silent vacuum upright at his side.

"Oh goodness. I'm so glad you found it. That could have hurt someone. Or even been some type of lawsuit. Don't let me bother you anymore. I'll talk to you later, Mr. Garcia."

She waved and left.

He watched her flee with the information. He worried about her. She was getting up there in age but still buzzed around like a busy bee.

• • • •

~DAN~

Dan heard a knock. He was back in his office to get some privacy and quiet.

He knew it was Linda by her gentle knock. She was the only person he would let in at that moment.

"Come in."

"I hope this will help ease your stress a little bit." She eased into the chair in front of his desk. "I found Mr. Garcia vacuuming up broken glass. That must have been what you heard."

She stared at him. He could tell she wanted the source of the sound to erase his pain, but they both knew it wasn't that easy.

He grimaced. "Oh, yeah, that would be a pretty gnarly sound." He turned in his chair and looked out the window.

"Dan?"

"Yes," he replied without turning around.

"Have you thought more about talking with someone? I want to help you, but I don't think I have the right things to say to you. You matter to me, and I want you to be okay."

"I know, I appreciate that, Linda. I really do." He turned back around to face her. "I'm just scared. I already have all this trouble—I don't want to talk about it and pour more salt on the wound."

She softened her eyes. "Yes, that makes sense. I can see how you might feel that way. But does it have to turn out like that? You were out there in the battlefield—wouldn't you rather try to help heal a wound rather than let it fester and get worse?"

His eyes felt moist. "I don't want to give up..." He trailed off and wiped the tear from his eye before it could fall.

"Then don't, honey." Linda grazed his hand, as she got up to leave.

Chapter 19
Making Amends

~ARLETTA~

"But it's been a year." Arletta shook her head while standing on the front porch.

"I'm sorry, I don't think it's a good idea," Deb muttered, as she closed the front door.

Arletta put her hand up, stopping the door mid-swing.

"You can stand on the front porch all day, but I'm going inside..." Deb left the door propped open and disappeared inside the house.

Arletta waited a moment and entered the foyer. She took a quick inventory of things. No clutter. Only a thin layer of dust lining the shelves and knickknacks. She was surprised a twelve-year-old lived there.

Stepping into the living room, she observed Deb sitting at her desk, positioned by the window overlooking the creek in the backyard. As she moved closer, the floorboard squeaked and broke Deb's empty stare. Deb grimaced and rustled some papers around to ignore her.

"Lincoln home?" She didn't push the issue from the porch.

Deb shook her head oddly.

"You shakin' yur head yes or no, dear?"

"I don't know." Deb sighed a big, long sigh and gasped as if she was going to cry.

Arletta pulled over a chair and put her arm around Deb's shoulders. She was surprised Deb didn't shudder away her touch.

They sat in silence for a minute.

"It'll turn out fine. Eventually de natural order takes its way."

Deb looked up, her eyes bloodshot and saggy. "I don't think so..."

"Don't say dat, 'specially if Lincoln's 'round ta hear. Ya gotta be strong for 'im. Ya gotta be strong fur yur-self. Dere's no otha choice. Ya gotta just keep telling yur-self dat and ya gotta start believin' it."

Deb didn't move.

"Listen, I know ya ain't fond of thee idea of visiting Beau, but I think it'll be good fur ya. And it'll be good fur Lincoln. I asked yur permission since yur his mom, but I'll take him if he wants ta go."

Deb took a big deep breath. "I know you're right...but..." Her voice faded away. "But I'm scared..."

"Of what? I'll go with ya. It'll be fine."

"I'm scared of him...as silly as that sounds.... I know he won't approve of the way I've been acting and the way I've been looking after Lincoln. I've been a mess, and I've been a terrible, shitty parent. I can't go there. I'm not ready yet...just give me some more time."

"My child, ya need ta let it go. Ya need ta let yur-self breathe and grieve. He knows ya gotta grieve. He wasn't the judging type, ya know dat. He'd never judge ya. He'd want ya ta visit; he'd want Lincoln ta visit. He's waitin' for ya. Ya know what de right thing ta do is. Ya just gotta do it."

Deb inched her head in acknowledgment but not agreement.

"Did I ever tell y'bout when I was a lil girl?" She pulled her chair closer to Deb.

Deb nodded her head no, but drew her eyebrows up.

"I was prolly 'bout four years old when it started." She paused and grasped the rosary hanging around her neck. "Lord, dat was so long ago..."

Deb shifted in her chair, leaning in closer.

"I didn't even know what was happenin'—all I knew was it was wrong but dat I had no way of protectin' myself." She looked down at her chest, rolling a single rosary bead back and forth between her pointer finger and her thumb.

Deb leaned in again, close enough that Arletta felt Deb's hand on her knee. Arletta felt the coolness of Deb's skin through her sheer auburn dress covered in beige flowers with bright green stems.

Clutching the beads, she looked up and stared out the window into the backyard.

"How was I supposed ta face my granddaddy? Every time I saw 'im I flinched, afraid he's gonna take me fur 'play time' in his room."

Her gaze shifted and she refocused on Deb.

"Ya see, I told my momma but she didn't believe me—she said Granddaddy Mack would never do somethun' like dat. She told me ta stop tellin' lies. But years later, I was prolly 'bout nineteen or so, my momma got the gumption and told me she was sorry. She told me dat Granddaddy Mack confessed to her after he stopped doin' it—which was when I was eleven—and she was scared ta talk ta me. She was scared I wouldn't love her no more because she didn't protect me. But child, ya should never be afraid of the ones dat love ya. The day she said sorry—I loved my momma more on that day than I ever did be-fore. It took me a bit of time ta completely forgive her, but her apology opened da door and I saw her in a whole new light. I saw dat everyone's scared and just tryin' ta do the right thing and dat everyone's just doin' da best dey can."

Arletta put her hand on top of Deb's hand that rested on Arletta's knee.

"Darlin', ya got nothin' ta be afraid of—ya loved my baby Beau and he loved ya more than anything. Ya can't be scared of dat. Ya can't be scared ta love yur son. Ya got yur own special way ta love him and he needs dat. And ya aren't gonna be perfect at it, but he'll know dat yur tryin' and dat's all dat matters."

Arletta took a breath so not to release the thin sheath of tear water stretched across the tops of her eyes.

"I'm so sorry," Deb whispered, looking into the depths of her eyes.

"Like I said, dear, it was a long time 'go."

"That doesn't mean it still doesn't hurt? Thank you—for sharing this with me." Deb squeezed Arletta's knee and touched her own heart with her other hand. "I need some time, though, to think about what you said. And to think about going.... I'm just not ready yet. I will be...it's just not today. But...you go on ahead with Lincoln."

· · · ·

~LINCOLN~

"Grandma!" He leaned his crutches against the end table, threw his bookbag on the couch, and gave Arletta a big bear hug.

"Oh, my baby. Yur foot any better?"

"Yeah it's about healed, I think." He put some weight on it to show them.

"We'll see about that. We have an appointment in a few days before you get the all-clear," his mom said.

"How was school today?" Arletta asked, wiping her eye with her hanky.

His cheeks turned red. He ran his fingers through his hair. "It was fine."

"No more detentions?" His mom smiled.

"Nah." The pit of his stomach ignited. Did she know about what happened with Mr. Hudson? Or maybe she had a newfound sense of humor?

"Hey listen, we gots somewhere ta go. I'm takin' ya on a little trip."

Arletta rose off the couch and put on her jacket. She checked her rosary beads once she was upright.

"Where are we going?" He crutched himself to the front door, following Arletta.

"You'll see. Let's git goin' before it gets too dark."

Once they were in the car, Arletta turned down the radio. She leaned to her right toward him. "Say, what really happened at school ta-day?"

"What do you mean?" He knew he could not lie to her. She was too good at sussing out lies. Just like his dad.

"Ya know what I mean—now out wit it." She kept her eyes on the road.

"It's this one teacher. I feel like he's kinda out to get me. Or I'm just always in the wrong place at the wrong time."

"I see." Arletta tapped her fingers on the steering wheel. "Well, ya probably gotta start makin' an effort ta be in da right place at da right time—ya know what I'm sayin'?"

He nodded. "Yeah, you're probably right."

As Arletta turned the corner, his stomach dropped. He saw the cast iron gate marking the cemetery entrance. She inched over the sleeping ground. The headstones stitched neat rows up and down the soil and green grass. As the names and dates came into view, his heart beat faster. His eyes peeled for Beau Peterson.

He wondered why he'd never thought to go to the cemetery on his own after the funeral. The distance was a long walk, but nothing he couldn't handle. He wondered how many times Arletta had visited his dad alone.

He took a deep breath as Arletta pulled the car over, straddling the pavement and the grass as she parked it.

"Honey, ya okay?" She looked at him.

He nodded as he released his seatbelt.

Arletta gave him a reassuring nod in return and opened the car door. She led the way. He followed on his crutches through the maze of granite squares, crosses, and circles—so many shapes. He glanced at the years and the messages etched on the stones. Some born long ago, before 1900. Most living long lives but some all too short. The whole of a person's life summed up in two numbers.

"Here." Arletta stopped and knelt by a brown granite rectangular stone.

He remembered the last time he was there. The day of the burial. But he never saw the stone.

The appearance of it—*Beau Jeffrey Peterson, 1954-1995*—chiseled in time forever.

He swallowed hard.

Next to it—*Deborah Lillian Peterson, 1957*—her life open-ended. If only she could see it that way.

He put his hand out toward Arletta, reaching for her guidance.

"It's okay, dear." She took his hand and squeezed it. "Beau, I have someone very special here."

He smiled. "Hey, Dad," he whispered.

"Good. Go ahead, he's listening."

He laid his crutches on the ground. He knelt on one knee, still holding Arletta's hand.

"I miss you, Dad," he whispered. "And Mom misses you too. She misses you a lot." He took a big breath. "All I want to do is figure out what happened to you. I'm not going to give up."

Arletta raised one eyebrow. "Okay, that's probably enough for now, honey."

"Okay, Grandma."

"Ya did good."

"I did?"

"Of course. You spoke from the heart."

Back at home, his mom yelled from upstairs. "Lincoln? Is that you?"

"Yeah." He closed and locked the back door.

"There are leftovers in the fridge."

He pushed over the leaning tower of mail littering the kitchen table. The collage for his English assignment needed a lot of space to spread out and work on. He'd put it off until the night before because he struggled to think of any ideas.

A few of the letters toppled onto the floor. He bent over on his crutches to retrieve them. He knew she would yell at him if she'd found him making a mess of her paperwork.

One of the letters was open, a tri-folded bulk of papers from the hospital. He sifted through the sheets discovering his bill from the emergency room trip. He couldn't believe the amount—$700! No wonder his mom stressed out all the time.

His eyes jumped down the page where it showed his patient profile. The boxes for Caucasian and Black were ticked under ethnicity.

"Mom! Mom, I need you to come here. Now!"

He heard her footsteps descending the stairs.

"Look at this. Why have you lied to me my whole life?" He shoved the paper in her face.

She smoothed out the rustled paper and held it out in front of her.

"Well?" He knocked his crutch against the table.

She pulled out a chair and sat down. "Lincoln, I'm sorry. Your dad didn't want to tell you until you were older." She looked him in the eye and reached her hand out to touch his arm.

He retracted it out of reach. "I just can't believe that. Why would he want to keep a secret from me? And why would you and Grandma let him?" His eyes dampened with tears.

"He...we...thought it would be best, honey. He wanted to protect you. So you wouldn't need to worry." The words stumbled out of her mouth.

"Worry? Why would I worry?"

She shook her head. "Because the world can be unfair sometimes. I'm sorry you had to find out this way."

"Grandma told me a little while ago, when she got sick. I found the picture on her mantel."

"I see." His mom squinted her eyes.

"I just don't want to be lied to. How can I trust anything you say?"

"I'm so sorry, honey. I understand that you're upset. I understand you might not trust me. But I'm always going to try and do what's best for you. You're my boy. And I love you."

She looked down at his arm. They both saw his hairs standing on edge. "Nothing is going to change that."

"I just can't believe Dad wouldn't tell me."

"He was going to, trust me."

"I don't know. I think I need to think about it." He gathered his crutches.

"Wait, what happened at the cemetery? Are you okay?"

"It was good. You should go."

She blinked.

He saw the tears flicker in her eyes.

"Yes...you're right...I should."

"Remember what Dad always said? There can be glory in failure. You gotta just go. It'll help."

· · · ·

~DEB~

She blushed and sniffed in her tears. Lincoln had quoted President Lincoln.

"Your dad would be so proud of you." She held her hand over her heart.

"I know he is." He clopped out of the kitchen.

The rhythmic pumps of blood like warm milk soothed her soul as she took a deep breath. She realized it was possible to see Lincoln as a loving reminder of him. To see her son and feel happy and proud, not sad and resentful.

She looked at the cupboard door under the sink. There was too much to process, too much to hold on her own. Arletta's story about her grandpa broke her heart. But in a strange way she felt closer to her. She was not alone in her grieving or pain or blaming herself. But why hadn't she given her the courtesy of a heads-up about Lincoln finding the picture on her mantel? And why wouldn't she have hidden it better?

The anger had curdled on her lips as she took the brunt of Lincoln's disbelief. But that moment was about Lincoln and she was proud of herself for staying present. However, that didn't stop the aches that ran up and down her body as her son faced so many recent harsh realities about the adult world.

She looked at the cupboard door again.

No, she told herself. As she got up to go to her bedroom, she caught a glimpse of Lincoln's homework assignment in the middle of the mess on the kitchen table. Assemble a collage of what happiness means to you.

Chapter 20
Gaining Courage

~LINDA~

"Good morning." Linda kept her back to the filing cabinet. She knew Dan's gait and didn't want to stop mid-alphabetizing.

"Morning," Dan mumbled over the tap of his familiar footsteps.

She found the "LO" and filed away the folder for Low Income Lunches. She turned and looked around. Dan was gone.

"You okay?" She leaned on the doorframe and peered her head into his office.

Dan sat with his head leaning in his right hand, staring at the stack of papers on his desk. "Uh, I will be. Right as soon as I get some coffee." He stood up.

"Oh, you just wait there. I'll get you some."

"That's okay, you don't have to do that."

She heard him but proceeded to the teacher's lounge.

After a few minutes, she reappeared.

"Here you go, one cream and no sugar, just the way you like it."

She gingerly set the hot coffee mug on his desk. Her hands wobbled a bit. A constant reminder that age added new ailments, never subtracted. She watched the steam slither into the air from the beige liquid.

"How'd you know how I like it? You've never gotten me coffee before?"

"Oh, I pay attention." She raised one eyebrow.

"Oh boy, I guess I better be more careful around here." Dan laughed as he took a sip.

"Joking aside, you seem a little different today. Something on your mind? I don't mean to pry, but you know you can always talk to me."

Dan held the mug in one hand and rested his chin in the other. "You do pay attention, don't you?" He laughed and put the mug down. "I finally took your advice."

"Oh?" Her eyes perked up.

"I spoke to someone about...you know..." Dan inched his head up and down.

She nodded. "Of course," she said, as the tension in her body she stored to worry about him relaxed.

"It was only one session. I have a long way to go, but it helped." Dan took a healthy sip. "It's a lot to process. I didn't get much sleep.

She batted her watery eyes. "One step at a time."

"But thank you. You gave me the little push I needed."

She nodded and smiled, as she put her glasses on and went back to her desk.

• • • •

~DAN~

As Linda left, he pulled up the shades despite the blinding sunrise that always hit that side of the building. His head throbbed and begged for sleep, but he had to focus. He had to keep moving forward.

With someone there to help him dissect each memory, they weren't as alive anymore. He felt like he'd regained some sense of control. He could feel the fear and look past it at the same time.

He had a lot to think about. His experiences, although gruesome and painful, represented an opportunity to grow. Something he never thought possible. Shame used to have him by the throat and wouldn't let him speak.

• • • •

~DEB~

Deb knew that if she waited too long, she wouldn't have the guts.

She had finished her day—a good one finally, showing two houses and getting one offer. All she wanted was to go home and collapse on the couch. Maybe have a drink or two. She hadn't touched her vodka bottle in a while, and then the thought of it latched in her brain and it was all she could think about.

She stared at the methodic setting of the sun through the windshield, as she winded along the tree-lined road that followed the creek. Daylight would last another twenty minutes or so by the shallow height between the sun and the tops of the trees. The cemetery was five minutes down the road. Enough time to stop and not too much time to wallow.

She pulled onto the tiny gravel road with a strip of grass growing in the middle. The old iron arches loomed down at her, whispering; *it was about time.*

As she passed by the headstones the air seemed to change. She rolled her window down a crack and listened to the tires crunch underneath her. His headstone was all the way in the back. She remembered the day he made her sit down and look at the paperwork.

· · · ·

November 13, 1984

"Here, just sign here, then we'll be able to rest together for all eternity." He handed her a pen.

"You make it sound…not good." She laughed as the pen slipped through her fingers and onto the floor.

He bent down and handed it back to her. "Well, I like to think that there is something good for us after. I mean, we're all gonna go sometime. I want to know that whatever comes next, I have you with me." He leaned in and kissed her on the back of the neck.

"You're too good to me," she whispered as she crunched her neck, receiving the kiss, and reaching up to cradle his head with her arm.

· · · ·

He had been too good to her. Why else would he have been taken from her so soon? God probably thought he'd made a mistake and decided he'd end her lucky draw.

She switched off the engine and tiptoed through the grass, the sun just below the tree line.

She knelt in front of the grave and laid her hands on the stone. The coolness seeped through her. Tears welled, then poured. She coughed and choked on the wetness.

She leaned over to let gravity take control. Her tears rained on the stone. The splashes painted circles across the surface until too many overlapped and the salty liquid drained into the little crevices of the letters. Watching the tears fall gave her something to focus on. The ever-changing pattern of the wet drops on the stone allowed her to keep crying and not feel pressured to stop.

A gush of wind whipped across the graveyard and slapped her wet face. She shivered. The sun had slipped behind the horizon. The night sky was enclosing above her.

She whispered "I love you, Beau" through her sniffles. At the sound of her own voice finally saying his name, she smiled.

. . . .

~LINCOLN~

He stared at the clock all afternoon. When the bell rang for the end of the day, he raced outside. He was skilled with his crutches now. He leaned on them as he waited for his mom on the sidewalk in front of the school. As the car came into view, he saw her park and get out.

"Hi, honey, I just need to go inside and talk to Principal Murphy about something really quick. I'll be right out."

"Ma'am!" The crossing guard barked at her. "Ma'am, you can't park there in the loading zone."

"I'll be just a minute," she replied, not even turning around.

The crossing guard then noticed him on his crutches and backed off, making eye contact to apologize. He nodded in acceptance.

"Mrs. Hoffman can be awfully ratchety, can't she?"

He turned around and saw Lizzy.

"I mean, if school crossing guard is her power trip, I feel a little bit sorry for her."

"She didn't mean it," he said.

"Okay." The warm spring wind whipped through the trees on the front lawn of the school. Lizzy tucked her blowing hair behind her ears. "How's your foot?

"It's doing better, almost healed." He looked down to avoid eye contact with her. He knew if he looked into her eyes, he would see himself and his armpits plugged with the ridiculous crutches.

"How much longer, you think?" She kicked a stone down the sidewalk.

"Hopefully not long."

"Hey listen, I know you probably don't want to talk about it, but I wanted to tell you something."

"Okay." He swallowed hard.

"I'm sorry my dad wouldn't let me stay in the ER with you. I started arguing with him about it even and he just got more and more upset, so I had to go home. I just didn't want you to think I just left you, 'cause I didn't."

"It's okay, you don't have to be sorry." He stopped and pivoted to face her. He wanted to show her the same respect he felt. No one had really cared for him like this before—well, at least no one but his dad.

"Well, I am. So you'll have to accept it." She bobbed her head to the side and smiled. "So now that I have your attention...can I ask you something else?"

He squinted his eyes, as the afternoon sun escaped from behind a puffy white cloud. "I guess so." He wanted to trust, but his throat clammed up. He knew what she would ask.

"What're all those envelopes? Is there some secret party that I'm not invited to?"

"Ha." His throat squeezed tighter, but he managed to eek out a dry laugh. "No, there's no party. Secret or otherwise."

"Okay, is that all you're gonna tell me?"

He closed his eyes and shook his head with tiny back and forth movements. "I'm sorry. I just can't." He swiveled on his crutches and turned back toward the school. Where in the hell was his mom? The one time she was not in a hurry.

Lizzy sighed and darted across the school lawn in the opposite direction.

• • • •

~DEB~

"Is Principal Murphy in?" Deb asked.

"No, he's down at the gym. Is this urgent? I can page him on the loud speaker." Linda peered at her over her wide-rimmed glasses.

"I'll go find him," she said without any hesitation.

Linda waved her out of the office.

She took the cue and speed-walked down the hall, looking for the gym.

"Oh hi, Mrs. Peterson," Trent said.

"Oh, Trent, hello. Can you point me toward the gym?"

"That-a-way."

"Thanks!" She smiled and went on her way, despite the confusion on Trent's face.

She heard the squeak of tennis shoes and rounded the corner toward the gym at the back half of the school. As she peered inside, she saw the teachers playing a pickup basketball game.

She spotted Dan with a cut-off T-shirt that said "ARMY" in block letters across the chest. He leaped off the ground for the rebound. He snatched the ball right out of the hands of the shorter man in front of him. One of his teammates called for the ball. He passed it up the court, but the ball skipped out of bounds near the doorway. Everyone stopped and looked toward her.

Dan ran over. "What's wrong?" he asked, out of breath.

"Oh, sorry, I didn't mean to interrupt." She blushed. She felt foolish making everyone stop playing.

"It's okay. What's up? Is anything wrong?" Dan wiped the sweat from his brow with the back of his forearm, and she glanced at his triceps engaging.

She shook her head and looked away, trying to refocus on the task at hand.

"I would like to hold up my offer." She smiled. "Have dinner with us Friday night. I'm cooking and I insist."

Dan paused and tugged at his shorts. "Well...I guess you leave me no choice, it seems?" He returned the smile.

"Okay, we'll see you at 7." She turned and exited the gym without looking back.

Back at the car, she slammed the door shut in a hurry and turned the ignition.

"What took you so long? Why did you have to see Principal Murphy? Am I in some kind of trouble again? I swear I've been good."

"No, you're not in trouble. I was just inviting him to dinner."

"Oh...okay."

They rode in silence for the rest of the ride home. She had a lot on her mind. She was trying to find the right words to say to Lincoln about visiting the cemetery. Nothing seemed right. She decided to keep it simple and say something instead of nothing.

As they pulled into the garage, she reached for his leg as he put his hand on the door handle. "Wait." She took a deep breath. He stared back at her, wide-eyed. "I did what you said."

He questioned her with his eyes.

"I went to the cemetery yesterday."

"It's about time," he snarked and stumbled out of the car.

She couldn't move, but a tear dripped down her face. She knew he was right.

Chapter 21

The Dinner

Dan shifted the small store-bought vegetable tray to his left hand and pushed the doorbell with his right. He heard a symphony of three chords through the door.

The door opened revealing Deb, apron-clad, barefoot, with cheeks glowing from the heat of the kitchen.

"Dan!" She waved. "Please, come in!"

"Why thank you." He stepped into the foyer. Towering a foot above her, he could see down her blouse. While he wanted to linger, he lifted his head and cleared his throat.

"Oh, you didn't have to bring anything, but how nice, thank you. I'm still finishing up—make yourself at home on the couch with Lincoln." She disappeared with the vegetable tray.

He sat next to Lincoln, leaving one cushion between them. "So how's the foot?"

Lincoln sat silent for a few minutes, his injured foot propped up on the coffee table and his head buried in his comic book.

Dan hung his head and looked to his right at the pile of magazines on the end table. He picked up the *Sports Illustrated* with a thin layer of dust fading the shiny veneer cover into a dull opaque mask. The mailing label on the bottom right corner said, "Beau Peterson." The words hit him like a lightning bolt.

"What are you doing?" Lincoln shot a glare in his direction.

"Sorry." Dan shuddered, as if the magazine gave him an electrical shock, and dropped it back onto the stack. He wondered if he should even be there. He waited a minute until Lincoln resumed reading his comic book. Then he made a break toward the door, and as he unlocked the deadbolt, it clicked.

"Dan?" Deb's voice filtered out of the kitchen and into the main foyer. "What's going on?"

"Oh, sorry." He stumbled. "I forgot something in my car." He sighed, pleased he was able to think of an excuse that made some logical sense. The sight of Deb in her apron and her hair pulled up with just a few stray hairs framing her rosy face made him woozy.

"Okay, well don't be too long. We're ready to eat very soon."

He stepped out the front door and sprinted down the driveway to his Mustang. Driving down the hard gravel country road toward town, the speedometer hovered around 70. The trees flew by the window, witnesses to his coward's departure. Suddenly the road turned to sand.

• • • •

September 2, 1990

Inside the Humvee, sweat dripped down his forehead.

He swerved.

A line of explosions snaked through the sand on their flank.

Orders to retaliate blasted through his walkie-talkie radio. "Fire for effect, over!"

The artilleryman grabbed the mounted weapon overhead.

"Shoot and scoot!" the artilleryman hollered. "Murphy, turn!"

• • • •

Dan bumped up and down in his seat. The Mustang careened onto the shoulder. He slammed on the brakes. The car stopped, the engine letting out a sigh of relief. He laid both hands on his chest, feeling it heave up and down.

What was he doing? He had to stop running. He was safe. He felt his shoulder blades against the back of the seat. His feet on the floor. His hands gripping the wheel. The birds and clouds in the sky stretching out in front of him. The voice of his therapist echoed in his head. *You can heal from your trauma.* He backed the car onto the road and headed into town.

Knowing he couldn't return to the house empty-handed, he stopped at the liquor store and grabbed a bottle of wine.

"Let's try this again," he whispered to himself as he retraced his steps up to the porch from fifteen minutes ago. He cracked the front door just enough so he could slide in.

"You came back?" Lincoln said, still uninterested and immovable on the couch.

"I guess I did." He shook his head and walked into the kitchen.

• • • •

~DEB~

"Oh my, another surprise!" She blushed and took the bottle of wine. Holding it up, she read the label. "A Syrah, this is lovely—thank you, Dan."

She shuffled across the kitchen to open the top cupboard and retrieve two wine glasses. She slid the glass she had already been drinking behind the toaster without Dan noticing.

"Cheers," said Dan. He wiped his brow and took a big sip.

"Cheers." She looked him straight in the eye, searching for something.

The timer on the oven dinged.

"Okay, we're ready to eat!" She announced loud enough for Lincoln to hear from the other room. "Lincoln, come get the salad bowl and put it on the table, please."

"Mom!" Lincoln raised his voice louder than hers, followed by an audible growl.

"Oh, silly me. You have no hands." She smacked her forehead. Her face turned red. She started to wonder if this dinner was a good idea, but her thinking was fuzzy. Maybe she should stop drinking, she pondered as she took another sip of wine.

"This looks really good, Deb. I love lasagna," Dan said as he pulled out a chair for her.

"Thank you, Dan." She smiled and took a seat.

They ate and silence filled the room aside from the periodic clang of a piece of silverware touching the ceramic plate.

Dan cleared his throat. "So how's your foot, Lincoln? It must be tough having to sit out of baseball. I heard you had one heck of a game not too long ago?"

"Yeah."

Dan looked to her. "You must be very proud of him?"

"Oh yeah." She swallowed another big gulp of wine. "Did I ever tell you the story of how Lincoln got his name?"

"No." Dan leaned in.

Lincoln glared at her and crossed his arms, but she couldn't help it. The story sprang from her lips.

"Well obviously—or maybe not so obviously—he's named after President Lincoln. Beau was a huge history buff. One of Beau's favorite quotes from Lincoln was 'Every man's happiness is his own responsibility,' and he wanted Link to always remember that he was in charge of his own destiny." She stopped. Fire burned in the bottom of her belly. Her dry throat spasmed.

Pushing back her chair, she went to the kitchen. She opened another bottle of wine and refilled her glass to the top. She chugged until there was a normal amount of wine in the glass and returned to the table.

"Sorry about that. I just had to check on the dessert."

Dan and Lincoln stared in opposite directions, neither of them looking at each other nor at her.

Dan broke the silence again. "It sure smells heavenly. What's for dessert?"

"It's a surprise." She closed her eyes and rolled them into the back of her head as she tipped back more wine.

Lincoln sniffed and glared at her.

Her hand floated toward Dan's.

He accepted and held tight.

Lincoln noticed.

"Can I be dismissed?" Lincoln's voice pierced the room.

"No-you-may-not," she replied, slurring the words into one.

She wobbled up from the table to the kitchen, chugged some wine from the bottle, and brought dessert from the kitchen. She put a tray of molten chocolate lava cakes on the table, doing her best to keep her balance. The room spun around her.

"What a special treat," Dan said, as the smell of chocolate filled the room.

"It sure is," Lincoln said sarcastically. "This used to be my dad's favorite dessert."

She put down her fork, and everyone froze.

"Yes, it was Beau's favorite, and it's about time we enjoyed some." She took another swig of her wine and then took a big breath. "He was the best man I'd ever met. He made me feel alive. He was the most wonderful father. I can't believe I haven't been able to say these things until now." She paused and wiped a small tear from her eye. "But I finally feel safe, like it's going to be okay and I am allowed to feel and have happiness without him."

She looked at Dan and squeezed his hand.

"He's not here anymore," she said, "but my happiness needs to be. I need to talk about him and remember the good times. Like when we would all go down to the creek, and he and Lincoln had cannonball contests off the dock. Or when the Christmas tree fell off the top of the car that one year on the highway, and we had to rent a truck to finally get it home. The way he smiled at me when he got home from his twelve-hour shift, even though he'd seen horrible things. All these things are okay to think about and remember and miss. It's okay to miss him. This cake tastes bittersweet tonight. I know he is watching us, hoping we'll save him a one."

She took a deep breath and exhaled. A small tear pattered from her eye. She wiped it before anyone could see.

Lincoln's face burned red. "I can't believe you, Mom!" he yelled and grabbed his crutches. He bounded away from the table and hopped up the steps to his room.

They heard the door slam.

"I'm sorry," she said, hanging her head. "I give up."

"It's okay." Dan got up and put his arm around her.

The touch frightened her. She smacked his arm away and immediately said, "I'm sorry."

Dan stepped back, frozen.

"I've had too much to drink. Why don't we have some coffee?"

"Yes, that sounds like a good idea."

She stumbled as she got up to make it.

"No, let me do it." Dan stopped her. "You go sit down." He helped her to the couch.

She just sat there. She couldn't think. She couldn't feel. She just couldn't anymore.

"Here." Dan handed her a mug.

She wrapped both hands around the warmth of the mug. Glimpsing into the liquid to breathe in the aroma, she shook her head as the smell struggled to penetrate the dullness of her senses.

Dan sat on the couch next to her. "How are you feeling?" he asked.

"Okay."

"I know this is so hard. I have no idea what you are going through, but I can imagine it's terrible."

She nodded and took a sip. The heat and acid cut against the alcohol.

"Are you gonna be okay? Do you want me to stay?"

"No, I'll be okay. You can go. I'm sorry about all of this."

"Don't be sorry," he said. He bent over to kiss her forehead.

She reached up and put her hand on his cheek. They locked eyes for a moment. Then Dan leaned in and softly kissed her lips.

"You are a strong person, Deb," he said, turning to go.

"I sure don't feel like it." She shook her head. Glancing up, she saw Lincoln peeking over the upstairs railing.

• • • •

~LINCOLN~

Lincoln pushed off the banister the instant his mom's eyes met his. His body filled with venom. He didn't know how to rein it in. He wanted to throw his crutches over the railing and hit Principal Murphy square in the head.

Instead, he kicked his injured foot against his bedroom door. Pain shot up his leg, and he hunched over. His face pressed against the carpet and he breathed hard, tiny synthetic fibers collecting in his lungs. He planted his hands in front of him and pushed up on one leg to hop into his room.

He couldn't believe she'd told Principal Murphy the story of his name. His dad had picked his name. His dad had always told the story.

And why in the hell did she call him "Link"? She'd never done that before. Of all the times he'd wanted her to open up, she chose to open up to a stranger.

The whole night was like a bad dream, nothing like the hope of a new future he'd envisioned for the past year. He slammed the door hard enough so they could hear his disapproval from the front porch.

All he could think about was his dad. The throbbing in his foot was nothing compared to the hole in his heart. He pictured last June, his dad's final birthday. How different everything would have been if he'd known it was the last time.

• • • •

June 29, 1994

"What are we gonna do for your birthday this year?" his mom said.

He overheard his parents discussing the subject in their bedroom one morning.

"I don't want to make a big deal. Just a couple of people, maybe down by the dock. I'd rather they have a good time than it be all about me."

"We'll at least have lava cakes?"

"Of course. I can't go without those!"

He heard them kiss.

They all gathered down by the dock on a Sunday afternoon—his mom, his dad, Arletta, and his dad's paramedic buddy, Jake. His dad and Jake sat on the dock, fishing poles in one hand, beers in the other. Arletta fussed after his mom about the napkins blowing away in the breeze. His mom stood arguing while Arletta fetched two rounded rocks and set them on top of the stack.

He pumped his legs higher and higher on the tree swing. When the height of the swing reached a ninety-degree angle, he launched himself into the creek. A splash rippled across the silent water.

"Nice form!" his dad called out from the dock. "That's my boy."

His dad's smile was the first thing he saw when he surfaced. He gulped a mouthful of fresh air and swam to shore.

"Why don't you get dried off? Join Jake and me? Maybe you can catch something." His dad laughed. He always made light of everything.

Lincoln shimmied his wet swim trunks off behind a tree and slipped into a dry pair of shorts. He pulled up a camping chair next to his dad.

"So how's summer break?" Jake asked.

"Oh, it's fine. Playing a lot of baseball." He cocked back his fishing pole and strung out the line.

"Thata boy!" His dad patted him on the back. "Link, you're going into the seventh grade now." His dad paused and rubbed his forehead. "I have something I wanted to tell you."

"Oh?" He looked at his dad with a wrinkle between his eyes.

"Mr. Hudson, he teaches in seventh grade, doesn't he?" His dad looked out over the water.

"I'm not sure. I haven't got my schedule yet." He turned.

His dad continued to stare ahead. Like there was something out there, someone walking on the water.

"Well, just be careful around him. He's an angry man. He's got a right to his anger, but it's best not to cause any trouble, you hear?"

"Sure, Dad." He leaped back as his pole locked. "Oh wow, I think it's a big one." He stood up, pulling and reeling.

His dad jumped up and stood behind him. With a smile painted ear to ear, his dad mimicked his arms in the air like a puppeteer. When the fish appeared, wiggling and waggling for its life, Lincoln hollered at the success with the two grown men. He felt grown now too.

"Boys!" Arletta motioned from the picnic table downstream. "It's time for cake."

They all sang happy birthday, and his dad smiled at Arletta, her deep baritone vibrating across the water.

As his dad blew out the candles, he wondered what he'd wished for. Lincoln watched his dad hook his arm around his mom. He pulled her in for a kiss. He dished out cake for everyone else and then sat down with his own. His dad clinked forks with him before he dug in.

• • • •

He wiggled his tongue around his mouth. The taste of the cake from dinner still lingered. He felt sick. He didn't deserve that cake anymore, not without his dad. No one deserved it, especially not Principal Murphy.

He also couldn't believe he'd forgotten about what his dad had said about Mr. Hudson. No wonder he was always on his case at school. But what was making him so angry?

~DAN~

Dan grunted as he returned the bar. It slammed against the weight bench, the two forty-five-pound plates on each side clinking together. The sweat dripped in his eyes, stinging.

Lying flat on his back, he wiped his forehead. Tiny fighter jets crisscrossed above him. This was new. He knew he should pause and think about what it meant.

Instead, he picked up the fifty-pound dumbbells. He pumped them in a running man fashion. He could use his body to overpower his mind. As he looked in the mirror, his T-shirt transformed into his camouflage jacket. His tennis shoes morphed into combat boots.

He put the weights on the rack with a giant thud and stormed out of the garage.

The cold Gatorade splashed down his throat, easing him for a moment. He sunk his back down the door of the refrigerator and sat on the floor, hunched over.

He glanced across the room and thought about the dinner with Deb. Should he have kissed her? Did he take advantage of a vulnerable woman? He cringed that Lincoln saw. What was he thinking?

But there was an emptiness in his bones—he longed for her.

Scenarios flashed in his head: He would apologize and one day propose. He pictured a wedding with him wearing his green beret and his dress blues, Deb walking down the aisle, and Lincoln standing and smiling as his best man.

He dismissed his fantasy and put his head in his hands, sighing. He stood up and got ready for work. Time to face another day.

• • • •

~LINCOLN~

"I bet your armpits feel better," laughed JJ. The other boys standing on the infield joined in on the laugh.

"So?" Lincoln jabbed back. "At least I can play again."

After two weeks on crutches, his foot was cleared for activity. He never felt better, at least physically.

"Yeah, we missed you too, Prez," Trent said. "Especially your pitching. JJ here just couldn't get his curve to curve like yours."

"Hey man, I have a great curve." JJ threw his mitt at Trent.

Trent walked away.

"I do." JJ followed Trent into the outfield.

"Let's go get warmed up," Lincoln said to JJ. "Practice is about to start."

Lincoln saw a group of kids walking just outside the outfield fence. They must be leaving detention, or maybe band practice? He shrugged and grabbed his mitt to begin the team warmup—playing catch. As he stood with his mitt raised in the air waiting for JJ to get in line across from him, he noticed the group head into the building. One silhouette remained in view, looking through the chain-link outfield fence. He squinted and saw Lizzy. He waved, keeping his arm close to his body to make it a low-profile wave. She noticed and waved back. First with her arm held high, but then she lowered it, mimicking his body language.

"Hey, Prez, are we gonna play some ball? Or are you gonna flirt with your girl?" JJ teased.

"Let's play." He hurled the ball toward JJ.

"Okay, geez." JJ caught the ball and took his hand out of his mitt, shaking it.

He smiled. JJ ought to get a little sting for all the shit he dealt.

The rest of practice went smoothly. He felt great being back on the field with the team. His arm was a little sore from pitching for the first time since his foot injury, but everything else was back to normal.

On the way into the locker room, he stopped in the hallway. The framed photo of Jackie Robinson caught his eye.

He heard Trent shout from the showers, "Hey, cut that out!"

"What's going on?" Lincoln popped his head into the shower room. All five showerheads sprayed out warm water from the silver tower in the center of the steamy room. He saw JJ waving a wet towel around. "JJ, knock it off."

"You're not the boss of me!" JJ snapped.

Trent scooted out of the shower while Lincoln distracted JJ. "Thanks, man," said Trent, as he hurried past.

Lincoln waited for JJ to finish his shower before going in for his own. Afterwards, he found JJ on the bench, his face hunched into a towel in the corner.

"Hey man, what're you still doing here?"

JJ looked up at him, his eyes bloodshot and his cheeks burnt red.

"I thought everyone else was gone." JJ rubbed his face, trying to erase evidence of his tears.

"I thought everybody was gone too. Are you okay?" Lincoln sat next to JJ on the rackety wooden bench.

JJ looked down and shook his head no.

"You don't have to talk if you don't want."

JJ looked up at him. "I don't know how to talk about it." He cringed over crying again.

He waited for JJ to regain his breath.

"It's impossible," JJ said through the tears.

"What's impossible?"

"Living."

He looked at JJ confused, and then realized what he meant. "Hey man, it's not impossible. We need you in the lineup..."

"Eh, you don't need me. No one does. Not my dad, not my mom. They want me to be someone I'm not..."

"What about your brothers? Who would they have to pick on?" Lincoln chuckled a bit, trying to lighten the mood.

JJ didn't respond. JJ had three older brothers who picked on him nonstop. They were very macho and athletic. His dad expected JJ to follow in their footsteps. Instead, JJ struggled a bit with sports and wasn't the all-star on the team.

"You don't understand..." JJ picked the towel back up and buried his face in it. JJ pushed Lincoln's thigh away, trying to create space.

Lincoln moved back and waited.

Then JJ put the towel around his neck and pulled. Lincoln lunged and wrestled it away from JJ.

"Hey, man, it's okay," Lincoln said, as JJ surrendered the towel to him. "Tell me. What don't I understand?"

"I'm a loser. I don't even have the courage to say it..." JJ looked at him with fearful, pleading eyes. Whatever it was, it was something JJ seemed to be praying for him to piece together.

Lincoln studied JJ's face with the same depth and concentration he would put on a picture. He looked deep into his eyes. He thought about JJ's dad pushing him to be a sports hero, JJ's constant acting out, his incessant tagging along with Trent.

It all made sense now. JJ liked Trent. And JJ would have a pretty close to impossible time if people knew that in their town.

"It's okay, JJ...I understand." Lincoln put his hand on JJ's shoulder.

JJ looked back at him. He took a huge deep breath, sighing out all the tension and anxiety from having to put words to the situation. "Thanks, man."

"I got your back."

JJ's shoulders tensed up "...and you won't..."

"Of course not. This is your life. You get to decide."

JJ relaxed again. "Thanks, man, I can't tell you how much it feels to have told someone. It's like I can breathe again."

"No problem. Thanks for telling me. You're a good guy, JJ. You don't have to fight against the world on everything. Just try and go with it a little more...and just be yourself."

"I'll try. It's pretty hard."

"Yeah, I get that. But if you ever need to talk about it..."

JJ nodded and packed up his stuff. "I'll see ya at school tomorrow, okay?"

He nodded back. "Yeah, see ya tomorrow, JJ."

Lincoln sat alone in the locker room for a while. He knew what it was like to hold a secret. In a way, he was envious of JJ for letting it out. But in a bigger way he was sad. What if he couldn't like Lizzy? What if he couldn't tell anyone that? It seemed impossible, just like JJ had said.

He walked down the hallway to leave but caught a glimpse of the Jackie Robinson photo on his way. He sat across from it, leaning against the cinderblock wall.

He stared. He blocked everything else out.

His eyelids dropped.

The hallway turned black.

Still.

Shifting to gray.

Tiny beams of light.

He opened his eyes.

There he was, Jackie Robinson. Standing in the middle of Ebbets Field. He didn't know what to say. He stumbled a bit in the dirt with his feet, stalling.

"You wanna throw the ball around?" Jackie asked.

He froze. This couldn't be real. "But I don't have a—"

"Mitt? Here, borrow one of mine."

He reached out and caught the mitt. Jackie's mitt looked and felt different from his own. Bigger, with wider fingers, and smelled like leather and tobacco.

"Go on, put it on. Let's play." Jackie pounded his fist into the mitt, waiting for him to hurl the ball his way.

He wound up and threw him a curve.

"Oh, so you are a pitcher?" Jackie laughed. "I thought we were gonna play catch."

"I'm sorry." He swallowed the lump in this throat. "Force of habit, I guess." His heart jumped into high gear.

"Say, if you're a pitcher, why don't you try and strike me out?" Jackie walked to the dugout and came back with his bat. "It'll be fun—don't be shy."

"I can try." He trotted out to the mound and took his position. He hoped his heart would calm down, but it continued racing.

"Hey, Pee Wee!" Jackie motioned a teammate from across the infield. "Come catch for this little fella for a minute. He's gonna try and strike me out." Jackie smiled.

"Oh sure." Pee Wee winked back and crouched down behind the plate.

"Okay, let's play ball!" Jackie called out.

He clutched the ball with his wobbly, sweaty fingers. Hall of Famer Pee Wee Reese was behind the plate catching for him and Jackie Robinson was at bat! Adjusting his cap, Lincoln looked for the sign and nodded, trying to concentrate over the beating in his chest. He wound up and let the ball go, holding his breath.

Jackie took a big, healthy swing. The bat cracked, sending the ball sailing over his head. He turned and watched it loft higher and higher until it bounced in the seats in center field.

"Wow." Lincoln's jaw dropped.

Jackie walked out to the mound. "Not bad, kid. Get a little more heat on that curve and you're gonna be lethal." He patted him on the shoulder.

"You really think so?"

"Of course I do!" Jackie winked at him and handed him an envelope. "Open it up."

His sweaty hands did the best they could to open the envelope. Inside, the card read, *Fear*.

He looked up and Jackie nodded at him.

He nodded back. His eyes felt heavy.

He closed them.

Darkness.

His portal.

He breathed deep.

The hum of the fluorescent lights.

He opened his eyes.

He was back in the hallway.

. . . .

~ARLETTA~

"You awfully quiet." Arletta looked over at Lincoln, riding in the passenger's seat. "Tough practice? I bet it was tough goin' back after ya been away so long."

"No, it's not that."

"Oh, then what?"

He sighed with hesitation.

"Ya can tell me...in your own time, honey."

"I'm mad." He folded his arms and looked out the passenger side window.

"Oh?"

"Yeah."

"Mad 'bout what?"

"Not what, who."

"Who den?"

"Mom."

She was stunned. Then not surprised at all. Then upset along with him.

She glanced at him, inviting him to share with her eyes.

"She was so stupid."

"Okay..."

"She invited Principal Murphy over for dinner. She talked about Dad. She told Dad's story about my name—only he can tell that story!" He raised his voice. "She made lava cakes and I saw them holding hands and kissing! She's forgot about Dad!" He huffed and started crying, putting his head between his legs.

She put her hand on his back. "It's okay, baby. It's okay." She whispered and rubbed her hand in a circular motion, waiting a minute for his crying to subside. "Lincoln?" She tried to get him to sit up. "Lincoln, I need ta see ya for a sec. Can ya look up at me?"

He sat up, his eyes bloodshot.

"I'm so sorry yur upset. It's okay. I'd be angry too." She paused and wiped away her own tears. "But she ain't forgotten 'bout him. Everyone grieves in der own way, honey. As much as dis hurts, I think dis's actually a good thing. I think yur mom might be comin' ta acceptance."

"I don't know." Lincoln grumbled and looked away. "Can we just go home?"

She knew not to push and put the car in drive.

They rode in silence, trying to come to grips with grief. Arletta had been waiting for so long for Deb to come to this moment. While she'd processed Beau's loss faster, she'd pushed away the final pieces because she knew she could never be at complete peace until Deb was. Deb's struggle reminded Arletta that the process was not 100 percent over.

But now the end was there. What now? All the emotions she had gone through before flooded back. She looked over at Lincoln. She could tell he felt the same way.

. . . .

~DEB~

"Hello?" Deb called from upstairs. "Who's there?"

She heard Lincoln come in through the garage and some rummaging downstairs.

"Lincoln?" She heard the door shut to his room.

She knew he was upset, but she didn't know what to say.

She knocked on his door. No reply.

She lifted her fist to knock again, but instead unclenched it and dropped her hand. She went to the kitchen and fished her vodka bottle from under the sink.

. . . .

~LINCOLN~

Lincoln grabbed the shoebox under his bed and studied his growing collection of envelopes.

Dinner. Car. Rain. Dark. Eyes. Deer. Guardrail. Tree. Glass. Blood. Seatbelt. Smoke. Fear.

Fear of what? Whoever was sending the messages, did they know about his heart? He was worried about being able to continue finding clues. The pain got worse and worse with each jump. He remembered his dad suffered from a heart defect; maybe he should stop pushing?

He sat cross-legged on his bedroom floor looking over the array of envelopes. Maybe he just needed to go faster?

Scanning the books in his bookcase, he pulled out a book about famous pirates. This should be fun. He flipped the pages. His mind raced with possibilities as he stopped on a page with a treasure chest. He stared.

His eyelids got heavy.

He held his breath.

The room filled with shadows.

Then darkness.

Only his heartbeat.

Then shades of gray.

He opened his eyes.

He sat in front of the treasure chest along with several other pirates. They were giddy with excitement and fawning over the loot they'd captured.

"Ahoy there, matey, look at these gold coins and diamond-studded knives," one of the pirates said, nudging him. "This is one of our best loots yet, doncha agree?"

He nodded. This was a dream come true. Here he was, among real pirates!

"Go on, take your fair share," the bearded pirate said, handing him one of the diamond-studded knives. "This is probably worth the most."

"Thank you." Lincoln took the knife and slid it between his red satin belt and his body. He wore a puffy white shirt tucked into baggy black pantaloons with a leather vest. His heart flinched and burned. *Oh no, not so soon,* he thought.

"Why lookey there! A ruby necklace." Another hand dove into the chest and pulled out a necklace. The hand belonged to a rather pudgy pirate who appeared like he'd had a bit too much rum. He held up the necklace and stumbled around the deck.

"Hey be care-fill, Slimy Bill, ya almost knocked da boy over!"

"Oh, e'm sor-eee, son."

"No troubles, fellas." Lincoln dodged out of the way. His breaths quick and short.

He went below deck. The narrow passage was lit with a flickering candle affixed to the wood plank wall.

"Stop right dere!" a voice called out from behind him.

He froze. This was not in his plan. He tried to shut his eyes to escape. There was darkness, but he felt cold, clammy hands twisting his arms behind his back.

"Boys, what do ya say? We got one to walk the plank tonight?" The voice spit in his ear as he pulled him up the stairs to the main deck.

"Oh, quit yur jokes, Rit. He's just a boy. He ain't hurtin' no-buddy. We done already gave him some loot." Slimy-Bill held up the necklace again.

Rit let go and pushed him across the deck in protest.

Lincoln looked over the rail at the dark, choppy water below.

"Don't lean over too far, ya might fall in." He felt a friendly hand on his shoulder. "It's mighty wicked cold."

"Thanks."

The bearded pirate reached into his pocket. "'Dis here's for you...'" He handed him an envelope. "Some kinda secret treasure map, maybe?"

"Maybe." Lincoln shrugged. "Say, maybe you can help me.... Where did you get this envelope? What do they all mean? Do you know how many more there are?" Lincoln looked up to find the pirate had vanished. The pain in his chest deepened.

He felt a gust of warm air, peculiar for that time of night.

His eyelids descended.

He yawned in the darkness.

The smell of the sea faded.

Golden shadows sparked in his periphery.

He opened his eyes.

He sat on his bedroom floor with a new envelope in hand.

The card said, *Knife*.

Chapter 23

Desperation

"—ello?" Deb slurred as she picked up the cordless phone. She was sprawled across the couch, the almost empty vodka bottle cuddled up next to her.

"Are ya drunk?"

"No..."

"What're ya thinkin' bein' wit another man in front-a Lincoln?"

"Excuse me? Who is this?" She perked up and could magically form full sentences.

"Deb'rah. Ya *know* who dis is." Arletta's voice expounded her headache. "And ya know I wan-ya ta move on." Her voice softened. "But please don't make it any harder for Lincoln than ya already 'ave. I'm sorry—"

"Okay, I thought I was starting to understand you, but I see what's going on again. You juuust can't stop accusing me. Nothing I do is right. Nothing I do is on your timeline. Why doncha tell me how I'm supposed to get over my husband's death? Huh? Come on! Out with it! You seem to know everything! You're the expert on trauma. Don't you miss your son?"

"Of course I do—" Arletta said quietly, but Deb cut her off.

"And you leave me high and dry! Lincoln asked me about his race. He said you already told him! I can't believe you would put me in such a position!" She paused to catch her breath. "I can't do this anymore."

She hung up the phone.

Her blood boiled. Her head throbbed.

She wanted to throw the phone across the room. But she also knew Arletta was right. She should have went out with Dan alone, without Lincoln. Why did she bring him over for dinner? The three of them sitting down together when she didn't even know what she had with Dan. How could she be so stupid? Lincoln probably hated her. All the progress she'd made with him—gone.

. . . .

~ARLETTA~

Arletta heard the all too familiar dial tone beeping in her ear. She shook her head and took a deep breath. She didn't blame Deb for hanging up on her this time.

. . . .

~HELEN~

"Oh hi, honey, I'm so glad you came over." Helen opened the door.

Deb stood on the doorstep. She opened her mouth to speak, but nothing came out. Instead, she burst into tears.

"Oh honey, come inside." She put her arm around Deb and ushered her inside. "What's wrong?"

"I don't know what to do," Deb tried to say through the tears and sniffles, pushing Helen's arm away. "I had another man over for dinner. Lincoln's principal at that! I was stupid. I had him come over for dinner with the three of us. God, what was I thinking?" Deb smacked the base of her palm against her forehead. "I thought I was doing the right thing. To get back out there. But I think I did the exact wrong thing." Deb shook her head, her hand still connected to her forehead.

Helen paused for a long bit and stared at Deb with still eyelids. "I think you did what you wanted. I hate to say it, but you've always done that."

"What?" Deb's tears came to an abrupt stop. Deb glared at her.

"I could never keep you contained." Helen shook her head, surrendering. Maybe the truth would help her change? Or maybe it wouldn't? Either way, she no longer could stand idle and watch her daughter keep lying to herself.

"Excuse me?" Deb's words shot like sassy rockets across the room.

"Think back to high school. Every time I would tell you not to do something, you would go do it—like the smoking and the drinking and the sleeping around—yeah, I knew. And when I tried to help you—you pushed me away. Like that night you came home at 2 a.m. with your clothes ripped, and instead of punishing you for missing curfew, I tried to talk to you—you sent me away like I was a stranger. I couldn't stop you or your reckless behavior. Hanging around with the wrong crowds—you were lucky you didn't get pregnant. You were lucky you kept your grades high enough to go to a good college and put all of that behind you. You've been awfully lucky most of your life, but now life has caught up to you, and you have to suck it up and get through this. You need to be a mother. Lincoln needs you."

Deb was silent for a minute, her jaw clenched and her eyes blinking at double pace.

"I don't have to take this." Deb jumped off the couch and headed for the door. The room was silent aside from Deb's heels click-clacking across the hardwood floor.

Helen watched Deb, feeling the urge to stop her but not acting on it. She couldn't. Deb had to figure this out on her own.

• • • •

~DEB~

Deb slammed the front door of her mother's house. The brass knocker on the outside bounced and clanged. She thought her mother might come after her. She might say sorry. Or at least a small part of her hoped.

She revved the engine and peeled out of the driveway. She cranked the tape deck as loud as it would go. The empty seatbelts clinked against the back seat with each thud of the bass. Picking up speed, she was going almost 100. The chassis of the car bounced with every small crack in the road.

Tears ran down her face, blurring the road. Through the fog, she detected the outline of a big cement barrier left over from some road construction. As the wall got closer and closer, she aimed for it. She imagined the impact. The crushing metal and debris flying every which way. And the blackness. The end.

She jerked the wheel back to the center line. The cement blockade whizzed past her window and over her shoulder. She took a deep breath, as memories of high school flooded her mind.

The night of the ripped shirt was a memory she'd locked away a long time ago. How dare her mother bring it up. She had no idea. How dare she talk about all her past mistakes. Hadn't she been through enough? Wasn't the past year of pain enough penance? When would she stop paying for her sins?

She tapped on the brake. She needed a destination. A purpose.

She made a hard left at the next crossroad. She thought she remembered where Dan lived but wasn't quite sure. Hadn't he mentioned a little subdivision outside of town about half a mile from the middle school? A new development that he got for a really good deal, she remembered him bragging.

Pulling into the subdivision, she saw four identical houses on each side of the curated street with a cul-de-sac at the end. The shine of the streetlight bouncing off Dan's black Mustang, parked in the last driveway, caught her eye. The second-story window had a light on. Phew, at least he was home.

She tapped on the front door and waited. A minute or two went by. She knocked again, louder this time. No reply. She noticed a doorbell and pushed it. The chimes sung and she took a step back, one foot on the porch and one foot on the sidewalk.

"Deb?" The door creaked open.

Dan stood in the doorway in his boxers, shirtless. He had more tattoos than she thought. His dog tags hung around his neck, clinking a bit, as he opened the door wider, realizing it was her.

"Oh..." Deb tripped, as she stepped up to put two feet on the porch. "Yes...I'm sorry to come so late...it's just..." She blushed, as the curvature of his chest emerged from the shadows as he flipped on the porch light.

"Why don't you come in?" He rubbed the stubble on his chiseled jaw.

"Okay," she said, following him inside. She didn't want to stay long; she wanted to get this over with.

"Do you want something to drink? I can make some coffee or tea." Dan pulled a coffee filter out of the kitchen drawer.

"No, thank you, that's all right. I'm okay." She pinched at the sides of her sweater. Her body was on fire. "Well, actually I'm not okay." She took a deep breath. "I'm sorry. I was wrong about the other night. I should have never invited you over, and definitely not in front of Lincoln. I don't know what I was thinking." She dropped her head. "And we can't do that again."

Dan dropped the coffee filter. "Uh...I'm sorry you feel that way..." He picked the coffee filter off the floor. She could see him crumpling it in his fist behind his back. "I had a really nice time with you, but I understand." He turned his back to her and started rearranging a big stack of mail on his kitchen table.

"It's just not right—at least, not right now. I'm sorry." She felt relief and sadness at the same time. She turned to leave. Another minute and she'd do something she'd regret.

"Are you okay?" He studied her face. She felt like he was looking right through her. Like he could see inside all the pain and longing she wanted to share with him.

She didn't know how to answer. She was nowhere close to okay, but she couldn't articulate her feelings into words. She walked to the door without answering.

He stepped in front of her. "Deb, I'm worried about you. Are you okay to drive at least?"

She nodded, stepped over his leg, and didn't turn back.

. . . .

~DAN~

Dan watched her walk like a zombie to her car and drive away. He stared at her taillights until the red glow disappeared into the night.

Why? Was she doing the right thing? Was she getting out before she could hurt him even worse? Or was she using her son as an excuse to avoid her real feelings?

He wiped his eyes. He wished he could do more to help her. But now she had made that nearly impossible.

. . . .

~LIZZY~

Lizzy turned the corner and saw Lincoln at his locker. She was apprehensive to talk to him. But she couldn't quiet the contentious voices in her head.

Had she pushed him too hard for answers? Did it really matter what the mysterious envelopes were? Maybe she should've minded her own business? Wasn't spending time with him enough? Did she have to push for more and risk their friendship?

She wished she didn't care so much. She could tell that Lincoln had secrets that were eating him up, secrets beyond the grief of his dad. All she wanted to do was help. If she were him, all she would want is someone to talk to. But how do you help a person who doesn't want to open up?

"Hey." She brushed up behind him. "How was practice yesterday? It must feel great to be back on the field." She cracked a small smile, hoping she could comfort him.

He closed his locker. "Yeah. My arm's a little sore, but I don't care. I just want to be back out there." He turned to walk away. "I have practice now. I gotta go."

"Wait." She grabbed his arm.

He winced but waited for her reply.

"Oh sorry, is this the sore arm?" She let go.

He shook his head. "It's fine."

"Listen, I'm really sorry about the other day. I shouldn't have pressured you."

"Thanks."

They both stood silent, side by side for a few moments.

"Are we okay?" she asked, trying not to sound desperate. But the truth was, she didn't want to lose him.

"I don't know. I just need some time to think." He swung his backpack over his shoulder and walked away.

She watched and hoped he might turn around, but she stood there until he disappeared.

"Hi, Lizzy, everything okay?" Principal Murphy sauntered by her.

She looked up, startled. "Oh...yeah...fine. How are you, Principal Murphy?"

"I'm well, thanks for asking." He turned around and circled back to her. "What were you looking at?"

"Oh nothing." She twirled her wrists and put her hands behind her back as her face reddened.

Principal Murphy stared back.

"Okay, I was watching Lincoln." She dropped her hip and head to the side.

"He's okay?"

"Oh, I don't know. I hope so, but I really don't know." Her face softened but remained blushed.

"You're a good friend, Lizzy."

"Yeah, I guess so. I just hope I didn't ruin anything."

"You didn't ruin anything. As long as you're honest, that's all you can ask for. The rest is up to him."

"Thanks." She nodded and shuffled along, dreading the likely chew-out session from her mom for not being outside for pick-up on time.

~DEB~

"Lincoln? Is that you?" Deb yelled from upstairs as she heard the back door slam.

Then from down the hallway, she heard his bedroom door slam.

The second slam set her off. This rift couldn't go on any longer. She put down her paperwork.

"We need to talk," she said, opening the door to Lincoln's room without warning.

"Mom!" Lincoln, bare-chested with his sweaty T-shirt from baseball practice in his hand, jumped behind his closet door.

She noticed the definition forming in his pectoral muscles. Her son was growing into a man. Her stomach clenched. "Just put a shirt on and come out here. We need to talk." She tried to stay focused.

"I don't want to talk!" he yelled from behind the closet door. "Especially to you! You never say anything that matters anyway!"

His words were like a gunshot to the heart, but she stumbled closer.

"What're you doing?" Lincoln grilled her as she sat on his bed.

"I'm sorry," she said. The framed picture of Beau and Lincoln on their last fishing trip was visible from Lincoln's open sock drawer. Their smiling faces nestled among soft white socks.

"I'm sorry I had your principal over for dinner." She cupped her hands and leaned over, cradling her face to hide the tears. "I'm sorry I said all those things in front of you. I know you deserve a chance to talk about those things with me first," she mumbled, her face still masked by her hands. "I loved your dad so much. My having feelings for another man doesn't change that."

After a few seconds, she unveiled her face and looked up.

Lincoln had vanished.

"Lincoln?" she cried out. The house was silent.

She ran downstairs to the kitchen, but the room was empty. The deadbolt was switched to the open position on the front door. She grabbed her keys and opened the garage door. As she backed down the driveway, she fought the tears that had started again. What kind of parent was she? She'd failed again, but she couldn't lose him. He was all she had left.

Out on the road, she turned her brights on to get a wider view. The moon, a tiny sliver of a thumbnail in the dark black sky, provided no light. As the road bent along the creek and through the trees, she kept her eyes peeled for Lincoln. She knew he had reflective strips on his running shoes, so she looked for that little glimmer.

Then she saw something. She couldn't tell what until it was too late. The whites of the eyes flashed at her like the devil. The big opaque body with horns towered over her. She swerved the car. The tires squealed and burned as the weight of the vehicle came to a stop no less than a foot from the trunk of a huge oak tree.

She gasped, staring out the windshield at the tree trunk inches from her. Gratitude infiltrated her whole body. She watched the deer in the middle of the road gallop away, hearing the faint click of its hooves on the pavement.

• • • •

~LINCOLN~

Lincoln's throat burned, as he swallowed the cold night air. He ran faster than he'd ever run. He didn't know where he was going. He didn't care. He just wished his mom would run after him.

The farther he ran, the harder for him to hold in all the emotions. Something inside him burst. The tears were cold. Like little knives cutting his face.

His chest tightened and he pulled up from running. His heart pounded and his breath raced. He listened and sighed as his body returned to its normal rhythm.

Then he walked. The act of putting one foot in front of another gave him purpose.

• • • •

~DEB~

As she sat frozen in the driver's seat next to the big oak tree, the hum of the engine registered into Deb's consciousness. She saw Beau's face. She saw blood, bent metal, and broken glass. The deafening sounds, the screeching tires on the road, the shattering of the glass, the crushing of the metal, her own screams. She smelled the burnt rubber, the blood, and the smoke from the engine. She tasted the salty tears running from her cheek.

Slapping herself in the face, she put the car into drive and eased back onto the road. The car jerked and bumped as she crossed the grassy berm transitioning from the gravel shoulder and back onto the smooth pavement. She gripped the wheel with a newfound confidence and determination. Her eyes, wide open, no longer cried.

She turned around and went back to their house to head in the opposite direction. She had been heading toward town, but now thought Lincoln ran toward Trent's house. The music playing in the background irritated her. She turned it off. The whooshing sound of the road filled the space around her.

As she approached Trent's house, she slowed the car and kept scanning. No sight of him. The blowing heat from the vents keeping her warm inside the car made her feel bad, knowing that Lincoln was probably shivering outside.

● ● ● ●

~LINCOLN~

Lincoln felt like he didn't belong anywhere. The darkness hushed his thoughts. He hung his head, the weight of it drawing his steps slowly forward. He fiddled with his hunting knife in his pocket. *Knife.*

Wait, maybe there was something more? The word stopped him in his tracks. He knew where he was headed now. To the site of the accident. He made a turn and picked up his pace. His blood moved faster and warmed him up.

Thinking back to Arletta taking him to the scene, what did he hope to find different this time? His dad had always told him that unless he did something different, things would always stay the same.

But he'd tried everything. He felt stuck. Even though his mom was acting so weird and pissing him off, it wasn't the change he was hoping for.

As he maintained his downward glance so he wouldn't trip in the dark, his shadow appeared in the approaching headlights behind him. His upright body sagittally split right and left across the white line on the shoulder.

The car slowed and pulled over. He stopped and turned around, shielding his eyes with his forearm from the blinding lights.

"Link?"

He saw the outline of the car. It was his mom.

He stood still, shoving his hands into the front pocket of his sweatshirt.

"Honey, I'm so sorry." She tiptoed toward him.

Reaching out, she put an arm around his shoulders. He didn't resist. He was too tired.

"I was so worried about you. I never want anything to happen to you. I'm sorry, honey. I'm sorry I've been making it so hard for you. I need to be there. I promise I will be now. I love you."

She looked over and saw a small tear running down his face. "You okay?"

He half nodded and wiped the tear from his face. She'd actually come after him. He thought he'd be wandering alone all night.

"I'm okay," he managed to mutter.

Then something inside of him shifted. The anger dissolved. "Oh, Mom, I miss him," he said as he buried his head in her chest and sobbed.

"It's okay," she said, stroking the back of his head. "I miss him too...I miss him too."

"I'm sorry." He picked his head up and looked her in the eye. "I didn't mean to make you worry. I just missed him...and you."

Chapter 25

Veritable Wounds

Deb rolled over. Her body ached. Her mind fogged. The night before had been a lot.

Hearing a faint knock from downstairs, she looked over at the clock—7 a.m. on a Saturday. A little early for visitors. She hoped it wasn't Arletta coming to talk to her about Lincoln again.

She wrapped up in her robe and went to the front door. Through the peephole, she saw Dan.

"Just a minute," she said, trying to be loud enough for Dan to hear but not loud enough to wake Lincoln.

Running upstairs, her body tingled. She threw on jeans and a sweater.

She cracked the front door, squeezed through, and shut it behind her. She stood shivering on the front porch. "Dan, you can't be here. I told you. It's upsetting to Lincoln. Please go before he wakes up."

"I'm sorry. I knew you wouldn't have talked to me if I didn't come over. I just want to make sure you're okay. I'm worried about you."

He leaned in.

She sunk back.

He backpedaled down the sidewalk.

"Dan, wait. I'm sorry. I didn't mean to..."

He gave her a little half wave, as he ducked into his Mustang and pulled away.

She stood limp on the front porch. This man cared about her. He came all the way over to check on her. She couldn't push him away, but she couldn't upset Lincoln anymore either.

Making breakfast might help. She got out the Belgian waffle iron and searched the refrigerator. She was excited to find a few strawberries and leftover Cool Whip. Cooking gave her something else to focus on, as she rinsed and sliced the strawberries and mixed the batter. The sweet smell of the vanilla extract lightened her senses and reminded her of baking with her mother when she was a little girl. Which reminded her of what her mother said to her. She sighed, but went on making breakfast. Lincoln was her focus.

. . . .

~LINCOLN~

Lincoln opened his eyes and smelled waffles browning. He swallowed and winced. The running around in the middle of the night had dried and sored his throat. Hunger tickled his stomach, but he was afraid to go downstairs. He wasn't ready yet.

He felt time was running out and he wanted to find more clues.

Grabbing his bookbag, he pulled out his history book. His class had just been tested about the signing of the Constitution. Being a fly on the wall in that moment sounded cool. In his textbook, there had been a painting of the Constitutional Convention where the delegates signed the document. He flipped through the pages and located it.

He stared at the painting. The room charged with hope and power. Hands raised in approval. Eyes filled with promise. All pointed toward the quill being passed hand to hand. Scribing history on parchment. He braced himself for the magnitude.

He focused on the page and held his breath.

He squinted.

Then darkness.

Black.

Silence.

His breath.

His drumming heartbeat. Already?!

Then light.

The room came into view. George Washington stood at the front desk looking out at the delegates. A quartet of flags and a drum hung behind him on the wall.

Lincoln itched his scalp and noticed he wore a wig with coifed white curls tied back in a ponytail. He stretched out his arms to look at the ruffles from his white undershirt poking through the ends of his burgundy suit coat. A drop of hot wax landed on his hand. He brushed it off, but the damage was done. His hand stung and burned. Looking up, he assessed the culprit. Candles dripped from the elegant chandelier hanging in the middle of the room.

"Here, it's your turn next." His heart lunged.

He turned and accepted the quill from a man. Gazing up, he realized the man was Benjamin Franklin. The round wire-rimmed glasses perched at the edge of his nose and stout frame.

"Thank you, sir." Lincoln obliged and stepped up where the Constitution rested. He gripped the quill as best he could with his sweaty fingers and dipped it in the ink jar. As he raised his wrist to sign, he stopped mid-air. What name should he sign? And what would happen if he signed? Would he change history? The quill slipped through his fingers and fell to the ground.

He ran out of the room, gasping for air.

"What happened?" he heard Washington ask the group as he scattered way.

The murmur of the crowd grew louder. Then shouts.

He hid around the corner, his chest heaving, but didn't know what to do. Then the hum of the room dissipated. Footsteps mounted toward him.

He had no choice but to run. He exited the building and darted into the cobblestone streets of Philadelphia. Bumping into a mail carrier, a satchel of letters flew into the air, floating every which way.

"Hey!" shouted the mailman.

But Lincoln ignored the mailman. His eyes fixated on the flash of blue. There was another letter with the blue seal. He snatched it and kept on running.

After he was in the clear, he ducked into an alleyway. He felt his body shutting down. He snuck a peek at the letter. It read *Love*.

This was surprising…

Darkness.

Eyes dormant.

Quiet.

A deep breath.

Light returned.

Back in his room, he looked at his hand. The bright red burn from the wax remained. And it hurt. He touched it and cringed in pain. He rushed to the bathroom to get some topical cream and a bandage to cover up the scar.

"Lincoln? Are you awake?"

The cream dropped on the floor. He grabbed the tube, rubbed some on, and tossed it into the medicine cabinet before scurrying back to his bedroom. He put on some slippers. The house was cold—there seemed to be a draft.

• • • •

~DEB~

"Are you hungry?" Deb turned and saw Lincoln standing in the doorway. "I made enough for both of us—come, let's eat."

Lincoln sat, grabbed a fork, and dug in.

"I hope you like it." She smiled, searching for his eyes.

"It's great, Mom," he said looking up and meeting her eyes. "Thanks."

"What happened to your hand?"

"Oh." He pulled his hand from the tabletop and buried it in his lap. "It's nothing. Just a little cut from practice."

"Okay." She nodded.

Lincoln continued eating. A crash of thunder struck and the two of them shuddered.

"I didn't think it was supposed to rain today," she said.

Lincoln shrugged.

"Say, it looks like we have a rainy Sunday indoors. What do ya say we watch a movie?"

"Don't you have a house to show?"

"Not today."

Lincoln's head remained hunched over his plate.

"Is something wrong?" she asked.

"No, I'm fine."

"Are you sure? Do you want to talk about last night?"

Lincoln sat still.

"I'm really sorry, honey. I know everything is really hard. What can I do to help?"

Lincoln got up from his chair and leaned his head into her chest. The connection felt natural, maternal. She felt like a mother again. She hugged him and felt his body relax. He sobbed, but they were both quiet. Being together was enough now.

A tear rolled down her face and fell onto a lock of his hair. She smelled his Teen Spirit shampoo released by the moisture. She breathed it in and sighed, strengthening her embrace around him.

· · · ·

~LINCOLN~

"Hey, Lincoln? What's up with you?" Trent asked, nudging his arm. "What do you want? Pizza or chicken fingers?"

The lunch lady plopped a rectangular piece of pizza onto his tray. "You're holding up the line."

"I guess I'll have pizza," he whispered sarcastically to Trent.

"I heard that," snapped the lunch lady.

"Man, you gotta chill out. She can be vicious if you don't tell her what you want. I heard about this one time when Tommy LaBounge had a sore throat and couldn't talk that great and didn't tell her what he wanted and she threw a hot dog at his head."

"That's not true."

"He told me himself."

"Okay, and you believe Tommy?" Lincoln slid his tray along the line.

"Whatever. But seriously, what is going on with you? That was a close call."

He walked ahead of Trent, attempting to avoid the question. Trent shuffled to catch up to him. They both sat down at the lunch table among the rest of the group.

Trent leaned in and whispered, "You're gonna tell me after school."

Lincoln glared back at Trent. "Hey, guys. What did you think of that math quiz today?"

The group murmured a bunch of replies, but he didn't care about the answer. He was lost in another world. His chest tightened as if he was in one of the pictures and he felt like he wanted to vomit. He stared down at the limp piece of pizza on his lunch tray and swallowed hard. He got up, tossed his untouched pizza into the trash, returned his tray, and headed straight into the bathroom.

The first stall was open. He knelt down on the cold, hard ground, clutching the toilet in front of him. The bowl reeked of urine and feces along with a faint smell of bleach. He tried to cough. Instead, his breakfast came up. He hunched over as the vomit splashed into the water with force. He sat back on his knees for a minute trying to catch his breath. A thin layer of sweat coated the back of his neck. Even though he'd just thrown up, he didn't feel any better. He whimpered and heard the door open. Footsteps shuffled behind the stall door.

"Prez?"

He heard Trent.

"Prez? You okay?"

He heard the bathroom door creak open again.

"Is he okay?"

He heard JJ's voice.

"Hey, I got this, all right?"

He heard Trent push JJ aside. His heart ached for JJ for a moment.

He tried to remain still, but it didn't stop Trent from bending down and looking under the stall door. Trent held his breath as he smelled the vomit.

"Prez, you okay, man?" he asked again, peering at him sideways. His knees on the dirty floor.

Lincoln wanted to run and hide but couldn't move or talk. His stomach churned. He reached up and turned the latch so the stall door could swing open and Trent could see the situation.

Trent sat down on the floor and put his arm around him. "It's gonna be okay, man. You don't have to say anything. Let's get you to the nurse."

"Okay, Lincoln, I'm going to call your mom to come get you," said the school nurse, as she removed the thermometer from his mouth. "Temp is normal, so that's good. I think you just need some rest and liquids to let the bug pass."

He nodded, still nauseous as he lay back on the small table in the nurse's office. He closed his eyes. He wished for peace. For his body and his mind. He wanted to know the truth and for his life to go back to normal.

• • • •

~DEB~

"Still no fever, but you feel hot." Deb placed the thermometer on the nightstand and brushed the back of her hand against Lincoln's forehead. "Can I get you anything else?"

She edged the cup of tea closer to Lincoln. She stared at him lying wrapped under the covers, a thin glean of sweat across his forehead.

"I'm okay." Lincoln's voice scratched.

"You don't sound okay, honey." Her eyes sunk. She fished his hand from under the comforter and held it. "I wish I could make it all go away."

She sensed his attuned but inaudible response and looked up to meet his eyes. Nothing got by him. She had an intuitive son.

One day, her statement would be true. All the pain, all the worry about a future without Beau. It would all have an answer, an ending. Lincoln would tell his future partner, his future grandchildren the story of his dad's life. She hoped he wouldn't be too harsh with her part, but so far, she had done little to earn herself redemption.

"Why don't you get some rest?" She slid his damp hair off to the side. "I'll get you a cool washcloth. I'll be right back."

As she ran the cold water, waiting for it to get icy cold, she glanced at her face in the mirror. *This is all I have,* she thought to herself. Skin puffy and thin, aged by the sun and alcohol. Tired eyes, cried dry. The scar above her right eye. What do people see when they look at my face—the sad, failing widow? *Wait.* What do I see?

She patted the skin underneath her eyes. There was still some life left. There had to be.

She wrung the washcloth and held it in a ball to keep the coolness in the center as she walked back to Lincoln's bedroom.

"There, that should make you feel a little better." She wiped his hair back again, making room for the cool rag, and unfolded it across his brow.

"Thanks, Mom." Lincoln pressed the washcloth into his forehead.

"Let me know if you need anything. I'll just be doing some paperwork in my bedroom."

Lincoln nodded.

She pulled the door shut. Please let him be okay.

• • • •

~LINCOLN~

Lincoln sighed as she left. His throat swelled and his body ached. He closed his eyes and tried to sleep, but kept seeing the image of himself on the floor in the school bathroom and Trent leaning under the stall. Even though Trent was his best friend, he felt embarrassed.

He opened his eyes and focused on the ceiling fan.

• • • •

January 18, 1991

"What I'm doing is very dangerous."

"But I want to help." Lincoln's neck was cranked back, watching his dad's every move.

"Okay, just wait. You can help in a minute." His dad knelt on the bed, reaching up toward the fixture.

Lincoln watched him unscrew the bulb, waiting so he could swirl it around in his hand, listening for the broken filament brushing the sides of the frosted glass.

"This one's burnt. You can hand me the new one."

Lincoln reached into the flimsy cardboard square and pulled out a new bulb, but as he made the exchange, the old bulb slipped through his fingers and cracked open on the hardwood floor.

"Oops, good thing that was the old one, Link. Get on the bed so you don't get glass on your bare feet." His dad twisted the new bulb in. "There we go. Wait here and I'll go get a broom."

. . . .

Lincoln missed how chill his dad was, no matter how big or small the crisis.

His dad must have been comforting to his mom at the accident, even though he was dying.

Lost in memory, he felt his eyelids tug. His gaze had been fixed on the opposite wall, but the image had not registered. It was his movie poster from the 1939 film *Stagecoach*, starring John Wayne. He and his dad had watched the movie together and that year he got a framed vintage poster for Christmas.

The poster depicted a sextet of horses pulling the stagecoach at full speed, trying to outrun the Apaches. The scene was set against a blue backdrop, the horses pummeling across the bright yellow block letters of the movie title. He blinked his eyes. Could his body take another trip? The image blurred.

The blue and yellow faded together into green.

Then gray.

Then black.

He held his breath.

His throat tightened.

Silence.

Then horseshoes clopping.

His eyes opened.

They burned with sand, whipped in by the gusty wind, as the coach bumped and galloped at full speed across the desert. He sat snug to Doc Boone, who was leaning out the window. The Doc aimed his pistol at the Apaches surrounding them atop a pack of horses.

"Take this, kid!" Hatfield, the gambler, tossed a pistol in his lap.

His hands trembled and fumbled the gun into shooting position to join the fight. He'd never shot a gun before. He didn't know what to do. Wrapping both hands around the weapon, he closed his eyes and squeezed the trigger. The gun kicked back despite his death grip. The heaviness sat on his chest, reminding him of the limited time.

"Curly, more ammo!" He heard a voice from the driver's bench outside.

Looking out the window amidst the dust cloud, he saw Indians falling off their horses, Indians shooting arrows, and Indians shooting rifles. He ducked under the window and held his breath. Was this chaos worth it? The clues weren't really leading him anywhere specific anymore.

Inside the stagecoach Mr. Peacock, the whiskey salesman, held a bloody rag to his chest. Mr. Peacock looked him in the eye for a moment. He went to Mr. Peacock and applied more pressure on the rag.

Lincoln heard the muffled cry of a baby. He turned his head to Dallas, the dance-hall maiden, huddled in the corner, an infant swaddled against her corset.

"It's okay," she said. "Just keep shooting."

So far, everything was happening like the movie. Well except for his intrusion.

He moved to the opposite side next to Hatfield to heed the call to be a man. He leaned out the window to take aim and saw the loveable outlaw Ringo Kid hopping along the backs of the horses until he saddled up on the lead horse. An incredible move!

Thudst.

The pierce of the arrow was unmistakable. He'd put his hands too far outside the window and had been hit. The pain radiated from the entry point in the back of his hand up and down his arm. He couldn't feel his fingers. He ripped the arrow out on instinct. Blood spurted everywhere.

"Here." Dallas had unwrapped the baby and put the blanket around his hand. "Lay down on the floor," she said, cupping the baby's head in her hand.

He glanced at the underside of the roof as the bullets and arrows pinged against the side of the metal coach, as he held his breath and prayed.

Mr. Gatewood, the bank manager, opened his small leather carpetbag and slipped an envelope inside his shirt pocket. "You'll need this," he said.

He couldn't respond. His eyes were closing.

Darkness.

Black.

Silence.

Fear.

Spinning thoughts.

Longer than usual.

But then the light.

His eyes peeled open.

He'd never been so glad to be sick in bed.

His hand throbbed.

There was a scar. The wound looked like time had somehow sped up and started the healing process. Maybe when he was coming back to reality?

How was he going to explain this? And where was the envelope?

He rummaged under his covers, bumping the tea. The warm liquid spilled all over his nightstand and rushed onto the floor.

"Shit," he whispered and tumbled out of bed. Yanking the sweatshirt off the back of his desk chair, he mopped up what he could.

"Lincoln? Lincoln, are you okay?" His mom's voice drifted down the hall.

He jumped to the door and locked it.

"Lincoln? You okay in there?" She tapped on the door.

His heart raced. He grabbed the shoebox from under his bed and dumped all the cards onto the floor. He added *"Courage"* to the mix.

Dinner. Car. Rain. Dark. Eyes. Deer. Guardrail. Tree. Glass. Blood. Seatbelt. Smoke. Fear. Knife. Love. Courage.

"Lincoln, we don't keep locked doors in this house. I need to know that you are okay. Please answer me at least." She didn't sound as angry as she usually would be.

"I'm fine," he stuttered, his throat burning.

"Okay, but I'm not okay with the door being locked. This is not going to be a normal thing, but I'll let it slide this one time since you are sick."

"Okay, Mom." He climbed back into bed and wrapped himself in a cocoon. Thoughts pinballed back and forth in his head, exacerbating his headache, but the darkness helped. He wrapped his hands around his knees to assume the fetal position.

Chapter 26

Determination

~LIZZY~

"Glad to see you're feeling better." Lizzy brushed up against Lincoln from behind, rubbing the small of his back for a micro-second. She didn't want to come on too strong, but she wanted him to know she cared. "Trent told me about the other day. It sounded like you were really sick. What did you have?"

"Oh, hey." He gave her a half smile and then looked away. Maybe she had come on too strong? "I think it was just a bug."

She noticed the bandage on his hand. Had something happened while he was sick? Maybe she was being too paranoid.

"Oh hey, Prez!" Trent approached Lincoln's locker. "You look so much better. Your face is a normal color." Trent laughed.

"Gee, thanks." Lincoln laughed back. She was glad they were such close friends. "What did I miss?"

"Nothin' much." Trent slicked his hair back and started to walk away. "Oh wait, Mr. Hudson gave out the assignment for the annual science fair. It's gonna be a lot of work and we only have two weeks to get it done."

"Ugh." Lincoln looked at her to make sure she shared his sentiment.

"It's 50 percent of our grade too," she chimed in, equally frustrated. She would be spending the next two weeks doing anything to avoid the daily grilling from her mother on her progress.

"See you at practice tonight?" Trent asked.

"Uhhh...I think I'm going to go home and rest tonight. Can you tell Coach? I don't want to be sick again."

"Yeah, sure."

"Where's JJ?" Lincoln asked.

"Oh, I don't know. He's been acting really weird and avoiding me, but I'm not complaining." Trent laughed.

"Huh? Maybe he could use a friend?" Lincoln said.

She watched Trent look back at Lincoln confused, Trent's eyes lifted up and to the side.

Lincoln's expression softened and as a result, Trent shrugged and said, "Yeah, you're probably right."

"How has JJ been acting weird?" Lizzy asked Trent after Lincoln was out of earshot.

"Oh, I don't know." Trent sighed and rubbed his head.

She turned away. She was disappointed Trent didn't feel comfortable enough to confide in her.

"Lizzy, wait." Trent caught her by her elbow. "Sorry, but I truly just don't know."

"It's fine. I just wanted to help." She wished she could help someone.

They stood for a few moments in silence.

"Do you think he's okay?" she asked.

"Who, JJ?"

"No. I don't know about JJ—I meant Lincoln."

"Got me again. A lot of strange stuff happening lately."

"Yeah." She felt helpless. Her mind drifted back to the science fair project. She needed to get home and start thinking about ideas.

"He'll be okay. Prez is the strongest dude I know." Trent's words brought her back to the present.

She shook her head in forced agreement. What else was there to do but believe that everything would be okay?

• • • •

~LINCOLN~

The smell of old carpet, hickory, and moth balls welcomed Lincoln into the public library. His mom had dropped him off on the way to a late afternoon showing so he could catch up on the work he'd missed being out sick. The librarian watched his every move, sending a glare his way. He ducked his head and stealth-walked to the encyclopedia section.

Unbeknownst to his mom, he'd already caught up on his homework. He was on the hunt for clues. This needed to end.

Sliding his fingers along the bindings, he picked out a random volume of *Encyclopedia Britannica*, "#19 Excretion to Geometry," and flipped to "Flight." There was an extensive section about the Wright Brothers and Lincoln wiggled onto the floor with the book wide-open in his lap. He focused on the picture with Orville lying down on the wide double-leveled skeleton, with Wilbur and Dan Tate holding the sides at the start of a glide on the banks of Kitty Hawk in 1902. Taking a deep breath, he prepared for however he might be injected into the scene. What if he was lying next to Orville? He waited for the wave of sleep and dark to sweep him inside. Closing his eyes, he concentrated on what he might see.

Eyes open. The bookshelf stood in front of him.

Lincoln tried not to panic. What was going on? Why wasn't he in the picture?

He stood up and held the heavy book in front of him, glaring at the picture with his eyes peeled open. Nothing.

Snapping the book shut, he walked over to his favorite leather chair. He sighed and gazed up at the atrium window. Maybe this was a sign? Maybe this was the end of the clues? He thought back to the last clue. *Courage.* Of course his dad had courage. How did this help tell him about what happened in the accident? But wait, Lincoln scratched his head. Maybe his dad was trying to tell him something?

He sprung up and shuffled to the microfilm machine. Having only used the contraption once before, he hoped he remembered how to use it. His heart drummed.

Searching the card catalog, he found the *Brightonville Gazette* dated April 6, 1995. He located the correct microfilm and propped himself onto the high stool in front of the machine. Flipping on the light, the print of the black and white paragraphs—organized like a patchwork quilt among the pictures and ads—flashed on the screen. His eyes darted to the picture of a charred and mangled vehicle in the lower righthand corner.

Accident On Wet Hwy 38—One Dead.

His heart exploded in his chest.

One Dead.

One was such a cold and empty word. Nothing to represent the entirety of his dad's life.

He read on, speeding through the words, hoping there was a magic answer...

A single vehicle crash left the driver, a thirty-nine-year-old male, dead last night. The only passenger, a thirty-six-year-old female, was treated for minor injuries and released from Mercy Hospital. The cause of the accident is believed to be wet road conditions while avoiding a deer. Authorities are still investigating. The identities of the victims have not been released.

He gasped and covered his mouth.

Before he thought too much, he took a huge, deep breath and stared at the picture with all his might as the warm wash of sleep dropped his eyelids.

This was it.

He squeezed his fists and eyes tight.

Black.

Like the night.

Cold.

A sprinkle on his nose.

He breathed in.

His eyes opened.

He stood on the wet pavement in the dead of night, but flashing red, blue, and yellow lights cast shadows on the trees that stood with a bird's-eye view of the wreckage. The rain was still coming down but had shifted from the downpour he remembered that night to a light mist.

He pulled up his hoodie, his hair already damp. He strained his neck and stood on his tippy toes, but couldn't see the car. The scene was encircled by a sea of fire engines, police vehicles, and ambulances. Something smelled like it was burning and he sniffled a bit, trying to withhold his oncoming sneeze. He ducked behind a cop car and peered into the back of an ambulance.

There she was.

His mom. Covered in cuts and blood. Her muddy clothes clinging to her wet body. Shivering in shock. Propped up on the stretcher. An IV laced in her arm. An oxygen mask cupped to her mouth.

He wanted to cry but he bit his lip and listened.

"Ma'am, can you tell us what happened?" A police officer stood next her with a pad and pencil taking notes.

She looked scared. He wanted to go take her hand, but he knew he wanted to hear what she had to say first. Listening was the only way he was finally going to know what happened.

She gulped back tears. "You know it was raining..."

The officer nodded.

"We were driving..." Her voice quivered.

"Yes..."

"It's all my fault—he couldn't get free..." Her breath quickened.

"It's okay." The EMT grabbed her hand. "Just breathe. I need you to breathe."

She followed the EMT's breaths.

"It's no one's fault right now. We just want to hear what happened. Can you do that?"

She gave her head a gentle bob. "It came out of nowhere really...the deer...just shot out right from the trees, from the edge of the forest right there...it was on his side...the impact...it was very sudden...and it spun the car...we crashed hard against the guardrail..."

She stopped to take a breath. A few tears dripped from her eyes. She wiped her eyes and continued.

"It's hard to remember every little detail, it all happened so fast...he only cared about me getting out of the car...we could smell the gasoline...his seatbelt was locked...he always kept a hunting knife in the glove compartment...I was able to reach it...he was in really bad shape...his head had been slammed against the window, there was shattered glass and blood in his head and everywhere...he told me to cut his seatbelt...I tried but I couldn't do it...my hands were wet and shaking...I couldn't hold the knife steady."

She hung her head and then picked it back up, fighting to get through the re-telling of the minutes-ago horror.

"Smoke started to pour into the car, and I couldn't breathe...I had a split second to make a decision..."

She shook uncontrollably.

"I pushed the door open and fell onto the road...I rolled away because my legs were too weak to stand...then I was in the ditch and then...then the explosion..."

Her head tipped. She fell backwards on the gurney.

The EMT sealed the oxygen mask to her mouth and listened to her chest. A sea of arms busied around her.

Lincoln closed his eyes and held his breath. He wanted out of the picture. But nothing happened.

Peeling his eyes open, he was still shivering beside the cop car. His mom was still lying motionless. The EMTs had stopped their activity.

He ran around the cop car.

"Mom!"

"Son, back away!" The paramedic grabbed him before he could get close.

He kicked and squirmed as a fireman appeared to restrain him. "Mom? Can you hear me?"

"Son, I think we need to give your mom a rest. She's been through a lot. She's going to be fine. Let's go over here." The fireman led him to the highway patrol car. "Here, this is for you," he said as he handed him an envelope.

He ripped it open. The card was blank.

And then everything went black.

Things never look the same after seeing them for something else. He had been running through what the accident might have looked like in his head for a year. Now it had come to life—and it was worse than he'd imagined. He had no idea what his mom had gone through. The horror she had lived. The finality she had witnessed on that dark, wet night.

Chapter 27

Unimaginable

~LINCOLN~

Mr. Hudson rolled the big TV in front of the chalkboard at the head of the classroom. "Trent, can you hit the lights?" His command blasted across the room. "Everybody quiet down. Today we're going to watch a video about plate tectonics."

The lights flipped off but the sunny glow from the windows infused the room. Mr. Hudson scoffed and marched to the back of the room to pull down the shades. "I said no talking." He returned to the TV and pushed the video cassette into the VCR. The screen lit up with white snow and the room filled with screeching loud static. Mr. Hudson lunged to press play. The Bill Nye theme song played.

Lincoln sank low in his seat. He'd seen the episode before while channel surfing at home. Resting his head on the back of the hard chair, he closed his eyes and thought about his mom. His head bobbed and...

"Wake up this instant!"

Springing out of his chair, he slammed his knees under his desk and winced. He blinked up. Mr. Hudson hovered two inches above him.

"Go to the principal's office right now!" he yelled so close to his face he could smell the tang of hot sauce on his breath from lunch.

Lincoln tried to gather himself but the dim classroom around him looked fuzzy. As reality became clear to him, he realized this was his final strike. He'd likely get something worse than detention with a visit to the principal's office. His stomach jumped upside down and tied up in knots. He stood up without a word and exited the classroom into the hallway. He turned to see if Mr. Hudson was watching, which he was, and he kept going.

. . . .

~MR. HUDSON~

"Everyone, keep watching. I'll be right back." Mr. Hudson closed the door to the classroom. He caught up with Lincoln in the hallway. "What have you got to say for yourself?"

Lincoln stood silent and frozen.

"That's what I thought. There's no excuse for sleeping in my class," he said with his arms crossed.

"What if I told you you could hold your daughter again?"

"Excuse me?" He unfolded his arms and opened his stance.

Lincoln paused and he watched his Adam's apple bob up and down with a hard swallow. "I said...what if I told you you could hold your daughter again?"

Fixing his glare on Lincoln, he hunched over for a moment, then straightened his posture. He put his hands on his hips and said, "You're crazy—that's none of your business. Get to the office right now!"

"I'm not," Lincoln said as he opened the door to go back into the classroom.

"Where do you think you're going?" Mr. Hudson squeezed his head into the doorframe and watched Lincoln approach his desk.

Lincoln picked up the only picture on his desk, a five-by-seven wooden frame resting landscape style.

He gasped. He wanted to scream, but his voice froze. He couldn't breathe.

Lincoln closed the door to the classroom and stepped back into the hallway. "Come, sit with me here." Lincoln sat against the wall and put the picture frame a few inches in front of them.

"This is ludicrous!" He managed to exclaim. "You have no right..."

"Just wait a minute...give me a second." Lincoln focused on the picture.

Mr. Hudson saw his younger self with his baby girl in his arms. The little baby's hand wrapped around his pointer finger. Their eyes locked on each other.

He felt Lincoln grab his hand.

"What're you doing?" He tried to shake his hand away.

Lincoln didn't let go.

The hallway turned pitch black. Did the power go out?

He tried to scream, but there was no sound.

Only silence.

He held his breath.

Was this the end?

He didn't pray anymore. He didn't believe it could help. Not after everything that had happened. But now he'd do anything. Anything to absolve his regrets. His sins.

A flicker of light.

The melody of birds chirping.

He was on his front porch in a rocking chair. His baby girl cooed in his lap. The exact moment from the picture.

His jaw dropped. He breathed in. He clutched his baby girl.

Every bone and muscle in his body relaxed. He felt all the toxins of anger and resentment release.

Bending over, he placed the softest kiss on her tiny forehead. Her skin, silk on his lips.

He looked up to the sky, wondering how this could be possible. His breath was still catching up. He gasped for air, trying to figure out if this was really happening.

"She's really cute," whispered Lincoln.

Lincoln's voice startled him.

"What..." He froze.

"Don't worry so much—just enjoy it," Lincoln said.

A tear formed in his eye as he swallowed the past and gazed at his baby girl. "Isn't she the most beautiful thing you've ever seen?"

"She sure is, Mr. Hudson."

"Please, call me Gene."

Lincoln hesitated for a moment. "Sure."

They both watched as the baby girl squirmed in his arms.

"How is this happening?" he asked.

Lincoln shook his head. "I really don't know."

"Is it real? Or is this some crazy dream?"

"It's as real as it feels."

The baby pulled her tiny fists toward her smiling mouth.

"She's so happy," Lincoln said.

"Happier than I've ever seen her..."

"Oh?"

"We'd only had her home for a few weeks, and one day she got a high temperature. We rushed her to the hospital, but never made it there."

"I'm so sorry."

"I wish it would have been me. I was the one driving. I ran a very questionable yellow light, and we got T-boned in the rear. You should have seen the car—it was a mangled mess.... I'm sorry..."

"It's okay." Lincoln put his hand on his shoulder. "I'm not afraid anymore."

They sat in silence, both staring at the baby for a few moments.

"I got to walk away. But my baby died. The two teens in the other car, they had some major internal injuries. My wife had a severe concussion and whiplash."

Mr. Hudson paused, caressing the baby's cheek.

"Nothing was the same after that. My wife divorced me. I lost everything." He looked down at the baby, nudging his finger into her tiny palm. "I wish there was something I could have done for you...I wish I could have saved you..."

Lincoln put his hand on his shoulder. "What's her name?"

"Samantha." He couldn't help but smile as Lincoln said her name.

"A beautiful name."

He nodded. "Listen, there's something I need to apologize to you for."

Lincoln raised his eyebrows.

"I've been unfair to you." He positioned Samantha over his shoulder and patted her back, focusing on Lincoln.

"It's okay...and now I understand." Lincoln tipped his head.

"There's more." Mr. Hudson closed his eyes for a few seconds, then opened them. "Your dad was the first on scene. I blamed him and I've been blaming you too. I'm ashamed of myself. I'm so sorry." A tear rolled down Mr. Hudson's face.

Lincoln swallowed and blinked rapidly. "I had no idea."

"I wouldn't think your dad would tell you something like that. Your dad was a fine man. He saved so many lives." He wiped the tear.

"He was pretty great. I miss him a lot."

"I bet you do, son."

"But don't be ashamed. It's okay," Lincoln said.

"You're some kind of special."

Lincoln smiled.

"How long does this usually last?"

"It depends, but not very long."

"I don't even have the words..."

Then the sky disappeared.

The black stillness returned.

Mr. Hudson took a deep breath. He opened his eyes and found himself sitting next to Lincoln, hands interlocked.

"Thank you," he whispered to Lincoln and squeezed his hand.

"You're welcome." Lincoln smiled back.

"Never mind about going to the principal's office."

"Oh," Lincoln paused. "Thank you. You're not going to..."

"Tell?" He finished Lincoln's sentence and took a deep breath. "Lincoln, you are some kind of angel. It should be yours to share, not mine. You've already given me more than I could have ever asked for."

• • • •

~DEB~

Deb sat on her bed surrounded by paperwork. A glass of wine breathed on the nightstand. She heard footsteps.

"What is it?"

"There's something we gotta do. Come with me," Lincoln said, out of breath.

She unfolded her legs and followed. "Be careful, you're going to fall." She watched him gallop down the steps two at a time.

Once she caught up, she found him sitting on the floor, holding a Polaroid Arletta had taken of the three of them at Beau's last birthday, standing on the dock.

"Okay..."

A shudder ran through her body.

"Here, sit next to me." Lincoln patted the bare floor next to him.

She didn't understand. The thought of looking at Beau, his smiling face within arm's reach while she sat next to her grieving son, her greatest shame, made her want to crawl under the couch and die.

But she promised herself she'd do anything to connect with her son. Now she had to follow through. She crouched down on the floor next to him.

Lincoln smiled and grabbed her hand. She squeezed back.

Lincoln took a deep breath and stared at the picture.

All of a sudden, the room disappeared into darkness.

Her chest hollowed.

She couldn't speak.

She felt the warmth of Lincoln's hand.

She held on tight.

Was this the end?

Was she having a heart attack?

She concentrated on her breath.

And prayed.

Then she smelled fresh water and fish.

The darkness faded to light.

"Wow..." Her jaw dropped and she let go of Lincoln's hand. Standing on the dock, she bent down and dipped her fingers in the water. "Wow...this is all real?"

"Yes," Lincoln sighed, a small smile cracked on his face.

"It's real if you believe it is...," a voice said from behind.

She turned.

"Beau!"

"Hey, Link," Beau said.

She ran to Beau and jumped into his arms. "I've missed you so much," she cried, burying her head in his chest. Her safe place. Like slipping into an old pair of shoes, perfectly molded.

"I've missed you too. I've missed you both."

She peered up from under Beau's chin and saw him wink at Lincoln.

"Mom, I just want to say I'm sorry. I've been such a brat and pushing you too hard. I didn't realize how terrible the accident was." Lincoln hugged her.

Beau looked at her, his eyebrows raised.

"What do you mean, honey?" She pulled Lincoln's head up gently.

"I mean about the knife and the seatbelt. I went to the scene of the accident, like Dad was trying to tell me. It's not your fault. Tell her, Dad."

Beau froze; just his eyes twitched back and forth. "Link, I never meant for you to visit the scene of the accident. I only meant to give you a little bit of closure about the things I remembered. With my head being smashed so hard, a lot about it was fuzzy." Beau rubbed his head and sighed. "I just wanted you to be able to let go...and to tell you how much I admired your mom's love and courage."

"I'm so confused." Small tears seeped down her face.

"But you, my little man." Beau pulled Lincoln close and stroked his head. "You had more courage than I imagined to visit the scene yourself." He turned to her and said, "For the sixteen lives I saved, I was able to send Lincoln sixteen one-word messages. When you tried the Wright Brothers and couldn't make it, that was supposed to be the end. However, the powers that be allowed me to let you into the scene of the accident because your act showed so much growth and courage."

"Yeah, Mom, I'm sorry," Lincoln interrupted.

"For what?" she asked.

"For not telling you...about the messages..."

She stared at Lincoln. His words passed right through her. Nothing made any sense.

Lincoln turned to Beau with puppy eyes, but Beau nodded and Lincoln continued.

"You see, I didn't even know what was happening the first time. I just wanted to escape." Lincoln hung his head. "You were yelling at me. It was the first day of school after spring break."

"I'm so sorry." She couldn't stand that she'd caused her son even more pain. She couldn't stand feeling like a failure of a mother, not in front of Beau.

"It's okay, Deb, let him go on." Beau put his hand on the small of her back.

Lincoln paused. She could tell he was taking in the moment, seeing his parents acting like a couple again.

"I knew you were upset. I knew you missed Dad. The day before at the house, you hallucinated or something when you saw my knife. Now it all makes sense. But at the time, I was scared. I asked Dad for help and that's when this all started to happen..." Lincoln trailed off. He started to look down.

She'd caught Lincoln's eyes and stopped them on their way to gazing at the floor. She was amazed at his synaptic look. What had she done differently this time? "What started to happen?" she asked.

"Well you see, I stared at that painting on the wall in the kitchen, wishing I was anywhere else but getting yelled at, and...all of a sudden...I was inside. I was sitting at the very same table at a cafe in Paris."

She took a step back, her hand frozen across her forehead. "You mean?"

"I know, it sounds crazy, but it really happened," Lincoln said.

"I don't believe it.... I mean I believe it because I'm here...now...but..."

"It's okay, I know it's a lot," Lincoln said. "It was a lot for me to figure out when it first happened."

"There's one more thing."

She and Lincoln both looked at Beau. "What?" Lincoln asked.

"You were selfless and took Mr. Hudson to say goodbye to his daughter. Because you did that, that's why you could bring your mom here...and you can bring anyone else in the future that needs to say goodbye."

"Really?" Lincoln asked.

"Yes, really." Beau wrapped his arm around the both of them.

"And it won't hurt?" Lincoln tapped his chest.

"No, that shouldn't happen. That was part of the message to tell you when it was going to be over. I didn't want to leave you abruptly without any warning. I hope it didn't hurt too bad."

"Nope Dad, nothing I couldn't handle." Lincoln smiled.

Beau smiled and hunched over. "We don't have a lot of time and I need to tell you both something. Deb, I'm so sorry I couldn't be stronger for you. But you...you had the courage to say goodbye and save yourself...to be there for Lincoln." Beau took her shoulders and turned her to look her in the eye. "I was not the man I wanted to be for you. I lost Mr. Hudson's baby and I could never forgive myself. Deep down, I always felt like I didn't deserve to live and I realize now how selfish that was. How much it hurt my chances of getting out of the car alive, and so I left you alone. The pain of regret doesn't go away. It's still with me, even in death. I want you both to know how important it is to forgive yourself here on Earth."

Her shoulders collapsed, and she leaned into Beau's chest. "I'm so sorry. I thought it was all my fault. I thought I chose me over you when I rolled out of the car, leaving you. I haven't found a way to forgive myself yet."

"It wasn't your fault. It wasn't your fault at all, babe. How can you fault yourself for surviving?" He pulled her tight. "You have to find it in yourself to believe that and to forgive yourself. It can only come from you."

She pulled away and looked at him, dreary eyed. "I'll try."

"It's hard, but it's the only way." Beau brushed her forehead with a kiss.

"But, Dad, it's not your fault either. Mr. Hudson forgives you."

"How do you know that?" Beau blinked a tear down his face.

"Because he told me what happened...when I took him to say goodbye to his daughter. He said you were a fine man and did all you could. It was his fault for driving recklessly."

"My boy..." Beau gazed at him.

The three Petersons leaned together and embraced. A moment Deb would freeze in her memory.

"Time's about up," Lincoln said, as his eyelids fluttered.

Her heart was on fire. She'd never felt so alive.

"But Dad, what did you have to tell me?"

Beau paused.

Her body felt hot and tired.

"It's about our family history." She watched Beau's Adam's apple bob up and down.

"I know about it." Lincoln looked away, rubbing his blinking eyes.

"I'm sorry. I should have told you sooner."

Lincoln looked back at Beau. "I know, Dad. It's okay."

The light dimmed, the sun temporarily eclipsed behind a cloud. The last thing she remembered was hearing Beau say, "I love you."

When she opened her eyes, she was seated on the dining room floor, weeping.

"Mom, you okay?"

"Oh yes, honey...I'm... I'm going to be okay now." She smiled.

Chapter 28

Coming Clean

Deb picked up the cordless phone and stared at the keypad. Her fingers shook as she punched the buttons one at a time, pausing in between each number. Upon completing her selection of ten digits, she waited for the ringtone.

"Hello?" The voice on the other end of the line picked up and sounded somber but joyful.

"Arletta?" she asked.

"Sweet Jesus, thank ya Lord! She lives!"

She cleared her throat and tried to ignore Arletta's incessant need to flamboyantly broadcast her emotions. "Listen, I just wanted to say I'm sorry about the other day...when I hung up on you. That was rude, and I apologize."

"Oh child, apology accepted!"

"It turns out..." She gulped down hard. "You were right...Lincoln was really upset about the way I brought Dan into his life. I was only thinking about myself."

"How's Lincoln?"

"He's okay." She was relieved and surprised that Arletta didn't give her a hard time.

"Glad ta hear it! It's 'bout time." Arletta laughed.

She felt the love Arletta meant with her boldness. "Yeah, I guess it was about time, huh?" Laughing with Arletta, she appreciated her vivacity; it reminded her of Beau.

"The good Lawd doesn't bless us wit enuf time. Ya gotta get out dere and make da most of it. Ya gotta live each day like it was yur last. And ya gotta appreciate what ya have. Lincoln's such a special boy—ya gotta be there for 'im and help guide 'im. He's lookin' to ya. Look back and see yur-self in dat child—and see Beau. He's there too."

She sniffled a bit as she wiped away a small tear of joy. "Yes, I have two wonderful men in my life."

"Doggone, ya gonna make me cry too."

"He actually wanted me to ask you something."

"Oh?" Arletta perked up.

"You mind coming by? He's got something really special to show you."

"Ya don't have ta ask me twice! I'll come on by right now."

• • • •

~ARLETTA~

Arletta hurried up the porch. *Go, legs, go,* she thought to herself, as her rickety hip joints tried to keep up. This was the first time Deb had invited her over since the accident. What had changed?

She reached the top of the landing, staring at the door handle as she caught her breath. She imagined the countless times Beau had grasped the handle with his warm hands. Resting her palm on the weathered brass knob, she knocked on the door with her opposite hand.

"She's here!" She heard Lincoln's muffled voice inside.

The door opened.

"Hi, baby, how are ya?" She wrapped him in her arms and felt palpable energy pouring out of him.

"I want to show you something. It's a secret, just for you." Lincoln led her by the hand into the living room. Her knees creaked as she lowered herself next to him on the couch.

"Oh my, a secret? Just fur me? Dis sounds suspicious."

"It's okay, Grandma, I promise." Lincoln leaned over and shuffled through the pictures sitting on the coffee table.

As he sorted, she saw the photo out of the corner of her eye. The picture came into focus, as Lincoln held the photo square in front of them with his outstretched arm.

She remembered that day, just like it was yesterday. The day hadn't begun as special, just an ordinary morning. But then Beau and Lincoln had shown up with a picnic basket—Beau having the day off and Lincoln on summer break. They took a blanket and spread it under the big old oak tree in the backyard. They sat around and joked about her neighbor's curious cats and spit watermelon seeds, the juice running down Lincoln's little hands. Lincoln was probably about seven years old? Her memory was dusty with the details, but she felt the spirit of that day alive and well in her veins. What was Lincoln doing with that photo?

"Here." Lincoln took her hand and held the photo in front of them.

She focused on Beau's smile. His head cocked to the side, watching Lincoln devour a triangle of watermelon, leaning over the side of the red and black gingham blanket so the juice would drip into the grass.

The memory must have been making her sleepy. The red and black blanket blurred and expanded.

Everything went dark.

She felt Lincoln squeeze her hand.

Was she still connected to reality?

Her breath quickened.

Was her blood sugar low again?

She squeezed back.

And held on.

Until the light.

The sun appeared and she saw the gingham blanket next to the oak tree.

"Boy? What ya gone done?..." Her voice trailed off as she saw Beau.

"It's okay, this is what I wanted," Lincoln said, as he stood.

"Dear Lawd Jesus!" She grabbed her rosary and leaned back so she could see the full profile of her son standing in front of her.

"No, it's just me." Beau laughed. He crouched down on the blanket and sat next to her.

She touched his face. "Are ya real?"

"Yes, this is real." Beau took her hand.

"My boy." She tried to hold back her tears, but it was no use. Taking the opposite corner of the blanket, she patted her eyes. "Ya don't say." She took a deep breath. "I've missed ya—boy 'ave I missed ya."

"I know, Momma, I've missed you too."

"How come we gettin' dis here chance ta talk? What kinda divine intervention blessed upon us?"

Beau looked over to Lincoln. "It's all because of Link; he gave of himself, and now he can keep on giving."

Lincoln blushed and smiled at them.

"I always knew you was special. Ya ain't no normal boy, you my boy's boy." She winked at Lincoln and opened her arms. Lincoln knelt to enter her embrace. She felt the same energy from him as before.

"He sure is. That's my boy." Beau sat down next to her. She added him to the hug.

This must be heaven, she thought. *If my time on Earth is over, this right here is all I ever need.* She took a deep breath before blurting out, "If only his mother would think like ya."

Beau put his hand on her shoulder. "She is. You gotta cut her some slack now, Momma. She got to say goodbye to me—Link made that possible. We talked about the accident, she understands what happened, and she doesn't have to blame herself anymore. I'm not the perfect man. I made some mistakes. She's got a right to make some mistakes too, right?"

She smiled at Beau. "Of course."

"Grandma, we gotta go," Lincoln said, his eyes blinking.

"I love ya. Yur a blessing. I'm always 'ere, wherever..." Her words trailed off as Lincoln grabbed her hand.

The backyard dissolved.

Black.

Peace.

Hand in hand with her grandson.

Gratitude in every breath.

Then light as they were back on the couch.

• • • •

~LIZZY~

"Okay, that's all for today. And don't forget to work on your projects for the science fair next week," Mr. Hudson said. "You can stay after class if you need help or have questions."

Lizzy closed her science book and tucked it under her arm. She had two science projects going. One that was risky but hoped would win her first place. Another as a backup, to ensure at least an A if the first one turned into a disaster.

"Geez, Mr. Hudson sure is a lot nicer these days," Trent joked, as they walked into the hallway.

"Yeah. He doesn't seem mad at the whole world. Or at least mad at our whole class." She laughed.

"I don't know. I didn't notice anything," Lincoln chimed in.

"You're crazy!" Trent patted Lincoln on the shoulder and pulled him back, stopping his forward progress. "He was the meanest to you and you think he's not nice now? I don't get it. You got a screw loose up there somewhere." Trent rubbed his fist on Lincoln's head of soft, wavy blond hair.

"Hey, knock it off." Lincoln swatted Trent's hand away.

"Whatever, Prez. See ya at practice," Trent said as he walked away.

Lincoln looked at her. "You have some time now? Before I have to go to practice?"

"Yeah, what's up?"

"Come with me." He led her down the hallway and into the empty auditorium.

"What are we doing in here?" She stared at the rows of folded-up red chairs. The stage was dark. The only light came from the dim glow of the emergency lights that dotted the aisles.

"This." Lincoln pulled an envelope out of his pocket.

She covered her gasp. Was he finally going to open up to her?

"I'm sorry I couldn't tell you about it before; it was too risky."

"Okay." She bobbed her head, urging him to continue.

"I don't know if you are going to believe me or not, but either way, you have to keep it a secret."

"I promise." She held up her pinky finger. Lincoln took his pinky and completed the link.

"Do you have your wallet in your bookbag?"

"Yeah." She let out a sigh. "Why? Are you going to charge me to tell me your secret?" She looked down at their feet in the shadows.

"No, nothing like that at all. You carry around a picture of your grandma right?"

"Yeah, how did you know?"

"I pay attention." He smiled at her.

She unfolded her wallet and slid out a small stack of two-by-three photos. She splayed them like a deck of cards in her hand and plucked out the one of her grandma.

"Here she is. I still miss her." She handed him the photo.

He gazed at it.

She could still remember her smell, a floral perfume, and her hands, as soft and spongy as a cloud.

"I'm going to show you my secret. Do you trust me?"

She nodded.

He took her hand and held the picture in front of them with his other hand.

She worried that someone was going to come in and find them. Her eyes darted around the auditorium.

The red emergency lights blurred.

Everything went black.

"Lincoln?" She quivered.

He squeezed her hand.

She held her breath.

She closed her eyes.

She opened them.

Darkness had swallowed it all.

She squeezed Lincoln's hand.

And held on.

Letting the stillness shift from scary to calm.

She lengthened her breath.

And then light faded into view.

She opened her eyes and saw her grandma, sitting in the rocking chair, a ball of yarn on her lap and a knitting needle in her hand, just like the picture.

"What..." Her tightened throat made speaking hard.

"It's okay." Lincoln rubbed her shoulder.

"My little Lizard. Come, give your gran-mama a hug."

The familiarity of her gran-mama's voice loosened her throat and the rest of her muscles. She leaned in, engulfed in her gran-mama's smell and softness.

"My, you have grown so much in two years."

She blushed. "I missed you."

"Oh child, I've missed you too."

"Gran-mama, can I ask you something?" She didn't know how she would ask, but this seemed like too good of an opportunity to pass up.

"Of course, anything. What is it, my love?"

"Can you send a message to Mom? She hasn't been the same since you died. She's so strict. It's suffocating."

"Oh, sweetie. I've seen. But I will see what I can do. Most of it is up to her."

"Yeah, I know, but I'd thought I'd at least ask."

"You always were my sharpest grandchild. So smart beyond your years. Don't you ever let anyone take that away from you."

"Thanks, Gran-mama." Lizzy leaned in and gave her gran-mama another hug. She didn't want this moment to end.

"And who is this fine young man?"

"Ah," Lizzy smiled. "This is Lincoln. He's hard to put into words, kinda like this experience."

"And he's responsible for all this?"

Lincoln nodded his head.

"Blessed child. Come get a hug for yourself as well." Her gran-mama grasped at the air, inviting him in.

"It's such a pleasure to meet you," Lincoln said, as he unlatched from the hug, a smile of nourishment stretched across his face.

"Same to you, Lincoln."

"Do you have anything else to say?" Lincoln's eyes blinked at her. She could tell time was almost up.

"Only that I love you." She pecked her gran-mama on the cheek and touched her soft hands resting in her lap.

The light dimmed.

Lizzy braced herself.

She drew in a deep inhale.

Darkness.

Stillness.

Peace.

Quiet.

She touched her heart.

And waited.

Then the dim red lights.

She had returned to the empty auditorium.

"I love you," she said as soon as Lincoln came into focus.

He kissed her on the forehead.

"I love you too."

They sat in the silence, hand in hand for a few minutes. She replayed the experience in her head.

"Wait, so what about the envelopes?"

"Oh. Those came to me one by one in trips like we just had. Until I had the full message. It was from my dad."

"What did he say?"

"He told me about the accident and to have the courage to move on."

"Wow, that's crazy. I mean, great advice, but all of this is so crazy."

"I know. The crazy part came when I took Mr. Hudson. It was my first time taking someone."

She looked at him confused.

"All of the time, I was doing it on my own and trying to get the message from my dad. But when I stopped to help someone else, instead of just thinking about myself, I was able to share the gift."

"So have you done this with anyone else?"

"Yeah. After I realized I could do it, I took my mom. She really needed to be able to say goodbye to my dad. Things were getting out of control, but now I think everything is gonna be okay."

"I can't believe..."

"I know, it's kinda unbelievable. But I'm not gonna question it. I'm gonna help people when I can."

Lizzy squeezed his hand and put her head on his shoulder.

. . . .

~DEB~

Deb wiped the sweat from her brow with the back of her forearm and brushed the flour from her hands on the front of her apron. An invisible cloud of warm air welcomed her as she bent over and opened the oven door. She slid the tray of banana-nut muffins across the wire rack. She wound the white egg timer to twenty-five minutes. As the timer ticked, she ran the water in the sink, watching the rising water lift the soap bubbles, until the pile of dirty dishes submerged. Washing the dishes, Deb breathed in the warm banana aroma filling the room.

"Hey, Mom," Lincoln said as he bounced in the back door from the garage. "Wow, it smells awesome in here!"

"You'll have to wait. They're not quite ready yet. How was school?" She dried the last dish, a big mixing bowl, and placed it in the cupboard on the bottom shelf.

"It was good." Lincoln hopped up on the stool.

"Say, it's kinda late. Did Arletta drop you off? I didn't see her car." She twisted her body to lean out of the kitchen and get an angle of the front window.

"No, Trent's mom took me home after practice. What got you in the mood to bake? I mean, I'm not complaining or anything."

She smiled. "Your dinner is in the fridge. You just have to heat it up. I'm taking a few of these muffins over to a friend."

"Okay, later. I'm going upstairs to finish my homework really quick before I eat."

Ding!

The timer chimed from across the room. She dumped the hot muffins into a basket lined with a blue and white checkered towel.

With the basket on the front seat, she backed down the driveway. The butterflies flinched in her stomach and tickled their way up her throat. As she switched on the music and Air Supply played, she grinned and turned up the volume. Remembering, not agonizing.

When she arrived, she put the car in park and trotted up to the front door. Her breaths left a trail of tiny clouds in the night air. She knocked at the front door.

The door opened. "Oh...hello, Deb." Dan stood tall, his T-shirt with a ring of sweat around the neck.

"Hey, I wanted to bring you these." She extended the basket.

Dan stepped forward to receive the offering, sliding both hands under the basket. "Wow, they are still warm." He took a sniff under the towel. "And they smell delicious!"

"I just baked them. I wanted to bring them over...and well...actually what I really wanted to do was have a reason to come and say I was sorry. I am trying to do everything right, but in the process, I got everything wrong. I upset Lincoln, and I upset you. Well, Lincoln and I are okay now, and I wanted to see if there was a chance you might be willing to see me again..." She raised her arm and interjected. "...if we take it slow. I don't want to involve Lincoln, not yet at least."

"Yes, of course." Dan's face lit up.

"Which part?"

"Both parts. I want to do this right too." He put his left arm behind the small of her back and pulled her close in a tiny little half hug, placing a soft sweet kiss on her forehead. "Tastes like salt." He laughed.

"Oh, that's the baking powder. It doesn't normally taste like that," she joked back.

· · · ·

~LINCOLN~

Lincoln heard the front doorbell. The house was empty, just him and his homework. He was not expecting anyone. He froze for a few seconds, unsure of what to do. The darkness of the night outside his bedroom window loomed. He needed to be the man of the house so he grabbed his hunting knife from his drawer, slipped it into his back pocket, and went downstairs.

Looking through the peephole, he sighed while seeing his Grandma, Helen.

"Hi, Grandma." He opened the door, surprised to see her.

"Hello, my precious grandson. Is your mother home?"

He watched Helen mosey inside. She was older than Grandma Arletta, but a little smoother. "She's not actually. She went out to give a friend some muffins."

"I thought I smelled something." Helen sniffed the air and unwrapped the silk scarf from her neck, placing it into her small side purse. He watched her scan the room and take note of the photo of them from the day they played hooky at Playland.

"Do you want one? I think she left some." He invited his grandma into the kitchen and hopped up onto the stool in front of the remaining stray muffins resting on the cooling rack.

"Thank you, sweetheart." She accepted the muffin and took a bite.

"How're you doing, son? You doing okay? I know things have been difficult lately. I know about your foot and I know about the dinner the other night. I know how hard that must have been."

He felt the love radiate from her heart into his. "Oh, it was hard—yeah I guess." He hung his head, his cheeks burning.

Helen reached across the island and took his hand. He felt her warm, soft skin covering his bright red, clammy hands like a little pillow. Looking up at her, he smiled.

"There it is, I see your smile. I knew it was in there."

He laughed and sat on top of his foot on the stool, making him taller and closer to Helen, so she could relax her over-extended arm.

"I'm sorry things have been so hard..." Her soothing voice trailed off, leaving him the space to think and respond.

He looked away to interpret the unfamiliar feeling running through his body. She really cared and wanted to know.

"It's okay, you don't have to be sorry. It's not your fault. I guess it's not anybody's fault...but sometimes it feels like the only way to move on is to blame someone. I was blaming my mom a lot...it wasn't fair..."

"Sweetheart, you've grown up so fast, facing all these adult issues." Helen smiled and sighed as she put her other hand on top of his. "You're right, it's no one's fault—I especially want to make sure you include yourself in that?" She looked at him with one eyebrow raised.

"Yes, I know." He nodded as the tiny cracks in his heart filled with love.

Helen smiled back at him. "So how is your schoolwork going? I know you're a smart boy, but are you applying yourself?"

"Yeah. I'm working hard. I have a science project due soon, and I'm going to test the acidity of different soda pops on nails. My guess is the Mountain Dew is going to do the most damage."

"Ah, I see, very creative," she laughed.

The two of them turned their heads, as they heard the garage door screeching open. He sat in silence listening to the sequence of the engine entering, the garage door halting, the engine switching off, and the car door swinging shut.

. . . .

~HELEN~

"Oh, Mom," Deb said as she stopped dead in her tracks in the entryway from the garage, an empty picnic basket dangling through her arm.

"Hello, Deborah," she said with a gentle undertone of authority mixed with love.

"I didn't expect to see you here."

"I'm sorry for coming unannounced, but I owe you a bit of an apology."

"Oh, Mom, you don't have to do this right now...in front of Lincoln."

"It's okay, Mom—I can go up to my room. You guys can talk," Lincoln said, as he winked at her.

"Okay, you want a muffin?" Deb offered.

"No thanks. I already had one with Grandma."

As she heard Lincoln trotting up the steps, she faced Deb.

Her daughter set down the empty muffin basket and pulled up a stool next to her.

Helen reached out and put her hand on Deb's hand. "I'm sorry I was hard on you before, but all I wanted was to help you. It kills me inside knowing all the pain and suffering you're going through and I feel helpless to do anything. I'd tried so many things and nothing had worked so I thought trying something more dramatic might make you think about things differently. But everything I try makes you run away. I don't know what else to do, honey. You are my only daughter and I love you. I only want what's best for you, and for you and my grandson to be happy. I'm sorry I've failed you."

Deb took her hand out from under hers and sat still, her head folded over. "I have failed my children more than once," she said, almost inaudibly.

Helen took a deep breath, unsure of what Deb meant. "Children?" she asked, even lower than Deb's voice.

Deb nodded her head, unable to look her in the eye. "Yes, children."

She paused, leaving the space for Deb to fill.

"You remember that night I missed curfew and you made me tea?"

"Oh honey, I think there were many nights you missed curfew and I made you tea."

"I only remember one night—I was probably too drunk all the other times. I was such a horrible daughter, I'm sorry." Tears erupted and Deb had to stop to catch her breath.

"It's okay, honey, it's okay..." She reached over and rubbed Deb's back. She was terrified but also filled with anticipation of what her daughter was about to say.

Once Deb regained her breath, she started again. "The night you made me tea, and I had the ripped shirt. I'm sorry I pushed you away. I'm sorry I didn't ask you for help."

"It's okay, sweetie. I'm sorry I left you when I could tell you were hurting." Feelings of guilt flooded her belly.

"And I'm sorry I never told you what really happened. You remember Tony?"

Helen nodded. She had feared Tony so much back then but didn't know how to steer her daughter away from him. He was bad news but movie-star handsome and a senior when Deb was a sophomore.

"Tony got me pregnant...and that night I told him about it..." Deb sobbed but took a deep breath. "...and he hit me...a lot...and I went a couple of days later and got an abortion." With the last word, Deb buckled over, clutching her throat.

"It's okay, honey, deep breaths. I'm right here," she said, rubbing her back again.

"I'm so sorry," Deb gasped.

"It's okay, it's okay. You just keep breathing. It's gonna be all right. I love you."

• • • •

~DEB~

"Hey, Mom, I made something for you." She heard Lincoln's voice in the kitchen.

"Coming." She pushed her papers across the bedspread and went downstairs.

"Here." Lincoln handed her a half poster board covered in pictures of their family. In the middle it said *My Happiness*.

She studied the images from top to bottom, hovering on the memory of each one. Beau holding baby Lincoln. Lincoln and Beau standing outside the baseball diamond, Lincoln's uniform covered in dirt. Lincoln crawling among the presents under the tree on Christmas morning. Deb and Beau toasting at an engagement party for Jake. The three of them huddled on the back of a hay wagon during the town's fall festival.

She stopped when her eye saw a Polaroid of Dan playing pickup basketball.

"I took that one," Lincoln said, following her eyes.

She pulled his head into her chest and hugged him. Her insides unwound. Her heart filled with potential. Their new beginning had arrived.

www.ingramcontent.com/pod-product-compliance
Lightning Source LLC
Chambersburg PA
CBHW071306140726
47996CB00005B/1652